LOVERS

AND OTHER

PENELOPE
KARAGEORGE

Print ISBN: 978-1-66786-032-9
eBook ISBN: 978-1-66786-033-6

1

Cass pulled on the black lace bikini panty, felt it move silkily against her skin, then the matching bra that made her breasts look even more voluptuous. Vance had reveled in them, adored her breasts. Tonight she would see her ex-husband for the first time in five years, and she still wasn't sure if she wanted to kiss him or kill him. She had refused his phone calls from Balaban Prison, and had not opened his letters, saved them so that someday she could toss them at him like a brick, tangible evidence of her disdain.

But last night she had dreamed of him, a dream so vivid that she woke up with tears in her eyes. When she was a child, her Greek grandmother Katerina told her that if you dream of someone, you must get in touch with them the next day. She had called Vance. Hearing his voice, years dropped away. He could have been asking her out on their first date. And once again – almost against her will -- she had responded eagerly to the reckless, charismatic ex-husband who had managed to turn Wall Street success into a five year prison sentence. Despite financial triumphs, he had fomented a Ponzi scheme that lost millions for friends, family and investors.

According to a psychiatrist who testified at his trial, Vance was not a criminal but the helpless victim of his own addiction to gambling, tougher to lick than heroin addiction. His mistake had been to play with Wall Street money. The judge granted him a lenient five-year sentence. And Cass finally faced the truth, that the husband she adored was a desperate gambling addict. His all-night card games and Las Vegas junkets were just tips of the degenerate's iceberg. Cass had accepted everything – his recklessness, his irrational spending, his moods -- as essential parts of the man who loved her and only her. But when the scandal broke, his affair with colleague Miranda Nightingale also surfaced.

Despite Vance's protests and remorse, Cass had gone through with a bitter and painful divorce. But she had never stopped missing him. Her hand shook as she used her lipstick to outline a red mouth. She struggled to get her straight black hair exactly right. From her days as a toddler, she had yearned for blond curls, but finally settled in adulthood to a look that was her own. Her hair set off high cheekbones, black eyes, a curvaceous mouth. She looked good, but how would she look to him?

She could use a drink. No. Not tonight. Tonight was too important. And God forbid that she have an anxiety attack. She dropped his favorite blue dress on over her head, a soft cashmere that hugged her body discreetly. She slipped into the red Jimmy Choo's with five inch heels that she wore on special occasions. A mist of Chanel No. 5 perfume, and she was ready.

Cass pulled her faux fur jacket out of the closet, grabbed her bag and keys, stepped out into a foyer, and rang for the elevator. Only one other apartment shared the elevator with her in her West 12th Street building. She loved her Greenwich Village apartment, an eight room treasure that she had been fortunate to keep despite the Ponzi debacle.

She whizzed down to the lobby from the 10th floor. It was a brisk November night. She stepped out on the sidewalk and took a deep breath of the crisp urban air, excited as always by New York's special undercurrent of grit and action, life happening. Two teenagers shared a joke as they walked down the block. Lights glowed in the apartment building across the street.

Doorman Jose wore his blue and grey uniform with the pride of an army officer. "A cab, Mrs. Cooper?" Two minutes later, a yellow taxi drew up in front of the building. Cass gave the cabby the East 63rd Street address and was on her way.

The cab moved past restaurants, shops, neon flashing, shouts, beeps. Hundreds of small lights decorated the bare branches of the trees in front of Bed, Bath and Beyond, a Christmas promotion but no less enchanting for it. In New York art and commerce melded and astonished.

The taxi drove across 42nd Street and up Park Avenue to the Sixties and its elegant, multi-million-dollar townhouses, architectural delights. Despite the new prominence of Soho and Noho, the East 60's had never lost their elan. Vance's best friend, lawyer Donaldson Frye, had offered Vance his four-story town house for two weeks, while Donaldson skied at his winter retreat in Stowe, Vermont.

The cab pulled up. Cass paid the driver and got out. She was breathless, as if she had run to this destination. She took two steps to the door. Before she could ring the bell, the door opened. Vance. Five years older, even better-looking. His face was thinner but still rugged, sharp, intelligent. The dark blond curly hair was now almost white at the temples. The slender nose, dark brown eyes, had not changed. And yet there was a difference. He smiled but it was a dark smile, a chastened smile. He drew her inside and closed the door quickly behind them. She could not stop smiling. A cry escaped from her lips. He put his arms around her and held her close, pressing her against him. They could never get close enough.

"You wanted to talk," he murmured. "But let's not talk." He took her hand and they went up the stairs to the green-walled bedroom.

"No," Cass said. "No." And then she was laughing. "Yes."

She had almost forgotten that amazing feeling of freedom that Vance gave her, the constrictions of being a dressed up grown-up falling away. They made love slowly. Cass savored every move, the incredible feeling of being joined to Vance, becoming one with the only man she had ever loved. She wanted it to go on forever, and she would keep coming, the orgasms pouring out of her as if she had stored them up for that night. There had been other men but those sexual encounters were just that. Sex. This was different, spectacular, the real thing. He pulled her close. "You are a miracle," Vance whispered. "You are mine. You will always be mine. Lie next to me. It feels so good to be next to you."

Lying side by side, the bright lights on, they dozed off.

Cass woke to a cell phone ringing. Vance stood next to the bed, phone in hand, a troubled expression on his face. "This is not a good time. Not for me." His voice dropped. Cass checked her watch. 2 A.M. "No. Yes. No."

Cass glanced around the room. Philip Roth's Sabbath's Theater was on the night table along with the Twelve Step Bible, the addict's study guide. Lemons and limes and a sharp, slender knife rested on the bar next to a cutting board. A note by the booze read "Help yourself to the good stuff."

Vance put down the phone and slid back into bed with Cass. She moved closer to him. He rubbed his cheek against hers. "In the morning I'm going to make you the incredible eggs you like for breakfast. And then we'll make love, and go for a walk and come back and light a fire. And make love. And go out to dinner. And I will tell you my plan for our future together. Do you know that prison was good for me? It was like a post-graduate course in living. But not easy. There's no such thing as a country club prison. It's hell – physically, intellectually, spiritually. Dante's Inferno is a picnic compared to prison walls."

"Oh, Vance," Cass hugged him. "I was a bitch. I wouldn't even speak to you."

"It's okay." He smiled. "I knew you loved me."

"I do love you and was happier being unhappy with you than anything, and I wasn't perfect and all those things. I've had plenty of time to stew."

"Let's get married again. Donaldson's loaned me his townhouse for a couple of weeks and promised to stay away. Perfect for a honeymoon, and a great place to avoid the press. Let's get married tomorrow."

"Shouldn't I be coy and say I'll think it over?"

"No. Life is not eternal. This is the new Vance. I was hoping you would like me."

"I adore you. As to your proposal of marriage, I say yes. Yes! Yes! Yes!"

And if it came back to Cass, the anxiety, the uncomfortable feelings she had during the last year of a twenty-year marriage, when despite his denials, she knew something was wrong, the left-out feeling, the pain, the doubting of her own sanity, she would put all of that away.

"Let me go back to the apartment and get my wedding ring and pack a small bag."

"How long will you be?"

"How about 7 A.M.?""

"Why so long?"

"If we're going to be on a real honeymoon, I need to send a few emails and polish up loose ends on a piece I'm working on."

"Don't be late." Vance kissed her gently. He gave her the key to the house. "I will miss you."

Cass hurried out the door, down out into the cold winter night and hailed a taxi. She had not had a drink and she did not need a drink. She was high on Vance.

3:30 A.M. She was back in her apartment, The dangerous hour of reckoning, a time to confront the bogies. She walked into the bedroom where she had passed so many lonely nights and looked in the mirror. She always looked better after making love with Vance.

"My passionate Greek," he would say. "I am good for you."

She had fallen in love with Vance on their first date and never fell out of love with him. He took her to a French restaurant where the chef created a masterful fillet of sole bonne femme and super-chilled martinis. They hit it off. Drinking. Talking. Knees touching. Hands. Most of the men she knew told her to slow down on the drinks. Vance stayed ahead of her. The pattern was set. The drinks. The love. The talk. They married three months later on the spur of the moment, she in a blue and white polka dot dress. She would never forget their reception dinner, Peking Duck in a Chinese restaurant with a huge bowl of sherbet and fruit, good luck symbols all around. She could not have been happier. She had never craved a big church wedding. Their only guests were their close friends and witnesses, book publisher Dev Lal and his wife Liv.

More than once, Liv been a sounding board for Cass after a particularly disastrous argument with Vance. In spite of their private language, their ability to get into each other's heads, they fought. And made up. They made love so frequently and so passionately. When did he have time to get involved with another woman? That was all in the past. She would have a drink to celebrate. Just one. She poured a shot, neat, and she stepped out on the terrace into the crisp cold night. The Empire State Building dazzled with a red and green display. Her first view of New York as a kid was cubes of light. This was her city, and Vance was a huge part of it.

She went back inside and opened her jewelry box. It was a huge tangle. She thought she had tossed the wedding ring there, but after taking everything out and putting it back, no ring appeared. Had she made some pseudo-dramatic gesture in an angry rage and tossed the ring somewhere? Maybe it was a good omen. She would have a new wedding band. She consulted her closet and found the off-white wool dress. She packed a bag. Finally she sat down at the computer to respond to the queries that she had set in motion for a piece she was developing on Cures for Cataclysmic Living.

After the divorce, Cass had thrown herself even more intensely into her work as a freelance journalist. Famous for her personality profiles, Cass had won a reputation for her daring exposes – and her willingness to go after celebrities who usually succumbed to her empathetic charm. She asked the bold questions and was likely to break down and weep along with the story subject.

She looked up from her laptop to see the sky turning from rosy pink to blue, with golden sun rays, heralding a beautiful day. It was already 6:30. She changed into the white dress, picked up her bag and jacket, hustled down on the elevator and outside. The doorman hailed her a cab and she was on her way. She did not want to be late for her wedding date with Vance She did not anticipate a life of ease. Because that would be boring, and easy had never interested her.

She unlocked the front door and walked into the hall, all black and white with a small crystal chandelier winking a welcome. She did not call out but went slowly up the stairs. The lights were off in the bedroom whose windows, even in the midst of luxury, faced a wall, making the room black around the clock. Hearing Rod Stewart blasting *They Can't Take That Away From Me* on the CD player, she groped her way into bedroom with the dark green walls, celery green bedspread and American Primitive paintings. The room reeked of marijuana.

She put her bag down and reached for the light switch. It looked like a party or rampage had taken place. The primitive painting of an elder hung askew, his enormous moustache pointing down to the floor where a small pair of black bikini panties embroidered with tiny red roses had been tossed. As Cass stepped into the room, an empty champagne bottle rolled away from her foot. The dresser drawer gaped out to reveal its ransacked contents.

In the midst of chaos, a small black vase holding one white rose had tipped over atop the bureau. It had not been there before. Cass righted it and mopped the spilled water with a tissue.

Cass walked to the bed and ripped back the cover. Vance lay on the blood-soaked sheet. He wore chinos and blue shirt open to reveal his naked chest. A dagger with an elaborate carved handle was buried in it.

"No!" Somebody screamed and screamed again. Herself. She flung herself on Vance's body. Her hand gripped the knife. Horrified, she pulled her now bloody hand away.

Better women might have prayed.

She called 911.

2

Vance's body was still warm. Cass sat back on her heels. She would do CPR. She interlocked both hands in the middle of his chest and pressed down. She blew into his mouth. Lips warm. Blow. Thirty moves. Count. His chest did not rise. Keep going. Rod Stewart continued to blast out *They Can't Take That Away From Me*.

Then she heard the wail, a heart-breaking lament coming from the center of her soul, all of the Americanization and Girl Scouts and Columbia School of Journalism washed away. Smelling Vance's lime after-shave, she yowled with grief. She wept and screamed like an ancient Greek woman tearing out her hair at the death of a beloved one, a primitive country woman who had lost purpose and the center of herself.

A blond police officer tugged at her shoulder. "Come now, Ma'am." Her dress and hands were smeared with Vance's blood. The officer reached up to forcefully pull Cass off of Vance's body and lead her into the next room. "Detective Adams is on his way."

Cass sat down in a green chair by a window overlooking a sunlit courtyard. Turning away from glaring light, she looked back towards the bedroom, now invaded by men and women, New York Police Department professionals. They photographed, measured, inspected, a small army equipped with cameras, tape, moving back and forth, collecting evidence, examining every inch of the floor, the furniture, the walls. Scientists. Technicians. Cold, objective strangers who did not know or care about the late Vance Elliott Cooper.

Cass shivered as the brutal sunlight blasted in her face. As she stood up to close the blind, a burly gentleman approached. He had a round face, a forehead etched with lines, a big nose, chubby cheeks, hazel eyes, wispy beige hair. A skeptical face, as if one eyebrow would always be raised as it was now. There was a slight paunch and the beginnings of a double chin. He looked weary, as if he had just been dragged out of bed or the local bar.

"I'm Robert Adams, homicide detective. You can call me Adams, because that's what everyone else calls me. I've seen your byline, Cass. Can I call you Cass? It's easier if we proceed that way, on a first-name basis. It facilitates communication."

"Of course." That weird, spaced out feeling was creeping up on her -- intimation of a dread anxiety attack. She took a deep breath. She would fight it. Inhale slowly. Exhale. This was not the time to whip out a small paper bag and breathe into it, or reach for a drink. "Please, I would like to call my lawyer. My bag with my phone in it is in the next room."

The young cop brought Cass her bag. She phoned Donaldson in Vermont, surprised at the level sound of her own voice. "Vance has been murdered. He was stabbed to death. Here. In your house. I found him. I am with the police."

"Vance dead." Donaldson's voice shook. "My God, no. Are you alright?"

"I would be lying if I said yes. I could use a lawyer."

"No more questions. I'm chartering a plane. I'll leave immediately. I'll come directly to the 67th Street Precinct station. Try not to talk to the police without me."

The police drove Cass to the 67th Street Precinct station, an imposing five story red brick and grey granite building that dominated the block. Adams turned her over to a team of technicians. First a young woman took swabs from her blood-covered hands, which she was then permitted to wash. As the blood mingled with water in the washbowl, she realized it was Vance's blood disappearing down the drain, felt it was a waste and a sin, a desecration. She did not want that to happen, wanted to bottle that blood.

Next the finger printing. "You'll want to get out of those clothes," the officer said, her voice cool and in-command. Cass took the big T-shirt, sweater and running pants offered to her, went to the bathroom and put them on as the justice system continued to methodically chip away at her persona. The officer put Cass's own clothes in a bag and labeled it with her name.

Detective Adams moved towards her. Despite the beginnings of a paunch and wispy hair, he moved gracefully as dancer, light on his feet. "Come." He led her to an elevator and then downstairs to an interrogation room, a grey room with a table, three chairs and a mirror that Cass knew one could see through from the other side. Another young police officer had joined them. "Meet Officer McGrath."

"Is there any new information?" Cass asked. "Anything you can tell me?"

"Everything's always new in a homicide case. We are constantly going back over evidence and finding new angles. Discovering what might have appeared insignificant at first and realizing that it is crucial. Or a new witness who has been holding back comes to the station and spills. A case is not inert. It is alive."

Cass was seated by the table, with the two men at a short distance away.

"First, let me read you your Miranda rights." Adams proceeded. "You have the right to remain silent. Anything you say can and will be used against you in a court of law. You have the right to an attorney. If you do not have an attorney, one will be appointed for you." He paused. "Is that clear?"

"Perfectly clear."

"Now let's begin. What's the last time you saw Vance Cooper alive?"

"Would it be presumptuous of me to ask for a cup of coffee?"

"Of course not. McGrath, get Mrs. Cooper a container of coffee. Cream and sugar?"

"Cream, please."

McGrath swiftly returned with a large cardboard container and handed it to Cass, who thanked him, gratefully opened the lid and took a sip.

"Better?" Adams asked.

"Somewhat."

"I'm not asking you to spill your guts," Adams said. "All I want are the facts."

Donaldson had advised her against talking to Adams. But she felt the need to reassert herself. She had nothing to hide. She was a practiced interviewer. She could hold her own. "I last saw Vance alive at 3 A.M." She looked up at Adams and the large mirror behind him

"Don't worry about observers. Talk to me."

Adams did not interrupt her as she recounted the night's events. He sat back in his chair, fingers hooked in his belt. "You speak of your late ex-husband as if he was a man you were just getting to know, not somebody you had been married to for twenty years. I'm not sure if that's charming or pathetic. You were divorced from Cooper. Why the reunion?"

"The night before he was leaving Balaban, I had this amazing dream about him," Cass said. "I called him and we made the date to meet at midnight. We planned to remarry today."

Adams stroked his chin as if there were a beard although not even a hair sprouted there. "Cass, I don't want you to get your panties in a tangle, but there appears to be a reality that you haven't been able to deal with. Your late husband was far from a perfect person."

"I was aware."

"In fact, he had been supremely lucky in having both a brilliant lawyer and psychologist defending him before he went to prison. He got five years. Bernie Madoff, another man who bilked people with a Ponzi scheme, got a life sentence. Madoff was short and ugly. Vance Cooper was handsome and charismatic. Women fell in love with him – including yourself -- and men related." Adams quirked an eyebrow at Cass.

"You have learned a lot about Vance in a few hours." The accusatory tone of her own voice surprised her.

"I am a New York police detective and a speed reader. You loved him but what kind of a husband was he?"

"He was my kind of husband." Cass felt as if she had to defend Vance and herself. "Our relationship was not straight out of the happily-ever-after books but it suited me. We talked, we cooked, we drank, we fought and made up." She would hold nothing back. "We had one physical drag-out fight when I emerged with a scar at the top of my forehead. There." Cass pointed to the scar on her forehead.

Adams mouth turned down. "I suppose you're going to tell me that you had great sex."

"I never discuss my sex life." Cass sipped coffee, now grown cold.

"Why did you divorce Cooper?"

"He had an affair. I couldn't handle it."

"And yet were ready to marry him again. Why?"

"We are all entitled to one mistake."

"Think of all the people Vance antagonized, the double dealings, the gambling debts. Cooper went through his life with the aura of a born winner, the American success story. Poor boy makes good. Scholarships to NYU and Wharton, plus his rumored charm led to dazzling success that acted like a cover for his dark side. If you did remarry him, what did you anticipate?"

"It might be difficult, but it's what I wanted."

"You decide to remarry Cooper. You leave and go home to pack a bag and to retrieve your wedding ring, you claim. But there was no wedding ring among your possessions."

"I could not find it."

"Is it possible that at your reunion he said or did something to make you angry. You left, returned to your apartment and had a couple of drinks."

"I had one drink."

"Then you decide to go back. There was unfinished business. You return to find bikini panties on the floor. Your would-be spouse is up to his old tricks. You explode with rage."

"That did not happen," Cass blurted. "No."

"Your fingerprints are on the murder weapon. Cassandra Cooper, you are our primary suspect in the murder of Vance Cooper."

She felt cold, sick, numb, cheated and used. Just a few hours ago she had been shrieking to God over the loss of her ex-husband and lover, about to be future husband. A brief dream, shattered. But the cynical part of her had been beating a message like a drum.

"I never really anticipated a happy ending today, Adams. Of course you didn't ask."

Donaldson Frye, New York's top criminal lawyer, walked decisively into the 67th Street precinct. He moved like a four-star general, his expression stolid. Square-jawed and bold, Frye was regarded as the Houdini of criminal lawyers. Armed with his tweed jackets and unique legal mind, he had rescued many falsely accused and helped them wriggle out of seemingly impossible situations.

Cass stood with Donaldson by her side. He pushed the arraignment through. He entered the not guilty to murder plea. The judge set bail and Donaldson and Cass walked outside into the cold, grey November day and towards his parked BMW.

This was a new Donaldson. Instead of his usual tweeds, he wore a loose-fitting grey shirt over a blue T-shirt. A small Buddha image hung around his neck. He had shaved his skull, not unbecoming. He touched his head. "Tired of the receding hairline."

He opened the door for Cass, then went around and got in the other side. Inside the car, his constraint collapsed. "Dear God, Vance dead. He was my oldest, my best and my closest friend." Donaldson's voice broke. "Did you talk with him?"

"We didn't talk, not really. We made love and I said stupid things and we decided to get married again today. I left and when I went back – it was over."

Donaldson gripped her hand hard. "Did you kill him Cass?" Donaldson's brown eyes turned black and anguished.

"Why would I kill Vance?" Cass pulled her hand back from Donaldson's vise-like grip. "First Adams accuses me of killing Vance, and now you suspect me."

"Rumors had it that you had it in for him – that the divorce set off a bitter aftermath – and it was payback time."

Cass felt her own anxiety building. "What rumors from where?"

"People are bastards. They know nothing but they talk. Sorry, sweetheart, I had to ask. I throw this at potential clients." Donaldson started the car. "I'm on your case, regardless. I need coffee. How about you?

"The Fourteenth Street Diner has big booths."

"Let's go."

3

Cass slid into the booth across from Donaldson. At 3 P.M. the Fourteenth Street Diner lunch crowd had dissipated, creating a spacious oasis. She glanced in the mirror. No lipstick. She always wore lipstick, felt naked without it. She need not worry about impressing Donaldson. "I know that I look like hell."

"You look fine, particularly under the circumstances." Where Vance had charmed, Donaldson reassured. Today there was a grim set to his wide mouth. He reached out with his large hands and encased Cass's hands in his. "Life sucks, doesn't it?" He pulled his hands back, looked down at the table, back at Cass. His mouth twisted in a rueful smile. "I loved the man, but I was aware of his flaws. I knew him from the time I was born. At age three he grabbed my precious Tootsie Roll and gave me the less desirable lollipop. And I happily took it. Around Vance I was always second best but I did not mind. He was my hero."

Cass felt the lump rising in her throat. A waitress brought water. She grabbed the glass of water, gulped. "What the hell happened? Did an old girlfriend stab him to death?"

"What brings that on? The bikini panties on the floor?"

"You saw the crime scene?"

"Adams described it." He signaled to the waitress. "And let's get some bacon and eggs with the coffee."

"I don't have an enormous appetite."

"When did you last eat? Starving yourself to death won't help." Donaldson placed the order.

"When did you last talk with Vance?"

"Yesterday. Dev Lal, the publisher, had driven up to Balaban to pick him up and dropped him off at my house. I had my bag packed and was ready to head for Vermont. He rang the bell. That was 3 P.M." Donaldson cleared his throat and continued. "I was so happy to see him out of prison. He looked fit, if subdued, but good. We didn't say a lot. It was all about feeling.

"I introduced him to Millicent, the housekeeper who comes in three days a week, gave him the keys and headed for the private airport. I always fly AirSki to Vermont, a chartered plane. It takes an hour. Vance called me on the plane to tell me that everything was fine and he had settled in. That night I joined my neighbors Betsy and Bill Coleman for dinner. You called me at 8 A.M. and here I am."

Cass listened to Donaldson but barely heard him. "Suppose I had stayed with Vance. The killer would have seen the two of us and might have backed down. It had to be someone who knew him – he would have fought off a stranger. Is there any other way into your house?"

"There's the door to the terrace. I do have an alarm system, but it's temporarily dismantled because of repair work being done. I planned to see to it on my return from Vermont and install a new and better system. I told Vance about it. Neither of us was particularly worried. There's a good strong lock on the door. Of course an expert could dismantle it, a really determined person."

The eggs arrived. Cass pierced a yolk with her fork. "Look at that, a potential chicken. Another life gone." Cass put her fork down.

"Easy, Cass."

"Did anyone else know that Vance was staying in your house?"

"Only Dev. And the housekeeper. Vance told me that he wanted time to think and relax and to avoid the press all costs. So I told no one."

"When I walked into that room for the second time, it looked like a party had taken place," Cass said. "A marauding party. Pictures askew. They were searching. Like what were they looking for and did they find it? There was a lingering whiff of marijuana. The reek of blood. The room was cold. And the flower. Weird. There was a slim black vase with one white rose. It had tipped over. I righted it. It's an odd little scenario, isn't it?"

"It's bizarre, suggestive." Donaldson frowned. "It could even have been staged."

"Interesting. To look like a bunch of people when there was only one person. Vance could have had one visitor, or there could have been a party. Perhaps the one visitor – his killer – threw around the other elements to throw the police off the track. The possibilities are vast but I am the suspect."

"At the moment."

"And then there's the knife, an ornate dagger. My fingerprints are on it."

"Why?"

"I threw myself on Vance's body. I reached out by accident and grabbed the knife. I clutched it and then pulled back, horrified." Cass suddenly felt depleted, as if energy had drained from her body and mind. She took a deep breath. "It does not look good, according to Detective Adams. The ex-wife returns with the expectation of remarriage and finds a woman's bikini panties on the floor. Enraged, she drives the knife through his heart."

Donaldson spoke firmly. "That story would not hold up in court. By the time the NYPD finishes going over the crime scene, there are certain to be a welter of footprints and fingerprints and DNA other than yours which will, I am sure, eventually yield the killer's identity."

"Do you have any idea who that might be?"

"No." Donalson mopped an egg yolk up with toast. "There are a slew of people out there with motives. People whose lives were destroyed when he lost fortunes for them – possibly waiting for revenge when he was released from prison."

"If a stranger came after Vance, he would have fought for his life. He seemed to lie back and take it."

"A stranger could surprise him – take him completely unaware."

Cass shifted to the other side of the booth. "I was so filled with anger during the divorce. I suppose the police and Detective Adams are pouring over those gossipy stories. New York magazine did a particularly scathing piece that made me sound like one of the avenging Furies. In one memorable line, the reporter wrote that I resembled Clytemnestra in the famous tragedy who plotted her husband's murder on his return from battle. Vance should beware of me when released from prison."

"False news. Despicable. But you're right to bring it up. We must deal with that kind of trash."

"With Vance, I had learned to look the other way. I adored him – then it all broke down. But when he said let's get married last night, I was joyous. I did not expect perfection. In fact, I anticipated difficulty. I did not care."

"We forgave Vance everything. Who could resist his charm?" Donaldson nodded his head. "You know somebody forever. You love them and then the shocks come. What hurts is the amount of betrayal in relationships. Did you know that Alicia and I split?"

"I heard that. I am sorry."

"Vance and Alicia. The two people I loved the most. I questioned my entire life, all the things I had formerly accepted. I discovered Buddhism. I began meditating. It's been a struggle, and an on-going one. It's not a joke."

"I'm not laughing." Pain was etched on his face, in the small lines around the mouth, the intense look of introversion.

"I only dress like this on weekends and while up at the ski lodge. During the week, it's the three-piece suit or the tweed jacket or the blazer. I never did approve of the no-tie look. But forgive me my personal trivia." He picked up his coffee cup and put it down without drinking. "I have something important to tell you. You have already been run over with a bulldozer, and I hate to pile it on, but you should know now."

"What is it?"

"Vance was putting your apartment on the market, and had talked with Branch Real Estate, who were eager to sell the property for him. It's prime real estate. Eight rooms, terrace with a view, two fireplaces. You know. You live there."

"It's my home."

"But Vance owned it."

"We were going to be married. Where did he expect us to live?"

"Unfortunately, you will probably never know what his plans were." Donaldson put his hand over hers on the table. "Now the apartment is yours, left to you as part of the divorce agreement. If he deceased you, you would gain the apartment."

"Yes. But why was he trying to sell it?"

"Apparently he needed the money." Donaldson hesitated. "Consider his situation. With the Ponzi scheme double dealing he owed and would always owe. Could he have been gambling from prison? I suppose anything is possible. Unfortunately, it does give you another motive for murder."

"Get real."

"You know the real estate market in Manhattan. Women have killed for less."

4

CASS WALKED INTO HER GREENWICH Village apartment, took a deep breath and looked around. Maybe she should get down on her hands and knees and kiss the polished floor, like an explorer on discovering the promised land. In less than twenty-four hours, her life had turned completely upside down. Her dream of love was destroyed, but she still had her home.

She remembered making love with Vance, and her body would not let go of that memory. She started to shiver. She hugged her body, as if she could hug Vance. She was acting like a mad woman, she told herself, and also told herself that she was entitled.

She pulled off the big pants and shirt given to her by the NYPD, stuffed them in a shopping bag and pushed them to the back of the hall closet. Then she took a long hot shower, wishing she could sluice away the ugly memories. No, she needed to hang on to them, every detail. She had not slept for twenty-four hours but she was wide awake. She dressed in jeans and a sweater, went into her messy but comforting office, her favorite place of retreat , and called real estate agent Charlotte Brand.

A top agent dealing with New York's luxury properties, Charlotte insisted on answering her own phone with the nasal Bronx tones that she had never lost. "Real estate is personal, it's emotional," she had once confided

to Cass. "People hear my Bronx twang or whatever you want tc
trust me. I get in their shorts. They tell me what they really wa⟩
their motor."

Charlotte had beautiful hands, the nails always polished in a deep red.
"Clients do not want an agent with purple nails. They don't want hippy. That's
not my brand. And I'm a brand. You have a business, you need a brand."

Charlotte sounded shaken when Cass identified herself. "I've been
reading all the papers. I'm sorry, really sorry. Of course you didn't do it. Kill
Vance? He was a sweetheart, wasn't he, in spite of everything. Forgive me.
My impression."

"We were planning to be married again, but it didn't happen. It's about
the apartment. My lawyer, Donaldson Frye, said that Vance had put it on the
market –"

"Not to worry. I took it off immediately when I read the disgusting
news this morning. Like sweetheart, are you alright? You sound too calm."

"I'm fine, Charlotte. Honestly. Regardless, the crazier I feel, the calmer
I appear. It's like a protective mask drops in place. Tell me about this trans-
action with Vance."

"He called me -- he specifically approached me because you wrote a
piece about me. And you had told him that if you were ever going to sell the
apartment you would come to me. So he called – and it was only three weeks
ago. He said he wanted to sell the apartment and he would take as little as
$5 million for it. That was nothing. But he wanted the money in a hurry. He
did not explain."

"You were aware that I still lived there."

"I asked him about that. He said that you might not understand. But
that he owned the apartment outright and when push came to shove, you
would go for it. That you would have part of the profits to spend towards a
new apartment. He was going to give you a million which amounts to bupkus
– like you could get a decent one-bedroom. Period."

"Did he say why he needed the money?"

"Not at all. And I did not ask. I never ask. I did ask him if I could find him another apartment, like a bachelor's pad if you will forgive me, and he said no, that he was not planning to stay in New York."

"Did he say where he was going or why?"

"Nothing. In our phone conversation, I had the impression that he was uncomfortable. Maybe even desperate. People get like that when they need a buck that badly."

"It was obviously a last-minute thing, his decision to sell the apartment."

"I found that unusual," Charlotte said. "He had all that time in prison to mull it over. Now you tell me you were going to be married again. So that would have changed everything, I assume. Unless he would want the two of you to head for the suburbs."

"Vance hated the suburbs."

"Honey, do me a favor and don't stay home and brood. You need a social life. I personally am always on the look-out for a new property and a new man. Sometimes I welcome the one-night stand. Slam. Bam. Thank you, sir. Here's your hat. What's my hurry. Sometimes a guy can feel insulted. Do I shock you, Cass?"

"I've always admired your enterprise."

"And now there's this new thing called Sexual Health. Like the MD's are worried if we're not getting some. Can you imagine? Like how we were brought up to be so proper – worlds go around. Forgive my chatter. My heart goes out to you."

Vance was leaving New York, but he was killed before he made his escape. If he was running, whom was he was running from? Had he been afraid to share his dark secrets with Cass? Had he been trying to protect her? He wanted them to remarry, to be joined together, and then would he tell her? He wanted them to take a road trip to destinations unknown.

Would their life have been like a grade B movie, driving at night through the rain, staying in cheap motels, dinner in the diner? Crazy, but she would have been up for it. Was Vance afraid she would turn away from him if he told her what was really happening, spilled the whole sordid and dangerous story. She was ready to go with him to the ends of the earth.

Vance had been flawed in many ways, but the one thing that rescued him for her, above everything, was the knowledge that he loved her. She had lost it, but that night he gave it back to her again. Cass wondered if she would ever become as inured to loveless love as real estate agent Charlotte. At the moment she felt that she would never be attracted to another man in her lifetime.

CASS SAT AT HER DESK in her office retreat, her comfort zone. Everything spelled safety, from the small bright Persian rug on the floor, to her books and her pens, her messy but workable environment. The phone was ringing. Journalists. She had no intention of responding to them.

Amidst all the phone calls, the three women she had become close to during the past five years remained silent, the Prime Timers as they dubbed themselves. Certainly Pru – Prudence Duluth – the chic former Vogue editor and media maven would want to commiserate, offer her a crying towel and shoulder to lean on. Cass had expected Angelina DeMarco, talented artist and mother of five, to be on her doorstep with a freshly baked lasagna and expression of sympathy. Jane Endicott, the clever research librarian, born John, had to be bursting with curiosity. She expected them to be flooding her with sympathy and concern. They might have tried. Her phone message box was completely full and her email was desperately overloaded. But she had expected them to push through and reach her somehow.

Of all the three women, Cass felt closest to Pru. They were both media mavens, in love with the printed word. Pru as an editor, Cass as a journalist. Pru had helped Cass build her career by throwing several juicy freelance pieces her way. Cass had appreciated her sensitive and on-target editing. They enjoyed going out to lunch, putting their heads together to relish the latest scandal and dish about the media's oversized, competitive personalities. Pru seemed to know everybody. Or they knew her.

Then her true life story broke. That glamorous Pru – the woman who vacationed with Prince Charles and Camilla -- had been raised in a trailer. "An actual double-wide," Pru had stuttered. "How can I ever show my face in public again?" Cass advised her to hold her head high and give interviews to the A-List media. "Your real story's great. It's colorful and American and rags to riches and even better than your pretend life." Pru took her advice and became a bigger celebrity. Ironically, her revelations of her early life as "trailer trash" – so she tagged herself -- bolstered her stardom. The press could not get enough of her witty interviews. "Vogue Editor Tells All About Life in a Double-Wide."

Cass picked up her phone and dialed Pru's number.

Pru answered on the first ring. "Darling Cass – I hesitated to call you – I mean – I didn't want to appear intrusive. You can be very private. I thought I would give you a day or two to nurse your wounds."

Cass was relieved to hear Pru's voice with its hint of a Southern drawl. "You *are* considerate. I'll confess. I'm totally wired. How about meeting for dinner."

"Are you really ready to face the public – after what's happened?"

"I feel trapped. Not only mentally and emotionally, but physically. I need to get out. The Bon Fleur's a new restaurant in Soho. We won't run into a lot of media people there."

"Then we must have dinner. The Bon Fleur. Perfect."

"I'll make the reservation. Eight o'clock.

"You're on."

Cass arrived at Bon Fleur restaurant fifteen minutes early for her dinner date with Pru. The new restaurant reeked of an interior designer's hand and the whiff of plastic. Cass preferred old French restaurants steeped in smoke and wine. As she pulled into the blue leatherette booth, she regretted having worn her dark maroon ultra-suede pants suit. It stuck to the seat and made her feel chunky. But she had chosen it because she did not want to appear the black-clad widow with Pru.

Cass found herself looking forward to Pru's familiar style of empathy, her tut-tutting, her views, and always her talk about her latest male conquests, because Pru was eternally driven to conquer, crushed if an attractive man did not make a pass at her, particularly if she had aimed the Pru brand of come-hither at him. "Tell me my style is Southern, corny and outdated and I say it still works."

Ten minutes late, Pru made an entrance in a stylish black suit. Tiny diamonds twinkled in her ears. Her streaked, tawny blond hair, tightly pulled back in a chignon, set off her elegantly boned face. An almost perfect face except for the too-full lower lip which, Pru claimed, men found sexy. Pru sat down across from Cass and plunked her over-sized bag down next to her. She squeezed Cass's hand as they air-kissed.

"What can I say, Cass? In spite of everything, you look wonderful. What's your secret?"

"I suppose it's ignoring the news." Cass attempted a laugh that did not quite make it.

"You can actually do that? You? The woman who eats news for breakfast? But you must want to know what they're saying about you." Pru's mouth drew into a thin line. Her lipstick rose above the lip line on the right side, unusual for the meticulous Pru. "It's a brutal business, and the press has utterly no respect for one of their own. I have been through it. I know."

"I do not want to know. I used to think that actors who said they never read their reviews were lying, but now I understand. It's hype and distortion and I hate it." Cass's voice rose. Maybe coming out for dinner wasn't such a great idea.

"Dearest Cass," Pru purred. "It's outrageous but you will get used to it."

"I hope not. I barely recognize myself the way some of these bastards have portrayed me – like a vengeful, murderous harpy." Cass took a deep breath. Control, she told herself. "If I were that bad, why would Vance want to marry me again?" Why had she told that to Pru? She had never shared her love of Vance with Pru or the women – quite the contrary.

Pru's eyes widened. "But you and Vance had not even spoken in years." She drew back. "That makes everything even more tragic, I mean – it's utterly." Pru signaled the waiter. "Why don't we order?"

Pru looked so together that Cass felt unnerved. Anxious. Ridiculous, she told herself, to feel at a disadvantage with Pru, her close friend. Why were women so much more intimidating than men?

A blond waiter in a blue bow tie and apron with a pink rose peeking out of his shirt pocket brought them over-sized menus and left. Pru drummed her red-tipped nails on the white tablecloth. Cass had a difficult time concentrating on the choices. The waiter had looked at her suspiciously, or was that her blossoming paranoia?

The waiter returned to take their orders. "That pink rosebud in your pocket is a nice touch," Cass said, sounding in her own ears as if she were trying too hard.

"The *bon fleur*," Pru pronounced in perfect French with a superior smile. "Charming. I will have the salmon," Pru ordered decisively. "Please don't overcook it. I prefer it on the rare side. And I would like extra slices of lemon on the side."

Cass ordered the special of the day which seemed easier than making an actual choice. "The trout almondine, please." She felt frozen. Nothing was working, including her brain.

"Drinks?" The waiter asked, pencil poised, directing his question primarily to Pru, whose personality had come to dominate the table.

"Not for me," Cass murmured.

"No, thank you," Pru said. "Perhaps I will have a glass of wine with dinner."

"Regular water or fizzy?" the waiter asked.

"Just regular plain old water, please." Pru smiled at the waiter, who finally moved away.

"Ordering salmon's terribly predictable, isn't it? Once women ordered cottage cheese and fruit. Now it's salmon."

"My least favorite fish."

"I'm glad we decided to come out tonight. There's so much happening. Angelina's big art opening is right around the corner. I am excited about that. And I'll be taking off for Saudi Arabia directly after the opening with Fazi Fakhouri– darling man – of course while I'm there it will be the best of everything, but I must avoid his wife and family."

"Does that make you uncomfortable?"

"Just a scootch. He's absolutely endearing. Even better, he's a billionaire. He adores experimental sex and is so appreciative, often expressed in gifts. I tell him, Fazi, this is not necessary. I enjoy being with you. Of course even when I didn't have two nickels I was of a practical nature. If I had a girlfriend who had struck up an affair with a rich married man I would advise her, at least get lamps."

"You are an original, Pru," Cass said. "You never let me down."

Pru shrugged and lowered her voice, now the confidant. "Do you know, Cass, that I enjoy sex and crave it more now than I did when I was younger." She examined a chipped nail. "But let's talk about you." Pru focused on the chipped nail. "That is just so annoying. The quality of life has definitely gone down, even with manicurists."

"I have always admired your long, beautiful nails." Cass questioned her own demeanor. What was she doing? Kissing up to Pru? She could not seem to find her emotional footing.

"How are you *really*, Cass? You poor darling," Pru gushed. "Let's talk about you."

"I'm okay. At least you have the decency not to say 'oh you poor thing.' "

Cass managed a smile but it felt forced.

"What a revolting phrase." Pru plucked a roll out of the bread basket, examined it and dropped it back in. "It's the sort of thing I would hear in the old neighborhood with the ladies in curlers sucking up beer."

"That's far in your past." Cass kept her mouth moving with feeble attempts at conversation. Coming out had been a mistake. Cass was turning into a blob with undefinable edges. Pru would understand if they cancelled the dinner. Cass would pay for the uneaten dinner orders, and they could retreat to a bar. This was the worst time to start drinking again, but she could use a double Scotch rocks and a change of atmosphere. "Pru, how would you feel about skipping this dinner? I'm feeling a little queasy."

"But you probably haven't eaten for days. You will feel better after you have a bite. Now I don't want you to go home and brood. And we've already ordered."

"True."

Pru briefly patted Cass's hand. "Did I tell you? I'm writing a memoir, just like you suggested, spilling the whole story, right from the beginning. How I made the good marriage from the right side of the tracks, then divorced Peter because being on top in Charleston wasn't enough. I needed New York and Paris and the world."

"You have done it all."

"But not enough. I'm excited about the memoir. I will load it with gossip and true confessions, and finally give those biddies in Charleston something to cluck about." Pru licked her lips. "Of course everyone's writing a memoir." She sat back, pulling away from Cass. "Even Vance was writing some kind of sensational confession."

Cass shifted in the booth. Her legs felt squeezed. "Who told you that?"

"Why, Vance did." Pru pursed her lips.

"Really?" Cass felt her face stiffen.

"Is that so remarkable?" Pru sucked in her mouth and fluttered her eyelashes.

"When?"

"I visited him in Balaban. I've always had a thing for the bad boys. Regardless, Vance and I had business things to discuss."

"Business."

"Back in the day when I left Vogue magazine, I had a chunk of money. I wanted some advice from an expert on managing my finances. It occurred to me that you had touted Vance as a whiz at investing. I called Vance up and introduced myself."

Cass hated the way Pru caressed Vance's name, as if she were stroking it with her tongue. Clever Pru. Ever the sophisticated predator.

Pru waved her hand at the waiter, who came swiftly to the table. "A dry martini, please, with two olives." She turned back to Cass. "Vance said he would try to help me. I suggested that he stop by my office on his way home and we could talk. He came to the office."

Pru's martini arrived in a thin-stemmed iced glass, two green olives glimmering at the bottom. She picked up the glass and sipped. She took another sip. She picked an olive out of the glass, chewed on it, plucked out a second olive and consumed it. "Vance gave me some good advice. Or course, it was part of his Ponzi scheme. I won and then I lost." Pru's voice flowed like warm syrup. Cass yearned to slap her. "After our initial meeting, we talked sometimes after work, sometimes at lunch."

In her black suit, her hair perfectly coifed, Pru could have been a lady warrior in armor. "I wanted to see him when he got out of prison. I thought you were finished with him." Pru paused to slug down another gulp of martini. "Now you're telling me the two of you planned to marry again. Are you sure that's not wishful thinking?"

"I'm anxious, but I'm not crazy."

"Let's try another scenario. Suppose you have the big reunion. You see the light and beg him to marry you. He says there's another woman in his life. You leave. You go home. You brood. You return in a jealous rage and deal him the *coup de grace*."

"You can speak English."

"I wanted to see you for myself. I'm not reading grief. You don't love him, not the way I love him. You would not read his letters. You burned them in front of us, and his picture, looking like a witch out of Macbeth."

"That's when I drank."

"And when we asked how you would kill an unfaithful lover, you said it would be a dagger straight to the heart."

"That was a game."

"You're not wearing black, like a proper Greek lady."

"Greek-American lady."

"You're not mourning. I'm surprised you're not sucking up Scotch."

"When did you get to be such a bitch, Pru?"

"Vance would come to my office but we never talked. We had sex, sometimes slow and sweet, sometimes hard and fast. Like the dirty sex I learned on the wrong side of the tracks."

"Apparently my feelings do not count."

"In this case, no." Pru spread her hands out. "I do have long red finger-nails, and I am not afraid to use them. They can scratch."

"This is ridiculous," Cass said. "You talk about Vance as if he were still alive."

"Isn't he? In my heart?" Pru took her gold compact out, opened it, reapplied lipstick, then licked her lips with satisfaction at her image in the mirror. She snapped the compact shut and dropped it in her bag. "You should know that I spoke with Detective Adams this afternoon. You killed him and I cannot let you get away with it."

6

CASS ASKED THE CABBY TO drop her off at Fifth Avenue and Fourteenth Street. She had to walk and dissipate the rage and hurt that flooded through her. Had Vance loved Pru? Or hated her? Was he ultimately sickened by her pursuit? Did he tell her that he was planning to marry Cass again?

Jealousy flashed. She felt robbed, as if her own private passions were being stolen from her. She and Vance had sometimes made love like desperate animals, particularly after a drunken argument. Occasionally when sober, having shattered everything – feelings, chairs – Vance once threw a favorite chair that she had found on the sidewalk and refinished into the fireplace – they would reach for each other. Sometimes it left her with an empty feeling. Or the realization that she desperately loved and belonged to this man and would always, always. Sometimes that scared her.

She and Pru had actually attempted to eat the dinners they had ordered, chewing silently. At one point Pru had said, "You look like you'd like to stick that fork in my eye." Cass felt bile rising up in her throat. She leaned over a garbage can and threw up. She stood up straight again, took deep breaths and walked. The streets were quiet. A couple strolled by holding hands, heads close together. A young woman in red tights bounced along with her dog, a miniature black poodle dressed in a red sweater.

Did Vance belong to her at all? He had struggled to make it to the top, using all of his brains, charm and imagination. He also drank and gambled to excess. Ultimately he chose to sabotage himself with Ponzi schemes and indulge in affairs including with one of his wife's so-called best friends. Face it. She herself was an addict whose life and soul had been entwined with another addict. Booze for her. Gambling for Vance. Addiction – that was the core of the piece she was writing. Cures for Cataclysmic Living. How in the midst of what seemed insuperable anxieties, addictions flourished.

Who owned the bikini panties? Was it Pru who killed Vance out of jealousy and rage, then went to the NYPD and tried to reinforce their suspicions of Cass? Clever Pru. If she had done something as insane as stick a knife into the heart of her lover, she would certainly manage to scheme her way out of it. Did she leave her bikini panties behind? Why? Terror and need to escape? Or did she take vicious delight in depositing an in-your-face souvenir of love gone wrong?

Cass felt suspended, out of the old reality with its familiar loves, hates, desperations, resentments and needs, surviving by the skin of her teeth. Had the killer had been waiting to wreak revenge on her? As if the killer not only hated Vance, but hated her. Perhaps hated her more.

Book publisher Dev Lal was a close friend of herself and Vance. She opened her cell-phone and called Dev.

"Cass, beautiful lady," Dev responded. "Thank God you finally got in touch. Lavinia has called repeatedly but you do not answer."

"I'll confess -- I haven't been picking up the phone," Cass said. "Mostly to avoid the press."

"Let me express my sincerest sympathy and heartbreak over Vance's death. His murder is beyond a crime. It is a desecration. He was one of the great human beings – for his charm alone he deserved a Nobel Prize. How are you really, Cass?"

"Hurt. Confused. Desperate. All those good things."

"How can I help you?"

"I heard that Vance was writing a memoir."

"Yes, and I was the editor."

"I would love to know more about it. To read it, of course, and it could even be relevant to my situation – you understand."

"I would rather we spoke about the memoir in person," Dev said. "In fact, there's an important question that you might be able to answer concerning it. On Friday we're holding a publication party for psychologist Noah Lazeroff and his new book – 'Everything You Will Ever Need to Know About Addiction.' You must know Noah – he testified in Vance's behalf."

"His testimony was crucial, but we never met. I'm not sure if I'm up for a party."

"Of course you are not in a celebratory mood. You are under a dark cloud, suspected of murdering Vance. But for that reason alone you must come. Let the world know that Lavinia and I support you totally and believe in your innocence."

"I appreciate that enormously." Touched by Dev's words, Cass walked slowly up West 11th Street. Tears streamed unbidden down her face. "But I don't know –"

"I hear tears in your voice. Wipe them from your eyes, love. Tough times are what friends are for. We will see you on Friday. It's crucial that we talk. Seven o'clock, Cass. Namaste."

7

SHE WAS DETERMINED TO MAINTAIN her daily routine, to not fall into booze and self-pity. In the morning, Cass made coffee and toasted an English muffin. She then slapped her body all over, jumped up and down three times, clapped her hands together, and sat down. This was considered "Chinese medicine." She bowed her head and meditated for ten minutes with her eyes closed. She did it every day, not yet certain if she had it right, but it felt right, helping to ward off anxiety and the alcoholic goblins.

She opened her eyes. Reality loomed. There was a killer at large who had set her up in what a noir film would define as a "frame." She loved those old movies, but she was no detective as played by Humphrey Bogart or Dick Powell. She would have to find her own way.

At age fifty Jane Endicott, the former John, had made the final transition into womanhood. Of the three Prime Timers, Jane could be counted on to be crisp, unemotional and objective. She had made blunt talk an art.

Jane answered on the first ring. "I hesitated to call you. It's a dark comedy." Jane's voice boomed. Despite all the hormones, in moments of stress she still burst forth like a baritone. "Maybe you're glad the guy's dead, whether you did or didn't kill him."

"Of course you're joking."

"I'm a librarian. I don't deal in subtext. Whoever did it, I am sorry. He was a good man, at least in my opinion. A real guy. Macho. All that bullshit. And smart, if misguided."

"Pru claims she had an affair with Vance. I'm suspected of murdering him, which you might have gleaned from the papers." Cass hesitated, not sure exactly sure what she wanted from Jane. "I'm looking for the real killer."

"I feel for you, Cass. But I don't know how I could help."

"Do you know anything about Vance and Pru – or something about Vance that I might not know?"

"Perhaps you won't like what I have to tell you."

"I'm not looking for like."

"I'll be over."

Cass lit a fire in the fireplace, and made a large pot of fresh coffee. She put out cheese and crackers, sliced a loaf of French bread, opened a tin of pate, and placed cups and dishes on the coffee table.

Jane lived four blocks away from Cass on West 16th Street in a rent-controlled studio apartment. She claimed it was all she needed. Room enough for herself, her cat, music and books. That was the charm of New York. Grandeur and low-rent charm dwelled side by side.

She arrived bringing a whoosh of cold air and a spark of electricity with her. Tall and slender, with a cap of curly black hair, pale green eyes, and a bony, hollow-cheeked face, Jane specialized in the good make-up job. She loved cosmetics and had studied with a professional to learn all the tricks of the trade. Her face was perfectly made up, and she had added dark glasses, which added a frisson of glamour.

She took off her Burberry trench coat and tossed it on the couch, then seated herself in the maroon chair by the fire. Jane beat her hands up and down on the arms of the chair. "Good to see you, Cass."

"And I'm glad to see you, as much of you as is visible. Dark glasses?"

"Oh." Jane reached up and took them off. "I forgot I was wearing them. They're new. You know, kind of like a toy." Glasses off, Jane now looked anxious and vulnerable. "I am ridiculously nervous. I'm not sure if I'm doing the right thing. I've kept my lip buttoned for so long – and what good is this information anyway. I mean, how could it be relevant now?"

"I don't know. You tell me."

"I don't want to disillusion you – to burst your balloon."

"I'm already jaded. Did you know about Pru and Vance?"

"She unloaded on me occasionally, told me more than I wanted to know. She was hell-bent to drag your ex to the altar. We all thought you were finished with him. Obviously she missed the boat." Jane moved her head around in circles, the relaxing motion, and stopped. "I think you should know that I knew Vance before I met you."

Cass poured coffee, relieved that she wasn't spilling it and handed a cup to Jane. "Tell me about it."

"I met Vance when I was still John, at P.J. Clarke's, that classic midtown bar. I'm a research librarian, but I enjoyed going in there after work and mingling with the glamorous elite. I enjoyed their boozy comradery. Vance caught my attention. He was a stunner, of course, but it was something else." Jane poured cream in her coffee. "I felt an instant kinship. He had an addiction that I shared with him."

"Oh? Gambling? You? Frugal Jane?"

"Not gambling. Sex." Jane's eyes glittered.

"Oh."

"Sex. It was all about sex. Just sex." Jane stirred her coffee, put down the spoon, leaned back and sighed. "I'm not talking about relationship sex, a dreadful term. I speak of a passion for the act all on its own. Unadulterated sex in its purest form. It's a look in the eyes, a recognition, not a flirtation, but excitement, a sense of danger, of here is another rule breaker."

"You could look at Vance and know all that?"

"Damn," Jane said. "It's one hell of a subject, isn't it, worthy of research. It's got nothing to do with lick lipping and tapping the palm with a secret signal or any of that nonsense. The true sensual adventurer is serious, committed, and as driven as any gambler. You study the face. You see the wounded look, because there is a wound. Ah, the Ancient Greeks knew, didn't they, about the Achilles heel, the great point of vulnerability." Jane paused. "By way of introducing myself, I invited Vance to an orgy in Hoboken."

"Aaaah." Cass expelled her breath.

"I was a guy inviting another guy to party. He accepted. We left P.J. Clarke's and drove over to New Jersey. We pulled up to this ranch house, exactly like every other ranch. At least it didn't have flamingos on the lawn. What boring people. They were naked and waiting for fresh blood. Their conversation settled on car routes and the latest sitcoms. Anyway, they dimmed the lights and somehow we got it on. The most interesting person there was a prostitute from Brooklyn with a lisp. We ended up giving her a ride home."

"What was I doing? I was married to Vance."

"I didn't know you then. I suppose you were building your career. I stayed in touch with Vance," Jane continued, "and we went to a few more parties. Then, while I made my serious transition, I lost contact. I had started my new life as Jane and hoped for a new lifestyle. But the itch was there. One afternoon I dropped by P.J. Clarke's. Vance was there in a grey pinstripe suit -- he knew how to wear a suit -- didn't he? He had the best ties –rich silk – gorgeous colors. I made myself known. He was excited to see me as a new person. I had become almost – chaste." Jane's voice dropped. "I was lonely."

"Vance invited me to swing. And I discovered that orgies as a woman exceeded anything I had experienced before." Jane rubbed a finger thoughtfully over her lower lip. Her voice broke. "I'm sorry. It was that meaningful to me. I was Columbus discovering America." Her eyes pleaded helplessly with Cass. "I knew that I could never turn back, regardless of the consequences." She reached out a hand and clutched Cass's hand. "I beg you to forgive me, please."

"For what?"

"For what I am about to tell you."

8

CASS DROPPED JANE'S HAND, AWARE of her own sweaty palm. She rubbed her hand against the surface of the couch, grasping for something familiar. Furniture. It doesn't let you down. Things. Stuff. She refilled Jane's coffee cup.

"Mind if I smoke?" Jane asked.

"Puff away."

"I mean smoke-smoke."

"What the hell."

Jane opened her capacious pocketbook, took out a small pipe, retrieved a tiny tin, opened it, and tamped marijuana buds into the pipe. She put the pipe to her mouth, lit it and inhaled. Jane held it a moment and released the sweet smell of cannabis into the air.

Jane offered the pipe to Cass.

"Thanks, no. I don't like to mix drinks."

Jane tamped the pipe. "This is an excellent blend. Mild. Mellow. No after-effects. That's the great thing about the new liberalization of marijuana. It's possible to identify brands. You know what you're getting. Do you indulge?"

"I'm not into it," Cass said. "Of course I tried it. Once I would try anything."

"For some of us, the need to experiment never goes away." Jane took another puff, breathed deep, and exhaled, releasing the distinctive sweet aroma of pot into the air. She leaned back and stretched her legs out in front of her. WQXR radio, turned low, switched to a lyrical Debussy prelude. "Debussy." Jane hummed. "Lovely. When I smoke I hear every note."

"Okay, Jane. You are killing me." Cass's voice shook. "We know each other well enough. I wish you would reveal whatever lurks there in your memory bag. No apologies."

"I'm trying." Jane's voice seemed to drop an octave. "When I smoke, my voice gets lower. I sound like John."

"Jane. John. I don't discriminate."

Jane took another hit on her pipe. "So let us begin. Stop me anywhere you want. Ask me questions. Push me to the limit, up against the wall. I don't want to hurt you. I don't want to hit you with more than you can take."

"I'm a journalist. There's nothing that I like better than a lurid tale. Spill your guts. I want to know about Vance's secret world. His milieu, hidden from me. How could I be married to a man and adore him and only be aware of half of his life, or a third."

"It must hurt like hell. Do you know how hard it was for me to admit when I was John, that there was another person Jane and that my true life was hidden while I brushed my teeth and pretended to be a functional human being." Jane released a stream of smoke. "There are so many realities."

"Suppose you give me a safe word, and when I can't take your revelations and want you to pause, I will say that word. And you stop for a moment and let me catch my breath, and then keep going. If there are any questions, I will ask them later."

"How about yellow roses?"

"Yellow roses," Cass repeated.

"I developed this huge crush on Vance." Jane rested her pipe in a dish on the table. "To me he was the epitome of everything masculine and wonderful. Sex-wise, Vance would have nothing to do with me. But I found that going to these parties or orgies or whatever you want to call them, I discovered a new side of my erotic proclivities. I liked to watch. In fact, I got off more on watching other people make love than doing it myself, or pleasuring myself along with them, like looking at a live pornographic film.

"And the one I loved to watch the most, in fact needed to watch, was your own husband Vance. Watching him thrust his hard cock straight into some chick, with a stamina that would never stop until he had her screaming for more. That got me going – I can't tell you."

"Yellow roses." Think like a journalist, Cass told herself. It's a story. She nodded to Jane, who relit her pipe.

"Vance was the star, regardless of the other men in the room. I needed to see him in action. Not wanted, needed. I would go home afterwards and pleasure myself like never before. Of course, I had my own encounters. Guys like me. Yes, they do. But I saw that I was losing Vance. At one of our women's gatherings, you had mentioned that someone had seen Vance having a drink with a red-haired sex vampire from his office. You asked Vance and he dismissed it as business. Her name stuck unpleasantly in my head, Miranda Nightingale. We all told you not to worry – this was trivial pursuit. After all, meeting guys for drinks was part of your work as a journalist. Wasn't Vance entitled? You seemed content to brush it away. I thought – why not?

"I made it my business to learn everything about Miranda Nightingale that I could. As a research librarian, such pursuits come naturally to me. I discovered that she was brilliant and driven. Determined to go from obscurity to the top. A total libertarian without a sexual scruple to call her own.

"I decided to get to know Miranda. I found the gym she used and joined that. I got on her schedule and chatted with her while we rode our stationary bikes. When I mentioned the name of Vance Elliott Cooper, she lit up. I invited her to an orgy. She was game. I also invited Vance.

"Miranda was unstoppable. She took to swinging like a fish takes to water. She went after Vance with a passion. He tried to push her away but she was like a sexual acrobat who seduces with her pyrotechnics. Watching them together was like viewing a ballet performance, a dance. They were on fire."

"Yellow roses." Breathe, Cass told herself. Breathe.

"And that's it. I was the catalyst. I got them going. Meanwhile I came to your house and made nice. I told myself I wasn't hurting you, that you were a different part of his life. When they locked him up, I hurt for him. I had thrown Miranda in his path. She was determined to get him for keeps, and when he would not leave you, she blew the whistle on him and his Ponzi scheme."

"Yellow roses," Cass said. "Yellow roses. How could you bring this woman into your life – into my life?"

"She was only an instrument for me to get close to Vance, your husband. Is that sick? Selfish? Rotten? When I became a woman, I experienced huge emotional changes. I became ruthless about guys. Vance didn't want me but I needed to be close to him in any way I could. Vance was searching for a new reality. I offered him orgies."

"I should hate you, but I sit here filling up your coffee cup and listening to your revelations, like group sex was the holy grail for Vance. Am I supposed to find this sex stuff useful?"

"Don't dismiss it. It has tentacles. It could matter." Jane recrossed her legs and leaned towards the fire. "I do love a fire, particularly in Manhattan. I never got close to Vance sexually but we talked."

"What did you discuss?"

"We talked about life. Identity. We talked about time. What is time? Just another artificial measure. Sixty seconds can be an intense, never-forgotten eternity."

"The oneness and the allness. Next thing you will be sitting on my floor and chanting om, and telling me to be mindful. When did you become so philosophical, Jane?"

"When? Perhaps in the womb. I grieve for Vance. He never got to take the trip."

"To where?"

"To his new reality." The room reeked of marijuana. "As we speak, I'm feeling high. Mellow now."

Cass whiffed the marijuana and wished she had a glass of Scotch in her hand. "He talked with you, shared feelings. I thought that Vance and I had years ahead of us –"

"I feel your pain." Jane nodded. "When I walked in I believed you had killed the guy. Now – I'm not so sure."

"Tell me about Miranda."

"She's not a big talker. She goes to a party, gets a drink, looks around and makes a plan. She's calculating, and guarded. If you ask her for the time of day, she won't tell you if it could give you some kind of an advantage."

"She sounds adorable."

"Her big interests are money and sex – and clothes. She grew up poor in Scranton, Pennsylvania, the youngest of seven kids, the smart one who everybody hated. She wore her sisters cheap castoffs and old underwear. When she won a full scholarship to MIT, she worked as a waitress to buy her college wardrobe. It consisted of jeans and panties in every color of the rainbow. She didn't need a bra. She's flat-chested. Later she spent a fortune on clothes in Bergdorf Goodman. She had a personal shopper."

"Where is she now?"

"She seems to have disappeared off the face of the earth. At least New York City. I did hear a rumor that she had some kind of serious breakdown."

"Just out of curiosity, where were you the night and morning of the murder?"

Jane tapped her pipe to empty the ashes into a saucer. "I spent the evening at a lecture on the historical novel at the Jefferson Market Library and went for a run at 6 A.M. the following morning. What interest would I have in killing Vance? I thought he was swell, really swell."

9

CASS MOVED BACK INTO HER office, put her feet up and pondered Jane's con-fessional bombshell. She felt like she should test her body for cuts and broken bones. But no, she remained intact. Despite the sex revelations, her heart did not feel crushed. Perhaps she no longer had a heart. She had to believe that what she and Vance shared was special and unique to them. The rest would remain in mystery, the life of a man she did not know – the other Vance.

Any one of the women -- Pru, Miranda, or Jane - - could have killed Vance for a variety of motives. Love and hate were close. Desperate desire could destroy, as well as madness. According to Jane, Miranda had a serious breakdown. Pru acted like someone on the verge of a nervous collapse. Jane, who appeared so rational, could have found time before her morning run to drive a dagger into Vance's heart. All three were slender enough to fit into the bikini panties found on the floor.

Cass dressed in her best status symbols: the black Missoni pants suit, gold earrings from master Greek jeweler Lalaounis, her red Chanel coat, and Saint Laurent dark glasses. She packed up her Valentino handbag, a gift from Vance, and took the elevator downstairs where doorman Jose hailed a cab for her.

Of all the Fifth Avenue stores, Bergdorf Goodman reigned as the top shopping experience for women. In TV's Sex and the City, it was the store of choice of clothes horse Carrie Bradshaw. Cass entered the store and breathed in a blend of expensive leather, satin and silk, the perfumed DNA of the clientele. Sensual. Rich. The special smell of luxury.

Cass rode the elevator to the Third Floor, and stepped into a phantasmagoria of lacy erotica. Cass thought of her aunt, Thea Heriklia, who would send her on a mission to find "snuggies" for her, stretchy pants that covered the thighs. Despite central heating, Thea Heriklia still recalled the chill of the stone house in Lemnos, Greece, and her girlhood. There was no place for snuggies in this world. Glass cases were filled with lacy thongs, displayed like Tiffany jewels. Plaster mannequins posed in bras, garter-belts and thongs created to be unveiled in super-wealthy boudoirs.

A young woman in a small black dress approached her. Heavy black mascara enhanced large blue eyes. "Can I help you with something today?" she trilled.

"I hope so." Cass smiled. "I'm looking for a gift for a niece –bikini panties. She specifically asked for black lace embroidered with red roses. Do you have anything like that? Size 2?"

A few minutes later, she returned. "These might interest you." She placed three pairs of what appeared to be doll-sized garments on the counter. A black lace bikini panty adorned with small black bows, a tiny blue lace and satin panty, and a black lace bikini panty adorned with rhinestone glitter.

"Not quite what she asked for." Cass paused thoughtfully. "Of course they are elegant. Do you have the blue model in size 6? I think I might like them for myself."

"Let me check." She returned in a minute with the blue panty in hand, and held them up for Cass's inspection. "They are sophisticated. And they are on sale, reduced to $110 from $125."

"I'll take them." Cass handed her an American Express Gold Credit Card.

"Perfect." She took Cass's credit card and returned a few minutes later with a small Bergdorf's bag and Cass's card.

Cass signed and tucked her credit card back in her wallet. She took the bag. "I have an associate, Miranda Nightingale, who does all of her shopping at Bergdorf's. Do you know her, perhaps?"

"Miranda Nightingale? No. That's certainly a name I would remember."

"She uses a personal shopper here and seems happy with her. Would it be possible to talk with her? I am interested in setting up an account with a personal shopper. I would particularly like to use her."

The young woman appraised Cass. "Let me ask my supervisor." Ten minutes later she was back. "Miranda Nightingale is registered with Regina, who happens to be here today. I will see if she's available. Your name?"

"Cassandra Cooper."

After a brief call, she directed Cass to go to the Fifth Floor and the office of Regina Diamond. "Room 508. You get off the elevator and you can't miss it."

"Thank you so much." Cass headed for the elevator, gratified that the young woman did not recognize her name as someone in the news. The door to Room 508 was open.

Regina Diamond stood up imperiously behind a huge silver desk that glowed against a setting of black walls. Her office looked like a box whose sole purpose was to display the owner. Her piled-up hair, emulating a pompadour of years past, made her appear even taller. Although her hair was white, it framed a relatively young, fine-featured, unlined face. Black eyebrows formed parenthesis for black eyes. Her slim body showed off an exquisite maroon suit, her only adornment a large gold cobra-shaped pin that sparkled with diamonds and rubies. Her five inch heels made her appear even taller.

Cass approached. "Thank you for seeing me on such short notice."

"Please sit down, Mrs. Cooper." She gestured to a low chair a few feet from her desk. She then sat down herself. Her melodic voice, tinged with some indefinable foreign accent, added to her exotic persona. "We need not fuss. If you were recommended to me by Miranda Nightingale, I am delighted to meet you. I would like to be in touch with Miranda again. You must give me her contact information before you leave."

"Actually my introduction to Miranda was indirect, through a close friend of hers, Jane Endicott."

"Jane Endicott." Regina licked her full red mouth. "Dear Jane. She has no taste whatsoever, but occasionally advises Miranda."

"Have you known them long?"

"Long enough." Her tone hardened. She swiveled back and forth, looking down at Cass. "I'm not here to fill you in on Bergdorf clients. Do you really need a personal shopper? From what I have read about you, you could be convicted of your husband's murder and your wardrobe will be provided for you."

"I'm not at liberty to discuss my case."

"For the price of a pair of panties, you expect to dig up the dirt on Miranda."

"For such an elegant lady, you do seem to want to go to the dark side. I'm not looking for dirt. I am genuinely seeking a shopper. Look at yourself. You have more than good taste. You have style. I was told that Miranda loved clothes and you helped her find the best."

"Clothes! She would spend and spend, and then spend more. She had turned one room in her apartment into a dressing room. She insisted that I come up to see it. She brought me into this room filled with racks and racks of garments, waved her arms and wept. 'Look,' she said. 'All this and I have nothing to wear!' She was never satisfied. And no matter what she wore, she did not look properly put together. She did not have the knack.

"Then she fell in love. She wanted to look like wife material. She went from extravagant to conservative. That did not work either. I believe he destroyed her, mentally and emotionally. Why would you, of all people, be seeking her now? She wrecked your marriage. You are suspected of murdering the man she loved. The notorious Vance Cooper. The hot guy. Those are the worst men to be involved with – unless your main interest in life is a hot fuck."

"Please." Cass started to get up and sat back down again.

"I love my job -- to take a woman who has no image, who looks like a pudding -- and give her a look. I don't think you need my help. I have done it for politicians and movie stars. Why seek Miranda now?"

"Because she gives me nightmares. Why did you agree to see me?"

"I wanted to meet the woman who killed the hot guy."

"Did I disappoint you?"

"Not at all. You wear your Chanel and Valentino well. They provide excellent camouflage. Most women are criminals at heart. You picked the right victim."

Cass walked out into blasting sunlight and swarming crowds, horns beeping, kids yelling, the overheated atmosphere of Manhattan at mid-day, a time of deals being made in over-priced restaurants, and affairs indulged in in luxurious hotels. There were worse ways to spend lunch, Cass thought, yearning for a drink. Instead she walked one block over to Madison Avenue and kept walking until she found a coffee shop. She sat at a small table, ordered coffee and tuna-fish on whole wheat toast with lettuce, her go-to lunch.

She could not imagine Jane Endicott advising anyone on clothes. Not because Jane had atrocious taste. But because she billed herself as an intellectual above such frivolous pursuits as fashion. Yet she had offered her views on Miranda's clothes choices. So the two were chummy after all. If Jane or Regina Diamond had any clue about Miranda's location, they were keeping it to themselves.

Cass walked up Madison Avenue, occasionally stopping to look in one of the windows at a fanciful display, enjoying the amazing variety and imaginative designs. This was work, but she enjoyed work. She had early defined herself as a Greek peasant who loved tilling the soil, but in her case, digging not for seedlings but for a story. She stopped by two high-end shops that sold lingerie and did not find black lace panties with embroidered roses.

The third and last shop on her list was Josephina's. Instead of lingerie, the windows displayed elegant lace blouses. Cass pressed a bell and was buzzed in.

A small woman in a bright yellow knit dress, with a halo of teased blond curls, round cheeks with rouge circles, a small turned up nose and rosebud mouth outlined in pink, most resembled a bright, chirping bird. She seemed to emanate cheer. A pencil was stuck behind her ear. She placed her small hands, the nails glowing with gold polish, on the counter.

"Good afternoon, Madame. How can I help you today?"

"I'm looking for a pair of bikini panties for a teenage niece. She specifically asked for black lace with red embroidered roses. Size 2."

The woman rubbed her small hands together, then lifted the gold-rimmed glasses that hung in a chain around her neck and fixed them on her nose. "I am telling you, just between you and me, that it's the rare young woman who can afford these garments. Some save. They cut corners because they know value." She bustled behind the counter, opened a drawer and took out several pairs of panties. "You asked for the small size."

The woman appraised Cass and winked. "We also have them in a larger size. But come. Take a look at these. Feel, but delicately. You must handwash the garments." She placed several pairs of panties on the counter. "They are silk."

Cass looked at the bikini panties. They were all black lace, but none were embroidered with red roses as the pair she had seen tossed on the floor in Donaldson's house. "I wonder – why does a woman crave silk lingerie?"

"It's a turn-on, darling. Have you ever tried it? You're obviously a woman who appreciates the better things. I doubt if you would insult your body or your lovers with cotton panties." The woman took a deep breath and smiled. "Silk lingerie is its own aphrodisiac for the wearer. She feels precious, sensual, valuable, desirable."

Cass gently touched the middle garment, black lace with tiny black velvet bows. "You are the poet of panties. How do you know so much?"

"Through study. I am fascinated by these garments. I have researched them through the ages. I talk to women, and to men. They tell me things."

"It's wonderful to meet a specialist, a person with in-depth knowledge and imagination."

"I design all the garments myself. You will not find duplicates anyplace."

"It's a lovely shop. I would like to walk around."

"By all means," Josephina said.

Cass strolled through the shop with its glass cases and photographs of exotic locales, stopping occasionally for a second look. She strolled to the back of the store.

"That section won't interest you," Josephina called out. "Those are garments I'm giving away to a charity auction."

Cass stopped in front of a glass case. It sat in the dark. She looked closer at the black panties embroidered with tiny red roses. "But these are exactly what I'm looking for."

"There is only one other pair like them in existence. I hate to part with them. I design everything in the store, and these are special. They were hand-embroidered by nuns in a convent in Tibet. They are the finest silk."

"Who owns the other pair?"

"Not a teenager, but a woman about your age. I didn't think they really suited her – the panties are so feminine, better for an ingenue. This woman seemed all business, and in a hurry. Last Thursday. I was almost tempted not to sell them to her. I take it all quite personally."

"That's beautiful," Cass said. "You are not just selling merchandise."

"Indeed. I am selling something more intangible. I am selling an accessory for desire. I believe in garments and their purpose. I am certain that nuns pray better in their habits, and can-can girls get inspiration from their swirly skirts.

"I designed the panties for twins. A gentleman ordered them. But then the twins would have nothing more to do with him, and I had this pair of delicious panties on my hands. I was hoping the twins would make up with him but he said no, it was never going to happen.

"This bone-thin creature came in. She wore a big hat and dark glasses, strictly pseudo Hollywood. I could not see her face. The glasses were enormous, and the hat. The little of her face that I could see was pale and without make-up. I objected to her foreign intrigue performance. I had put the pair on display. She insisted on buying. I raised the price. She was indifferent to the cost, which I had escalated to $200 for a pair of bikini panties. Even I, the designer, found the price ludicrous. She wanted them. She told me 'I like good things and money is no object.'"

"Do you remember her name?"

"She refused to give me her name. She paid with cash and ran out the door."

"When?"

"Exactly five days ago. In the afternoon."

"This woman, how did she sound?"

"Husky, strange. As soon as I met her, I wanted her to disappear."

"I would like to buy the pair," Cass said. "What is the price?"

"I was not going to sell them," Josephina said, "But for you, yes. I know you will treasure them. I am giving you a special price of one hundred dollars."

"I appreciate your artistry, Josephina." Cass handed Josephina her credit card.

Josephina returned swiftly with the card and the panties in a black bag with the Josephina logo. "Stay well, my friend. I recognized your name on the card. God bless and keep you. Have courage. You will win."

10

CASS WRIGGLED INTO THE NEW blue bikini panties from Bergdorf, topped them with her best black silk pants, added her favorite jacket, and she was ready for what had to be a sensational party. Because that's the only kind of party that Liv and Dev Lal gave. Reluctant about facing a crowd in the new guise of the notorious Cass Cooper, she chose her outfit as if selecting armor. She wanted to look smart rather than seductive. She decided to skip the perfume. Her red heels had a closed toe. She checked herself in the mirror, grabbed her coat and bag, and took the elevator down. Doorman Jose hailed a taxi and she was on her way to Sutton Place and the home of Dev and Lavinia Lal.

Visiting the Lal home was like stepping into a technicolor musical, and that night was no exception. Their vast apartment on East 55th Street overlooking the East River had once been owned by a legendary film star, who had transposed her glamorous Hollywood aura to New York. Dev and Liv had upped the charm. Their apartment glowed with art and color that echoed the palaces of Mumbai, along with brilliant crafts from the streets of India. Raised in a super-wealthy upper-caste family, Dev said that "life begins in the streets. Desire. Need. Desperation. Raw emotion."

Dev greeted Cass and personally escorted her through the crowd. His voice dropped to a whisper. "Nothing goes right. The samosas were burned. We have a new Norwegian gal in the kitchen and what does she know about Indian food? Zero. The Sixty Minutes producer cancelled. He had been making noises about devoting an entire program to Noah's book. But I'm talking too much." Dev stood back and appraised Cass. "You are beautiful tonight. Appreciate yourself. Thank your face for being so lovely. Good. You're not frowning. You must not do that. Even if you feel like shit, don't let it show. Don't give the killers satisfaction."

"I am supposed to be the killer."

"We need to talk."

"How about now?"

"Not here. A private talk. Later. It's important. Now where is Noah Lazeroff? I expected him about half an hour ago –" He smiled. The smile grew broader, and then the high beams turned on. He stepped towards a tall man with dark hair and eyes and a real chin. Craggy. She liked the look. Intellectual but not a bore. A man who could laugh. A black shirt. A colorful tie. Tailored, well-fitted tweed jacket. Grey slacks.

Dev moved towards him. "Noah, you bastard. In a few minutes, I will introduce you, and you can say a few words. No speeches. This is a party. Save the talk for the media interviews. The world needs your book. People are looking for salvation from their addictions. We are all addicts. We live in a troubled society."

Noah put his arm around Dev's shoulders. "You and I – we'll save the world, Dev."

"And why not? Once I worried about stepping on an ant. I was taught to harm no living thing. Now I am concerned with bloody murder, a subject that does not appeal to my literary sensibility. The horror. But come, no grim talk." Even standing still, Dev appeared to exude energy in action. He turned to Cass. "Cass Cooper, meet Noah Lazeroff, our star."

Cass was aware of Noah's appraising her. In the midst of tragedy, a man's appreciative glance still mattered. She was glad she had worn the red shoes, slim black pants, and jacket that her friends and enemies coveted. She had come to think of it as the magic jacket. It was black, covered with red and gold flowers. It always looked good and fit all occasions.

Before Noah and Cass had even exchanged greetings, Dev grabbed Noah's arm. "If you will excuse us, Cass, I'm going to spirit Noah off and introduce him to the crowd."

Time to plunge into the fray. Cass often congratulated herself for being good at working the room, finding her way in a party of strangers. She had made a rule for herself. Talk to at least three people to gain entry inside the social loop. It never failed her. Tonight was special. Tonight she was looking for anyone who could literally give her a clue. She found a drink at the bar, Perrier and lime, and appraised the scene.

Waiters circulated through the crowd of talented, controversial, and news-making party goers. To rate an invitation to a Lal party, a person need not be successful. It was more important to have a point of view. Difficult won over nice. Bland proved unacceptable. More than one friendship had ended at a Lal party, and a romance had begun.

Regina Diamond, earlier met at Bergdorf Goodman, stood by the window, framed by a sparkling bridge and full moon, wearing something long, draped and silver.

Cass approached Regina. "So we meet again," Regina said, giving Cass the up and down. "That jacket is magnificent. It becomes you."

"Thank you, Regina. That is a compliment, coming from you. Nice to see you in completely different circumstances. And what brings you here tonight?"

"What brings most people to a party?" Regina's eyes snapped. "The dream of making a connection that will change one's life. The desire to show off. To dress up. To be noticed. That is a ridiculous question, worthy only of a schoolgirl."

"Forgive my curiosity," Cass said. "You look exquisite, like a silver goddess in that dress."

"We try." Regina batted silvery eyelashes. "This was my husband's favorite dress. He had it designed for me in Paris. When I wear it, I think of him. Your late husband lost my husband's fortune for him. My husband was destroyed. He hung himself. He chose to do it from the shower in our bathroom." Regina's eyes were black in her silvery pale face. "I still have not pushed that image from my mind. It haunts me daily."

"I am sorry," Cass responded, aware now of the source of Regina's earlier hostility.

"Not as sorry as I am." Regina pointedly turned her back to Cass to gaze out on the East River.

Cass stood and took deep breaths. There were thousands out there whose tragic stories she had not heard. People with real motives for plunging a knife in Vance's heart.

Dev had returned to Cass. "My God, what happened? You look as if someone punched you." He linked his arm with Cass's. "Come." His voice was heavy with urgency. "A new guest has arrived. Detective Robert Adams. I actually invited him. I didn't expect him to come. He claims he's only here to socialize. He's strolling around in his baggy blazer, a real boon for the news hounds."

"How did he know I would be here?"

"He did not know. He came to study me in my natural habitat."

Dev's private lair overflowed with books that packed shelves and spilled over into piles on the floor. The comfortable literary cave glowed with its deep red paisley covered couch, bright silk pillows, dark green walls, mirrors and art. Cass and Dev sat in two chairs overlooking the East River, a phantasmagoria of lights, bridges and boats gliding by.

"I watch the boats move. Where are they going? Where am I going? I ask myself that question at least several times a day." Dev held his hand up. "No, do not protest that I have arrived. You are too smart for that kind of cliché."

"Where do you want to go? That is the question."

"Aah, now you are getting profound." He checked his watch. "This was not a good idea. We had better get back to the party." He started to stand up.

"Please don't run away, Dev. I am desperate to talk with you, particularly about Vance's memoir. And you had a question for me."

"This is it." Dev ran his fingers through his thick salt and pepper hair. "Do you have a copy of Vance's manuscript?"

"Unfortunately, no. I was totally unaware of Vance's writing a memoir until two nights ago. I am desperate to read it, not only because Vance wrote it, but it could be helpful to me. Is Detective Adams aware of the manuscript?"

"Totally. Vance wrote it, but destroyed the manuscript before myself or anybody else had a chance to read it. When he was writing it, it was all hush-hush. He wanted it that way."

Cass sat back. "Why would I have a copy?"

"Let me explain . While in Balaban, he had been working on the book. I was excited about publishing it. He was a great fan of the classics, and he was modeling it on the Confessions of Rousseau, the philosopher, and St. Augustine's tell-all. Vance would divulge all, and then some, with a flourish. He let me read the first chapter. I found it totally disarming. It displayed narrative brilliance. I yearned to read on.

"He would not permit me to see any other part of the book until he could present me with a finished manuscript. I went to meet him when he left Balaban. I had always been intrigued by the scenes in films when the ex-prisoner is finally given his freedom. I was disappointed to see him holding a small bag, obviously not large enough to hold a manuscript. He told me that he had given the manuscript to Donaldson to bring to the East 63rd Street house, where it would be safe and secure.

"I dropped him off at East 63rd Street but did not go inside. He went in, then came out and told me that Donaldson had put the manuscript in a safe in his house and taken off for Vermont. Donaldson had left a note for Vance. He would have to call Donaldson to get the combination to open the safe, and when he had it he would call me."

"But Donaldson told me he was there to greet Vance."

"And he spoke truth. I have talked with Donaldson." Dev got up and paced. "I had a series of meetings after I left Vance, and a dinner with a too-convivial author. Our dinner party lasted late into the night. We closed down the bars. At this point, I was wide awake, remarkably sober, and decided to visit Vance. I also had a present for him. I came back here to pick up the gift and then went to Donaldson's. I rang the bell. It was about 4 A.M., an outrageous hour for visiting but these were unusual circumstances.

"I gave Vance the antique Indian knife. He had admired a similar knife. I had searched for one to replicate it. He put the knife down on the table. He said that he was not worthy of this magnificent gift. He told me that there was no manuscript. I found this hard to digest, since he had spoken about the book with such enthusiasm.

"'I could not bring myself to tell you,' he said. 'I put everything in the book. Too much. Publishing it would be dangerous. I destroyed the manuscript.' He drew himself up and threw his shoulders back like a soldier preparing for battle.

"I pointed out to him that we could deal with the worrisome passages. Delete them and leave his story intact. 'You must have a copy, on your computer or whatever.'"

"'I have destroyed all copies and notes about the manuscript and just to be sure I wrecked the computer,' he said.

"I was speechless, and exhausted. Perhaps he had another book in him, I thought, but this was no time to propose such an idea. I went home. I woke up to learn that Vance Cooper was dead."

"Exactly time did you arrive that night?"

"4:15 A.M. I checked my watch. I came right on your heels. I saw you leaving, a woman in spike heels hurrying for a taxi, carrying a large pocketbook. I thought the manuscript might be in that bag. I marveled that you could stay erect in those spindly shoes. I rang the bell and Vance came down in jeans and an open shirt, as if he had dressed hastily."

"But the woman you saw was not me. I left at 3 A.M. "

"Oh. Then it was another woman. Sorry."

"Go on, please."

"I ran down the stairs, anxious to get away from Vance. I felt dreadfully let down and disillusioned. I was counting on Vance's book to be a best-seller. And it would be his redemption, telling the world how he had gotten into the Ponzi mess, his apologia. I did not tell him about my company going down the tubes because of other authors I had gambled on. Fine, brilliant writers who did not sell. And how he lost me a ton with his Ponzi games. No. That is not my style. I knew Vance's book would sell. The one chapter that I read proved that he could write. He had a voice, style, and a story to tell."

"Did you hear anything? Other people in the wings? It's a big house."

"I left swiftly, and I heard nothing." Dev sighed. "Suppose the woman I saw did have the manuscript, took it and read it and didn't like what she read and returned and killed Vance. It's a possibility." Dev continued pacing. "Somebody arrived between 4:30 when you left, and 7 A.M. when I returned."

"Perhaps more than one person. Unless they were already in the house and quietly waiting to strike."

"What are we talking about? I am no Sherlock Holmes. Nor are you. Two days ago, Detective Adams contacted me. He had traced the dagger back to me. And why would I want to kill Vance, I asked Adams. Don't I need a motive? Adams pointed out that I'm known for my occasional rages, as well as my lavish lifestyle. Book publishing is a mercurial business and, yes, Lal Publishing does happen to be in a bit of a bind. I was counting on Vance, but killing him would not produce a manuscript."

Dev smoothed his hair down and smiled wearily. "If we had Vance's manuscript, what a treasure that would be. We would discover him all over again. Even if I never made a dime on that book, I would hold it close to my heart."

11

Lavinia Lal burst into Dev's private lair, looking like a British enchantress. Slender and lovely, with a cap of golden hair, she wore a shocking pink satin gown with a huge bow at the waist and a slit skirt that showed off her exceptional legs. During her salad days in London, Liv had made a ton of pocket money by working as a leg model, something that her father the Viscount frowned on, and her mother found amusing. An Oxford graduate, Liv had also studied ballet seriously, and like her husband was the picture of grace. Together, they moved like two dancers. Photographers adored them, and their images frequently popped up in the media.

Liv had won renown for her magazine, Prima, that she founded after top jobs at Vogue and Vanity Fair. Her magazine was literate, contemporary, and offered the best of fashion and personalities. "People's main interest is other people," Liv would say. "That's the premise of People magazine, and it works."

"Hello, darling Cass." Liv's British accent floated into the room like a breath of spring air. She opened her arms wide to Dev. "Sweets. A hug. It's been so long. I've missed you."

Dev hugged his wife. "Tonight you look like a delicious bonbon. And you smell divine. Could that be Joy perfume teasing my nostrils?"

"Definitely. You have a good nose. You could be a perfume tester, or a wine tester, but tonight you are the host, and you are missing the party. I suppose you and Cass have been up here hashing over murder, a terrible idea." Liv turned to Cass. "And Cass, my love, you wouldn't be in this pickle if you had listened to me. Do you remember how I congratulated you on divorcing Vance?"

"How could I forget?" Liv had taken her to lunch and spent two hours pointing out to the still-doubting Cass that she had done the right thing.

"And didn't I tell you that not under any circumstances were you to speak to him again? That he would get out of prison and call you and be utterly charming – because that was Vance – and you would not resist and you would be right back where you started. And I was right. But I am sorry, really sorry." She reached out to press Cass's hand. "Can I do anything to help?"

"Your friendship helps everything, Liv, and your beautiful party. Nobody gives a party like you."

"Then come, Cass. You too, Dev. Let's not miss the occasion."

They walked back into the party, now peaking into a crescendo of laughter and clinking glasses. A famous musician had found the piano and was playing a new composition that rippled through the crowd. Deals were instigated. A young woman in purple velvet sat in a red chair and wept, as a short, plump man hovered over her. Regina remained in her post by the window, backed by the moon and glittering bridge.

"Reg knows how to frame herself, doesn't she?" Liv commented. "Of course you've met the famous Regina Diamond. She was once *the* top model and has never forgotten it."

"We spoke," Cass said. "I found what she said disturbing."

"About Vance and her husband? Regina's a bit mad. She quit modeling to devote herself to her super-wealthy husband. She worshipped him, but in truth he was both unfaithful to her and unstable. When he lost his fortune – let's face it he was greedy and should have known better, he fell apart. He hung himself from the shower. Can you imagine? Reg was reduced to living in a two bedroom apartment on Sutton Place, which she considers beneath herself but most people would die for. She converted the second bedroom to a shrine for the late husband, the repository of his ashes as well as photos, memorabilia, and even clothes. If she invites you for tea or cocktails, sooner or later she drags you into the Pierre room. So unnecessary! Do not trouble yourself about Regina. Look after yourself, and enjoy the party."

Liv brought Cass over to a small group. She introduced her to three British actors, two men and a woman, renowned on the British comedy stage who were in New York for a special British show of Saturday Night Live. Cass enjoyed talking with them. They knew nothing about her or Vance, or murder. For several minutes she totally forgot about everything that had been weighing her down. Occasionally she glanced over at Noah Lazeroff, but he was constantly surrounded by people.

Cass excused herself from the group, telling them honestly what a delight it had been to talk with them, and she looked forward to their SNL performance. She plunged into the fray, because that was the fun of a party. But did she deserve to have fun? If she were living this moment Greek-style, she would be home, dressed completely in black. If she were a widow, she would wear that black for a lifetime. As she turned, she directly faced Detective Adams, his face lightly covered with perspiration. He touched a handkerchief to his brow.

"Are you enjoying the party?" Cass asked.

"Mostly definitely. Yourself?"

"I do love a party, although I would not define myself as a party animal."

"I have so little leisure, that when I do have time I tend to seek other pursuits."

"Like?"

" I enjoy the opera. In fact, when we travel my wife and I make it a point to go to cities where we can indulge in an opera performance. Milan. Sydney.

Peking. Opera can take you around the world. It makes tragedy beautiful. It touches my soul and takes me away from the fascinating but difficult life of the police detective."

"Tonight you appear to be working overtime."

"On the contrary, my evening's quite social."

"Even though Dev Lal has joined your list of suspects."

"Tonight I have other pursuits." Adams smiled at Cass and pushed back his wispy hair. "Isn't the pianist wonderful?"

"He weaves a spell, doesn't he?" Cass's glass of Perrier was empty. "And what might your other pursuits be?"

"That is classified." Adam's face turned pinker and wetter. He mopped and turned away to immediately be taken up by a tall, bearded sociologist. "Ah, Doctor Roscoe…"

Cass returned to the bar. Her mouth was dry. She craved a Scotch. She asked for a Coke with lime. She took her drink and walked to find Donaldson standing against a dark green wall. Running into him was no surprise. He was a Lal author. He had written one book for Lal Publishing, *Mind of the Murderer*, and Dev had been after him to write a follow-up.

Donaldson detached himself and moved towards her. He looked particularly attractive, dressed in a navy blazer with yellow silk ascot and grey pants, a slightly more colorful Donaldson than the man she had known.

"You look wonderful," Cass said. "I hope you're enjoying the evening. How could you not in such a beautiful place."

"Beautiful place. Beautiful people," Donaldson responded. "It is a rare experience. But come. I must talk with you." He edged her towards the wall.

"Tonight everyone must talk with me," Cass said. "Why is that? Why am I suddenly so in demand?"

Donaldson steered her down and around the corner away from the crowd. "Would you like a drink? Of course not, you don't drink. I've been trying to get in touch with you but you seem to be constantly out. Or I'm calling at the wrong time. We have a problem – or perhaps I should say that I have a problem."

"Go on," Cass said.

"I have been getting calls from a man. He says that Vance wrote a book that libeled him. He wants to see the manuscript. I told him that I was unaware of the book. This low-life was so insistent. He said, well you were his lawyer, so wouldn't you know about it before anyone? Didn't you read it? I said I knew nothing. What do you know about it?"

"That he wrote a memoir and destroyed it. He was uncomfortable about some of the information he included in it. Dev was going to publish it. But it's gone. It was a huge disappointment to Dev."

"All copies?" Donaldson asked.

"All," Cass said.

"Damned." Donaldson's hands curled into fists. "It's a damned shame. His death was a tragedy. Now this." His hands opened and hung helplessly at his sides. "Are you sure every copy has been destroyed?" Donaldson asked peevishly. "Even if something has been erased, one can retrieve it from the computer."

"According to Dev, Vance destroyed the computer. Smashed it and threw it into the junk heap. Finito. Done. Gone."

"I suppose it's for the best," Donaldson said. "But how about his letters to you? Didn't he discuss what he was writing about?"

"I burned the letters, unread."

"Women!" Donaldson leaned back against the wall and laughed. "God help every would-be Romeo pouring his heart out in love letters."

"It's good to see you laugh," Cass said.

"I'll cop to it. I am a serious person." Donaldson straightened his cravat. "I have never been amusing, and I finally gave up trying. To thine own self be true. That is my credo."

12

CASS HAD NOT SLEPT WELL. When the phone rang at 8 A.M., she woke with a start. Far from gracious, Detective Adams issued a blunt directive to her. "Be here at the Precinct House at 10 A.M. today." Cass's head was still buzzing from the party the night before. What did Adams want to talk about? Had his interest been piqued by Vance's vanished manuscript? Or would he ask her intrusive questions about Dev Lal? If so, she would take the Fifth. She had nothing but positive views about Dev and Liv, but even those could sound distorted under a police expert's interrogation.

Once again Cass sat across from Adams at a small table, with McShane a few feet away. Cass pulled her coat tighter around her in the cold room. "I don't imagine that you invited me here to discuss the opera," Cass said.

Adams rubbed his hands together, and then slapped his thighs. "Not at all. Although a dramatist's interest might be piqued by this case. I ask myself – was the murder scene the setting for an orgy, a tribunal, a trial?" Adams finally had a change of wardrobe, from the baggy grey suit to a similarly shapeless brown suit. A striped green shirt. A brown tie. For him, it was almost dress-up. "At Vance's actual trial in court, the sentence was lenient. There was a public outcry. How did this bum get away with it? People guilty of a similar crime are put away for life."

"Vance was the golden boy, until he wasn't."

Despite the cold room, Adam's face burst out in perspiration. He took a large white handkerchief out of his pocket, mopped his forehead and put it back. "I'm taking some allergy pills that make me sweat. Also this case does it to me. Are you with me, Cass?"

"I don't know where you're going." Cass smelled mustard and onions, echoic of somebody's late, bought off a corner wagon breakfast. "I've never encountered a police detective before – despite all the stories I've covered -- except on TV and film, where they are usually terse and tell you nothing until the last scene. You, on the other hand, are voluble and throw me these teasers, as if you want to shake me out of complacency. I might appear calm, but it's strictly a façade. Inside I am jello."

"It's about the night -- or morning – of Vance Cooper's murder. You did not meet Vance until midnight. What were you doing earlier in the evening?"

"I met with three other women – close friends --at my apartment."

"Wouldn't you under normal circumstances be getting ready for this all-important date?"

"The meeting with the women had been planned. I did not want to shift it to another time. I did not want to tell them that I was meeting Vance that night. I had given them the impression that I was totally finished with him. I went so far as to throw a picture of him into the fire to demonstrate my feelings."

"If you despised him so fervently, why so eager to marry him again?"

"I never fell out of love with Vance, but that was my secret. I did not choose to discuss my true feelings with the women. I have never been given to girlish confidences. Vance meant too much to me – I could not share my emotions – including the hurt."

"According to Prudence Duluth, on the night of his murder, the four of you played a game. Each one stated how she would dispose of an unfaithful lover. You said it would be a knife directly through the heart."

Cass's face felt hot. "But that was just a dumb game. How is it relevant?"

"Because you are suspected of driving a knife through the heart of your ex-husband. Perhaps the so-called game inspired you."

"I am not so lacking in imagination that I would need a game to dream up a method for murder. Why do you take the word of Prudence Duluth?"

"I am listening to all comers. Because this is real life." Adams mopped his perspiring face. "We have calculated that there were four people on the murder scene that night. You and Dev Lal make two. Can you suggest any other possibilities?"

Cass dug her hands deeper in her pockets. "Prudence Duluth was in love with Vance. Somebody called him about 2 A.M. I believe it was Pru. You can check that on Vance's phone."

"His phone is missing."

"I leave. Pru arrives. She flings herself at him, goes so far as to do a strip tease. He tells her it's over, that he's marrying me. Outraged, she stabs him, then panics, leaves the bikini panties behind, takes his phone and flees."

"Ms. Duluth was not there that night. She spent the entire night and morning with a gentleman named Fazi Fakhouri. He backed her up as well as his body-guard. She has been crossed off our list of possible suspects."

"Did it occur to you that Fazi Fakhouri is protecting her?"

"I'm a New York police detective. I take nothing on face value. It's possible that Vance made love to another woman that night, besides Pru or you."

Cass felt her face getting hot. "Is this surmise necessary?"

"That's my job. I'm a cop. This is no time to play the blushing virgin. By now you know about Vance Cooper's extensive love life, if you want to call it that. Did you walk in on him and a woman?"

"No." Cass gasped for air, knew that she was having a dread anxiety attack. "No. No. No."

"How about your friend Dev. He was there. Was it orgy time?" Adams stood up and stared down at her.

She reached into her pocketbook, pulled out a small paper bag, inflated it, put it over her mouth and took deep breaths.

"Get a glass of water," Adams said to McShane, who returned swiftly with a tall glass of water and handed it to Cass.

She took the paper bag off her face and sipped water.

"Dev brought the dagger to kill Vance," Adams continued. "His sympathy was with you, and his fingerprints were on the knife as well as yours."

The interrogation went on. Cass left precinct headquarters bruised and confused. In Adam's hands, the truth twisted back against her.

Cass cabbed back to her apartment and phoned Donaldson.

"Did Vance ever discuss his affair with Pru Duluth with you? According to her, it was of long-standing and went back to before the trial and divorce."

"Never. He might have been too embarrassed to bring it up. It would make him appear totally unfaithful and degenerate. Although his sex life was not on trial – only his financial dealings – a jury could have been swayed by the blatant display of immorality."

"You are the murder expert. You wrote the book. Tell me what drives a person to murder. Is it money, passion –"

"It's desperation. It's the only way out."

Cass had planned to work on her piece Cures for Cataclysmic Living, but she could not write. She was living the subject, psychic survival in an increasingly bizarre world. Clowns governed. Whales beached themselves. Did Vance's drive to live to the fullest and on his own terms make him a target? The existential problem persisted. How does one endure in this world? Spiritually? Emotionally?

She needed to talk with Pru again, to ask her why she was so adamantly trying to nail her, Cass, for the crime. She would be there tonight at the Morris

Jasper Gallery for the opening of Angelina DeMarco's much-anticipated one-woman painting show. Pru had orchestrated the show and set it in motion.

Cass would take her aside. It would be the perfect setting for a private talk. Surrounded by people, they could not cut each other up.

Cass dressed with care. She wanted to appear sophisticated and in command. Forget the artist-jeans-paint-in-the-hair look, affected by some art hanger-oners, women with a superficial knowledge of art who went to openings to socialize. She settled on black pants and a black and white silk jacket that had worked in the past.

She went downstairs and grabbed a cab to Manhattan's Chelsea art scene and the Morris Jasper Gallery.

13

THE CROWD OF GALLERY GOERS massed on the sidewalk in front of the Triangle Building on West 21st Street indicated an important opening inside. The crowd buzzed in a chorus of anticipation. Cass pushed her way into the large elevator that emptied on the fifth floor. She flowed with the crowd to the Morris Jasper Gallery where Angelina DeMarco's show FLESH was happening, and stepped into the gallery. A palpable excitement filled the air. The room hummed and roared and buzzed as artists, art lovers, socializers, artists manque and buyers looked and talked and drank wine and talked.

The first painting inside the gallery – a woman's enormous breasts, topped by a mouth and a penis approaching – proclaimed what the fuss was about. The painting was raw, dramatic and socially unacceptable. It was not polite. It shouted. It was obscenely beautiful and riveted the viewer.

Frequently at gallery openings visitors barely looked at the paintings, or glanced at them, and proceeded to talk to each other. But for Angelina's FLESH, the subject matter absorbed the crowd. Cass moved into the melee and listened.

"Picasso did sexy but nothing like this."

"Crude. Are these her fantasies?"

"Magnificent. Like this is a break-through and the paintings are lewd and beautiful and they are about life."

"She's a genius."

"Strictly from pornography."

"Degas and all the great artists did sexy stuff that never made it into a gallery. I have a book with a collection of their work."

"Will anyone buy this work, put it on their walls?"

"She's already sold six of the paintings. Look at the red dots. Rodney Kramer, the real estate tycoon, bought 'Fellatio at Sunrise' and paid $60,000. Not bad for an artist starting out. He's going to hang it in his dining room."

"How utterly bizarre."

Cass worked her way through the crowd, aware as she moved that she had become a focus of attention, with nudges and remarks made. She was a murder suspect, and yet she was out and about. A few people who knew her nodded hello and smiled but did not seem to know what to say. Should she approach them? She would hang back and observe, a state of being she was inured to. It came in particularly handy when she felt overwhelmed. She could revert to being the journalist, taking notes in her head.

When Vance was riding high, making millions, many of his clients sank their money into art, going to auctions at Christie's and Sotheby's where incredible sums were made and continued to make news. A hundred million would be paid for a Picasso painting. Insane. But not for art lovers and serious collectors. Still, it reminded Cass of the Dutch tulip mania that collapsed in 1637, the first speculative bubble. People lost a life's fortune on the bulbs that reverted to being what they were, just bulbs. Picasso was unlikely to receive that treatment. But who knew what judgement future generations would pass on him and today's artists?

Angelina did not traffic in small, modest works. The paintings were immense and intense. She had painted them with a palette knife thickly impacted with paint, and attached objects to some of the paintings to create collages. Dried flowers. Bits of lace.

She had given them names that mingled hard-core sex terminology with occasional food images. Crème de Cunnilingus. Cass kept walking, mesmerized by the paintings. Not only the subject matter, the artistic execution. The use of color, shading and texture, the drama, the expressions on the faces of the people in the paintings.

Cass recognized by the atmosphere in the room that this wasn't just any opening. Angelina was a major talent to reckon with. The art world, always eager for the next original thing, had an important new voice. Welcome to Angelina, not only for her talent, but for the controversy she would engender. Now the critics had something to scrap about. Editorial writers could also weigh in on good and evil. Should the kiddies be exposed to this dubious form of art? On the other hand, Angelina was extraordinary, original, and impassioned.

Cass stopped in front of a painting, eight by five. Paint appeared to have been splashed on spontaneously. A man, centerpiece of the painting, engaged in an erotic game with four woman. The women were unrecognizable, their heads turned. The man in the center of the action was Vance, his face totally recognizable.

She heard a voice in her ear. "Seem like old times?" Cass turned around. Bugsy Fozer leaned on an elaborate red and gold cane. He looked, if possible, fatter, his moustache longer. "Long time, no see." His green velvet jacket topped checked pants and patent leather boots. As he drew closer, Cass observed the frayed edges of his cuffs, how his stomach protruded from the front of his jacket. But Fozer would squeeze himself into one of his flamboyant get-ups if it meant being noticed. Twenty years ago he had been an artist on the way up. He managed to ride a wave of interest in his star paintings, stars large and small, of dazzling colors, or black and white, and finally minimalist white, buoyed by his talent for self-promotion.

A client of Vance's, Fozer created a big-time image out of a small-time talent. He bought a loft and gave lavish parties. He promoted and hung out with young artists on their way up. But when Vance crashed, Fozer came down with him. In a recent article in The Wall Street Journal on artists whose work had precipitously lost value, "Artists Not Making a Splash," Fozer took the top spot. One former collector said: "I can't give them away. It's sad but true. I did a lawn sale and added my typewriter, and a Fozer. I finally sold the Fozer but I would be embarrassed to tell you what I took for it."

Fozer's nose flattened against his face. His enormous, bushy eyebrows hung over pale hazel eyes. "Sorry about Vance." Apparently noting her expression he added, "I mean it. He was a brilliant son of a bitch who screwed me financially for sure. But it was a wild ride while it lasted. I tried to hate him but could not achieve that. In fact, I must admit, I always wanted to be Vance Cooper."

"But then you would not have been an artist."

"Vance was the biggest artist of all, a master of illusion." Fozer took a couple of steps back, to gaze up at the painting that now commanded Cass's full attention. "Do you think he posed for it?"

"Anything is possible."

"Angelina has put Vance in an erotic scene with only the backs of the women showing. Could one of them be you?"

"I am not into groups."

"Are you shocked?"

"I am intrigued. Angelina has an amazing erotic imagination."

"She's brilliant, isn't she? I can't help but hate her because she's doing something at exactly the right time." Fozer's pink tongue protruded childlike as he put his head back and gazed up at the picture. "In the middle of the Me Too movement and women crying out that they have been wronged, and raped and mauled and in all ways sexualized and not liking it one bit, and screaming at the ramparts and sending men to prison and making them lose their jobs, and so much of it is absolutely justified because men can be pigs, nonetheless she is ripping the tissue paper of respectability away. She's saying this is where we live in our erotic lives and imaginations. That she's a woman who can paint a five foot vagina pleasured by a three foot man's tongue. She's important. She's not just a painter. She's a power. And that's what you need today to be noticed, to be sold. I should know. I certainly tried."

"What have you been doing with yourself lately, Fozer?"

"I'm embarrassed to tell you."

"We all have to survive."

"My stars lost favor with adults, but kiddies love my work. I have been doing paintings for children's rooms and nurseries. I spent a few years struggling and finally conceded that my bid for true artistic recognition was over. My shirts were frayed, as well as my nerves. Funny thing is, I'm having fun seeing kids really like my work."

"What could be better. You're making people happy." Cass felt that she could have been in a bubble with Fozer, despite the surrounding crowd. "Tell me, did you stay in touch with Vance at all after the debacle?"

"I was planning never to see or speak to him again. Then one day in my black and blue period, as I call it, I was mooning about and thought about Vance and wondered if he could possibly be as depressed as I was. After all, he too had come down from an enormous high, like having a huge hangover that does not go away. I craved commiseration. I went to visit him in prison."

"How was he?"

"Different, in unexpected ways. This was three years ago. He said he had been through a black period at first, grim and dark and hopeless. But he had done a lot of soul-searching and was beginning to see the light. He realized with his particular personality that he needed life's highs, that he was never going to be happy sitting with his hands folded. He was seeking a new high. Of course, he did not mention what the new high would be.

"He gave me the idea to do the kids' pictures. He explained that in prison, he had nothing. He had come to the realization that you work with what you have. Fozer, Vance said, you're not a no-talent. You have some talent. You're not Picasso. When did you first get this itch to draw and paint? Undoubtedly when you were a kid and you loved messing around with colors and drawing stars. So do pictures for kids. In today's world kids rule and parents will do anything to help their kids get on in the world. Like give the kid real paintings done by a significant artist. You have some credentials. Get to work. So I did."

"I wish you luck, Fozer."

"Thank you, dear. And all the luck to you." Fozer began to move on and turned back. "Vance said something in Balaban that piqued my interest. I thought you might know what the hell he really meant."

"Oh," Cass said eagerly. "Do tell."

"He was glad to be in prison. He was on a new path. But he did not elucidate. I suppose he was taking stock. You know, Dante, in the middle of the journey of his life etcetera. Perhaps you would like a star picture."

"Nothing would make me happier."

"I will paint one just for you."

"Thank you, Fozer. I will treasure it."

Cass walked away from Fozer and set out to look for Pru, who had set the gallery show in motion and then used all of her connections to attract a crowd that not only looked at paintings but bought them. Well-known TV personalities and more than one film personality. Cass expected to find Pru in the middle of a crowd, making introductions, helping to advance Angelina's artistic career as well as her own.

She did not find Pru, but she did bump into Mario, Angelina's handsome husband, the police detective, looking fit and sexy in a dark suit with red silk tie. A gracious charmer, he briefly bent over Cass's hand to bestow a butterfly kiss. Cass could not help but wonder if he had been told to keep his eye on her if she made an appearance.

At the far end of the gallery, Angelina stood surrounded by well-wishers. Angelina left the group and rushed up to them, her cheeks scarlet. She wore a long gold, blue and white brocade coat over black pants, the blue in the coat reflecting the blue of her eyes. Instead of overweight, Angelina looked impressive and in command. A few of her eager entourage trailed behind her.

Angelina hugged Cass and their words overlapped. As Cass offered her congratulations, Angelina gave her sympathy. "I'm so sorry, sweetheart. I am praying for you." Cass felt her sincerity. She could not begin to ask her why she had chosen to portray Vance, a man she had never met, at least not in Cass's presence, in such a grotesque fashion.

"Thank you, Angelina. Thank you."

"Have you seen Pru? I am going crazy because she was supposed to give the welcoming speech and introduce me. I'm so happy to have found the two of you together." She gazed up at Mario. "You look gorgeous, baby. This crowd fighting over a picture for enormous dollars amazes me. So have you seen her?"

"No way," said Mario.

"I tried to call her and text her and nothing." Angelina said. "So unlike Pru, who is always reachable." She threw her arms up. "What do I do?"

"Where does she live?" Mario asked.

"On the upper West Side."

"I'll go and look for her."

"I'll go with you," Cass said. "I know the doorman in Pru's building."

"Great." Mario took Cass's elbow and steered her towards the door.

14

PRU SPREAD THE CLOTHES OUT on her blue satin bedspread in her duplex apartment in the Alain, exulting to herself about her prestigious Manhattan address. She adored living in The Alain, second only to New York's famous Dakota in prestige. Address mattered, and it made Pru particularly happy to rub it in the snooty noses of the Charleston socialites who had once looked down on her. Now they envied her. Little did they know. She had everything and nothing. She had never been able to lure Vance to spend a night in her lovely bed. Dreaming of that occasion, she had bought magnificent silk sheets. At least Vance had not married Cass again. That would have killed her.

She eyed her main selections for the long weekend she would spend with billionaire Fazi. The long black velvet dress. The short blue she wore with ultra-high heels to show off her exceptional legs. The brocade one-shoulder stunner, hand-woven in India. Also exquisite underwear, ultra-thin and lacy items.

She gazed at Fazi's picture framed in thick gold on the dresser. A burgeoning belly. A double chin. A pointed beard. A fine moustache. Distinctly foreign, he could be deliciously sweet and endearing in his remote mogul way. Pru looked forward to fun and games with Fazi, to pleasing him, but as an actual lover he proved a major flop. Her greatest sexual experiences had been with All-American boys. Rich or poor, they could do it. They knew how and they had stamina and drive, undoubtedly beaten into them at some prep school playing ice hockey or on the high school football field. Of course, true sensuality was unknown to them, and their egos could get in the way.

Vance. Forget him.

At least Pru had Fazi. His zipper number annoyed her. It just seemed so ridiculous, but it caused her no pain and he rewarded her with a ruby bracelet the last time they played. She enjoyed accepting gifts from Fazi, and did not object to being a kept woman, if that phrase was still operative. She had spent years breaking her creative butt in the service of high fashion and glossy magazines. Exciting. Brutal. Thrilling. She had gone places and met people. Now she considered herself Emeritus. She could play at selected projects and with men.

She needed all those men. A coffee here. A cocktail there. A few small favors.

She was late for Angelina's opening. Her gold dress, a masterpiece in sequins and lace, had cost her a small fortune. Bergdorf's buyer Regina Diamond had found it for her. Reggie, whom she had known since her modeling days, had also slipped the news that Cass had been nosing around Bergdorfs. Sometimes the New York world was too small. But the dress was worth any small aggravation it entailed. Pru slipped the dress on and looked in the mirror.

Gorgeous. Simply gorgeous.

She was ready for anything and anyone including certain callers.

Hello world, here I come.

On Eighth Avenue. Mario hailed a cab, held open the door for Cass and climbed in after her. "Aaah." He leaned back. "I was glad to escape from that zoo. I don't enjoy the company of phonies and pseudos trying to get laid. They could care less about the art, just sucking up the wine. What do you think happened to Pru? Does she drink?"

"Not to excess."

"Sorry about this unhappy mess you're in, Cass. Sorry about Vance. I once considered investing with him. But I changed my mind. It just sounded too good to be true. When the Ponzi scheme scandal broke, I was not surprised. The defense impressed me. Investment fraud as addiction."

"Thanks for the sympathetic words. Donaldson Frye is a brilliant lawyer."

"He's considered the best criminal lawyer in the city. Maybe he should plead my case with Angelina. You know about Angelina and me and Dorrie."

"Somewhat. Angelina said that you want to live together in an open marriage. In our little group we tagged Dorrie, the other woman, as the bitch."

"Perhaps the tag is apt. Where Angelina's soft, Dorrie's tough. Where Angelina's emotional, Dorrie's a cool cookie. Angie wanted me to give her up. I tried. I couldn't. Finally I faced it – screw the world and its conventions. This is what I need. I made Angie see that I needed her and Dorrie."

"Angelina gave in."

"If I were a wealthy Roman, it would be considered a scandal if I didn't have a wife and a mistress. I told Ang to take it or leave it and finally she said she would take it. She missed me. I have been living on my own and she's been totally preoccupied with the painting and the opening. We will wait until after the opening to actually move back together. We will take a weekend away, like a mini-honeymoon to mark the occasion."

"And her painting?"

"She has a unique talent. Believe it or not, Dorrie was the catalyst. When Angelina learned about Dorrie, she was desperate to channel her rage. She rented a big studio and sent me the bill. I paid for it. I owed her, and I loved her. Tonight was the first time I saw her work. I was stunned, my wife -- I still think of her some kind of a Madonna -- creating these paintings dripping eroticism.

"I hate some of them and others I find strangely beautiful. I didn't know Angie had it in her. And that's who I am and who she is. And who are you, Cass? Are you the talented, never say die until you get that quote and hit the deadline on the mark journalist, or are you somebody else?"

The cab drew up to Pru's building. Cass and Mario approached the doorman, Ramon, who greeted Cass with a smile. She had made him the centerpiece of a story on New York's "personality" doormen that ran in New York magazine.

"Ramon, maybe you can help us. We're trying to find Prudence Duluth. My friend Angelina's having an art gallery opening tonight arranged by Pru. Pru's supposed to make the welcome speech and introduce Angelina, but she appears to be missing in action. Have you seen her?"

"Not today." Ramon frowned.

"Can you let us into her apartment?" Mario asked. "Could we talk to the super or the person who has a key?"

"Sorry but that absolutely never happens. We have the tightest security system. There are a number of celebrities who live here. Security's one of the building's attractions." Ramon rubbed his gloved hands together. "This building is like Fort Knox."

"I am a detective in the New York City Police Department," Mario said. "Doesn't that make me a candidate for entry?"

"Not unless you arrive in uniform, or with a partner and a permit. Or if one of the residents has informed me that you will be arriving." Ramon shook his head. "I appreciate your concern but it is out of the question."

Cass and Mario turned away from the building and walked across the street to Central Park. Cass called Angelina on her cell phone. "Has Pru shown up?"

"Not yet. I sure would love to see her. She knows this world. An M.D. just tried to buy one of the paintings for $75,000. I am overwhelmed. I should be thrilled. Of course I am, and yet I'm not. At this minute I want to run someplace and hide. I'm tempted to get out the rosary beads but that would really blow my image."

"Have a glass of wine and take a deep breath," Cass advised. "You worked hard for this. I understand the anxiety. Your life is changing, and it's happening so fast."

"Thanks, Cass. You get it. I'll see you and Mario when you get back here. Soon, I hope. I need somebody to lean on. Blow Mario a big kiss for me. He looks gorgeous, doesn't he. Tell him I can't wait to celebrate with him later."

Cass hung up. She delivered Angelina's message to Mario, who was about to respond when his cell phone rang. He leaned away from Cass as he talked into the phone, his expression changing from anxious to anticipatory. Cass did not have to ask who was calling him.

"Ah huh. Emn. Ah huh. But it's Angie's big night. Where am I? Two blocks away from your apartment. Just for a half an hour? I don't know." Then the grin, the low shared laughter. "Okay, okay, okay. See you in five."

Mario turned back to Cass. "I'm going to take a break." He held up a hand. "But don't worry. Tell Ang that I will be there and we will celebrate. Wish I could be of more help with the Pru problem. But you know her friends. I don't think that I can be of much more help."

Mario headed off across the street, leaving Cass to ponder her next move. The cold was beginning to press down on her as the sun faded. Probably the wisest choice would be to give up the search. Angelina's opening was already a huge success without Pru. But it was unusual for Pru to miss a chance to shine big-time. Unless something else wonderful popped up, just like that. But she would have called Angelina. Why should she, Cass, be worried about Pru, and the possibility that she had a heart attack or stroke or an accident. Old friendships die hard, Cass told herself, realizing that she had a residual affection for Prudence Duluth. She called Jane and left a message, to get in touch with her if she knew of Pru's whereabouts. Who else could she contact?

The Saudi billionaire Fazi who maintained a New York apartment? She did not have his unlisted number.

Cass opened her pocketbook and took out her keychain. There it was. The key to Pru's apartment with a sticker on it in pink and the initial P. At some juncture, she and Pru had exchanged keys with each other, should there be an emergency. They did it several years ago, during an awareness raising period. She fingered the key. Cass got up off the bench and walked back to Pru's building. There was the matter of getting past Ramon.

Cass shivered, her nose red from the cold.

Ramon greeted her again with a warm smile.

"Any luck?" he asked.

"Mario and I put together some phone numbers of Pru's associates." Cass pulled a reporter's notebook out of her pocket and held it up. "Could you do me a tremendous favor and let me sit in the lobby and make a few calls?"

"Well, it's not the usual thing to do." Ramon looked towards the empty lobby that beckoned with warmth and comfortable chairs.

"I realize that," Cass said. "But this is special. If Pru comes down I'll see her. I won't stay long. By the way, Ramon, I'm planning a follow-up piece on important New York doormen. I want you to be a major part of it. This time we will get even more intensely into your job and how it differs in the cyber age, if it does."

"Of course it does." Ramon looked around. "Okay, Mrs. Cooper. For you."

Ramon held the door open. Cass thanked him and headed for a chair in the corner. She took out her cell phone. Ramon returned to his post. Cass walked quickly to the elevator and pressed the button for the 20th floor. Suppose she found Pru in bed with a guy or some other awkward situation. She would make a swift apology and leave.

She inserted the key in the lock, opened the apartment door, and closed it behind her. She stood still for a moment and called out Pru's name, but the only sound she heard in response was the a low whirr of a vacuum cleaner from the floor above. Cass moved through the apartment. Elegant, but not too perfect, reflecting Pru's personality. She walked through the kitchen, and finally to the second floor of the duplex.

Cass smelled Pru's perfume as she approached the bedroom.

She walked into the bedroom, a phantasmagoria of blue silk and satin, ruffles and lace. Pru had designed it to replicate her adolescent dream of a girl's room that she had when she was squeezed between two unruly sisters in a double-wide.

An exquisite blue satin bedspread covered the canopied bed.

Pru was stretched out on the bed. Dressed in gold, she looked like a beautiful statue, except for the blood that spilled out on the gold dress. One arm dangled off the side of the bed.

A knife protruded from her heart.

15

Cass moved closer to Pru's body. Pru's eyes remained open. Cass bent over her, knew she should close those eyes. But she could not. Did not want to touch the body that had once been Pru. It could not be happening but it was. And then she collapsed, the world growing black, fading, knowing she was fainting but could not control it. She fell over Pru's body, came to on the floor, her hand smeared with Pru's blood.

She went into the bathroom and washed her hands. She should call Detective Adams. Now. The shoulds. But she could not. She looked about the bedroom. Everything was in place. On the dresser, one white rose filled a small black vase.

Next to it was a note on Pru's distinctive blue writing paper. The note had obviously been printed from a computer. Cass picked it up.

> *"Please forgive me. I killed Vance Cooper. I cannot live with that knowledge.*
>
> *Prudence Duluth."*

Cass put the note back down, feeling colder now than when she walked in. Pru could have killed Vance in a moment of insanity and perverted passion, but kill herself? Never. And if Pru were writing a suicide note, she would do it by hand in her distinctive script.

Cass hurried out of the apartment, rode the elevator down, and rushed past Ramon who was engaged in conversation with a tenant. She managed to offer him a quick "Thank you." When Pru's body was discovered, the police would question Ramon about visitors. He would have to give them her name. Or would he? He would be risking his own job if he said he had admitted her to the building.

Cass realized she was thinking like a criminal. She was being pushed deeper into an underground world. She walked quickly to the corner taking deep breaths. She would contact the police, but not from her cell phone. She spotted one of the outdoor phones on the corner. One of the purposes of the phones was to aid in emergencies. "If you see something, say something."

Cass dialed 911. "Please send the police to the apartment of Prudence Duluth in the Alain. It's an emergency. A suicide. A murder." She hung up. Her first impulse was to look for the nearest bar and get drunk. Instead she headed back to Angelina's opening.

Now the party was in full swing. The buzz had become a roar. Angelina, surrounded by press, appeared happy and preoccupied. Cass walked slowly around the gallery, returning to a portrait of Vance. Vance on his own, the study of a man in deepest introspection. He looked gaunt and troubled. A man of intrigue. He sat on a red velvet chair, his legs parted, his sexuality in repose.

The portrait stopped Cass. Had Pru killed him and then herself? There was no sign of a struggle. It's as if Pru had invited the killer to stab her. Come closer, darling, and admire me in my magnificent gold dress, but do not touch. And he had stabbed. Perhaps a she? Had the killer drugged her first? Had Pru identified Vance's killer and confronted that person?

Cass made another circuit of the floor, ever-aware of eyes on her and the chatter. Amazing how you got the vibe, how you didn't have to look over your shoulder to know when you were being scrutinized. She wondered how much she was giving away, if her face screamed about what she had just experienced. Life as nightmare. She had returned to Vance's portrait. As if a calming hand had been placed on her shoulder, a man's reassuring voice sounded in her ear.

"You look like you could use a glass of wine." She turned. Noah Lazeroff, all dark tweed and perfectly fitted jeans, a black turtleneck, and horn-rimmed glasses, held up two glasses of wine. "I always take two." He offered one to Cass.

"Thank you." Cass took the wine glass in her hand.

He took a step closer to her. She liked his style, which was bold and masculine but not overly flirtatious. Yet he seemed to acknowledge her as a woman. "I saw you standing there alone, Cass. You looked like you could use someone to lean on. You still do."

Cass attempted a smile that did not work. His sympathetic look brought tears to her eyes. She reached into her pocket for the ubiquitous tissue but knew if she pulled it out there could be drops of blood on it.

"Hey." He drew even closer, as if to shield her. "Can I help?"

Cass gestured to the portrait. "It's Vance."

"Your late husband." Noah studied the portrait. "He was such an out-going person, and yet so isolated. It captures him."

The gallery noise had become overwhelming. Cass took one step closer to Noah and smelled him, the unmistakable aroma of masculinity. After the tragic scene she had just witnessed, how could she be attracted to this man? Everything was heightened. She was alive.

She drank the wine, let it tease her tongue, swallowed, felt a buoyancy, a tingle.

Cass looked up at Noah. "How would you like to get out of here?"

"Let's go."

16

Cass felt giddy from one glass of wine. She linked her arm through Noah's as they walked down West 21st Street. When Noah pulled her closer to his side, she no longer felt the cold. The police would be looking for her. She wasn't ready for them. She needed time out.

"What would you like to do?" Noah asked.

"It's like this." Cass looked up at Noah. "I've had one glass of wine. I would love another glass of wine. I want to walk and and drink wine and walk and drink."

"Since I'm the responsible adult, can I suggest that I buy a bottle of wine and we drink it while walking on the High Line. There's an entrance near here on 23rd Street."

Cass knew the elevated park well. The converted railroad spur terminated not far from her apartment. "That's a perfect idea."

They stopped at a liquor store and settled on a bottle of dry white wine opened by the clerk, who also provided two plastic glasses.

They took the elevator up to the High Line. Across the river, the lights of New Jersey glittered, and all around them magnificent New York buildings rose above the trail's greenery, testimonies to architectural daring. Smaller buildings were tucked in between the skyscrapers. Windows offered glimpses of New York life like peeks through giant keyholes.

They strolled to the first bench and sat down. Noah opened the wine and poured. He raised his glass to her. "I have a confession," Noah said. "I came to Angelina's opening with the hopes of meeting you. We never had a chance to talk at Dev's party."

"Dev says you've written a brilliant book on the fascinating topic of addiction." Cass sipped wine, told herself not to gulp it down. "Congratulations!" She touched her plastic glass to his. "Unfortunately there's no merry clink."

"I'm glad you stopped shaking. You are safe with me."

"I have this crazy impulse to be absolutely honest with you, to blab on as if I were on a shrink's couch and just let it all hang out. Do you mind?"

"Mind? I welcome it."

"It's as if you're magnetized. I want to move towards you."

"Come closer. Please." Noah edged towards her. "We're feeling the same thing at the same time. So that means something significant, doesn't it?"

"Aren't you afraid of me? I'm a murder suspect. I could have a knife in my pocket. I might be a bit mad."

"I'll take my chances. I'm crazy myself. Why do you think I became a psychologist? Criminals fascinate me. How did they get bent? I could easily have become one of them."

"Did you get to know Vance well?"

"Yes. Vance belonged to my gambling addiction therapy group at Balaban Prison. He was an important member. He went through a lot of changes at Balaban. I planned to see him after his release."

"Ah, the brilliant psychologist will continue his study of the aberrant Vance."

"I felt a kinship with Vance. We had a lot in common and nothing in common. I grew up in Brooklyn, a city kid and a street fighter. Not the good Jewish boy, I rebelled against the Bar Mitzvah. I went to what's called reform school, and then other events happened on life's road. A scholarship to Columbia saved me. On to Johns Hopkins for my Ph.D.. But I'm talking too much."

"Please keep talking." Cass closed her eyes, and opened them again. "You are doing me a big favor, not making demands that I be charming and sane."

"Forget sanity."

"Do you mean that?"

"Totally."

"I learned recently that Vance had been involved in what I guess you would call the swingers life while we were still married. That he was addicted to sex the way he was addicted to gambling. Did that ever come up with him?"

"I can't say anything more. We do not repeat what we have shared with each other. Of course you already know about Vance's work with Gamblers Anonymous."

"All of these Anonymous groups." Cass extended her empty plastic cup and Noah filled it. "I am a serious alcoholic. This wine is the first in six months -- I had one Scotch the night when I met Vance -- but mostly I do not think about booze. Tonight was different."

"Vance's portraits."

"I never joined AA. I did go to a few meetings but it made me want to drink instead of the opposite. A friend of mine who is an AA fanatic calls me a dry drunk. That means I have not gotten the AA message. Vance and I drank together. And apart. Sometimes it's like I did not know Vance at all. Were we really married for twenty years? In a bizarre way, I'm angry with Vance. Did he love me? If he did, how could he let this happen to me. Are these normal feelings?"

"They're your feelings. Trust yourself."

Noah took her hand in his and they sat for a moment without speaking. Around them stars mingled with city lights. The world flashed bright. "It's so beautiful, like Van Gogh's painting, Starry Night," Cass mused. "It's all happening, the universe spinning. I want to jump out of myself and into that world."

"Life's changing for you. Let it happen, the good and the bad. When you think it's the worst, you could be moving towards the best."

Noah pulled Cass towards him. He kissed her lightly. His firm lips felt like a homecoming. She did not pull away. "I have an idea," Noah said. "Have you ever made love outdoors in New York City?"

"Never," Cass said.

"This is a special night. Why don't we make it a first -- the night that we made love on the High Line in Manhattan?"

"You mean jump into the Van Gogh world?"

"We can try."

They moved to a bench in the shadows. The moon mixed itself up with the stars and city lights in a dazzling show. Incredible. Cass could not stop laughing as they wrestled with buttons and zippers. His warm lips. His tongue. His hot hands on her buttocks pulled her close, closer. Amazing. Their bodies burned. Crisp, cold air surrounded them. Had anything ever felt so good? Nothing else mattered.

Cass could not believe all of this was happening. She felt like she had been away from herself for a long time and was just starting to come back. To actually feel something. Not the way she felt with Vance. That was the old Cass – this was the new and unknown Cass, new even to herself.

Afterwards they walked with their arms around each other, not talking, just occasionally looking up with a smile. They were both wearing enormous grins when Munro Brown of the New York Post appeared from behind a tree, flashing his camera at them. Pop pop pop.

Cass pulled away from Noah. "You bastard, Munro. What are you planning to do with those pictures?"

"They're for Page Six. Cass Cooper shares a romantic High Line interlude with psychologist Noah Lazeroff. A reporter will be calling you."

"Don't expect me to answer."

"I followed you from the art opening. You didn't waste any time, did you?"

"You are a crude son of a bitch."

"For a woman who loves to dig for the dirt, I would not play the coy maiden. Call it getting a taste of your own medicine. And like they say, a picture is worth a thousand words."

Cass watched Munro move swiftly away, hustling off to The Post with his pictures. "I'm sorry," Cass said to Noah, "to involve you in this mess."

"I was always involved." He took Cass's hand and they kept walking, moving down the stairs to leave the High Line and walk through the West Village.

"I have kept something from you." Cass looked up at Noah. "I found Prudence Duluth's body tonight. Like Vance, she had been stabbed to death. I went looking for her when she did not arrive to make the introductions at Angelina's show. I ran. I called the police. An anonymous call. I returned to Angelina's show. I met you. Am I a disgusting coward?"

Noah stopped abruptly in the middle of the block. 'You are brave. Thank you for finding me." He put his arms around Cass. He hugged her close. Under different circumstances Cass might have felt that she had been rescued, pulled back from the cliff, but even with Noah hugging her, she trembled in the cold.

17

INSIDE HER APARTMENT, CASS DOUBLE-LOCKED the door and turned on all the living room lights. There was a small blood stain on her coat sleeve. She went into the kitchen, found a new sponge and worked on the stain, the blood moving on to the sponge. Finally satisfied, she hung the coat up in the bathroom to dry. With every move, she felt more devious.

She checked her phone messages. News reporters, including one from Page Six of The Post, had called. Cass turned on the TV news. She did not have to press the remote far before she found the story about the police finding former Vogue editor Prudence Duluth dead of a suicide on the night of her friend Angelina's big art triumph. How Pru had helped set the event in motion. One newscaster interviewed Angelina. "I'm crushed." Angelina burst into tears. "If I could destroy every painting and bring Pru back , I would do it."

The buzzer rang. "Mrs. Cooper, the police are on their way up," the doorman said.Cass opened the door to Detective Adams. He knew that she had been in Pru's apartment that afternoon. She was on the video in the security camera and instantly recognizable. Despite the note, Pru's suicide was viewed as "suspicious." Would she accompany them to headquarters?

Adams found her coat hanging from the shower with the wet spot on it. He would take it along.

They were back in their familiar places at the Precinct House, Cass at the small table, Adams across from her with McShane. Adams' voice dripped with sarcasm and a new anger as he questioned Cass. "You appear to have a pattern of stumbling into bodies with knives sticking out of them. You have motive, opportunity and means, yet you remain in complete denial." They sat in the barren interrogation room with its rudimentary table and chairs. "For starters, you lied to the doorman."

"Guilty as charged. In this fiasco, Ramon is blameless."

"Why did you break into Prudence Duluth's apartment?"

"I was afraid something had happened to her. An accident. Mario and I went to look for her. And I found her. My first impulse was to call you. I passed out. I woke up on the floor. I panicked and left."

"Just try and level with me –you had a key to Prudence's apartment. You did not tell Mario. Why?"

"Pru and I had exchanged keys several years ago, so that if there were an emergency we could get into each others apartments. We were once close friends. I had forgotten that I even had the key."

"Now you were on the outs. You had the perfect opportunity to take revenge, stab Pru to death, and pin Vance's homicide on her." Adams raised his right eyebrow at her. "By the way, have you been drinking?"

"I had a glass of wine at Angelina's opening. Would you rather we continue this conversation tomorrow?"

"No. McShane, get some coffee for Mrs. Cooper and one for myself as well." Adams brushed at his wispy head. "I never cease to be amazed. The most buttoned down people have a couple of drinks and suffer a complete moral breakdown."

"I was sober when I found Pru. She looked so beautiful – like an exquisite painting slashed by a marauder."

"You can save that for the piece you will undoubtedly write. Was it murder or suicide? What I need are the facts."

McShane returned with coffee. Cass took the cardboard container, opened it, took a sip and set it down on the table. She described her moves after finding Pru's body. "Of course the suicide note was a fake. If I were trying to fool the world and pretend to be Pru, I would not have written anything that simplistic. Because I knew her. She would not have left a bland suicide note printed from a computer."

"What's the evidence?"

"Pru was proud of her handwriting. She called it Charleston Socialite Cursive. She had taken lessons to master the art. If she were going to write a suicide note, it would be in her own hand. Pru had style."

"She had that in abundance." Adams nodded his head. "She asked me with more than a hint of irony where I bought my jackets. And I told her --thrift shops. I don't want to be noticed. I'm not a shiny guy. I love my work but it's grim."

"Pru had been looking forward to Angelina's opening. She had planned it and set it in motion. Afterwards she was taking a trip to Saudi Arabia with Fazi Fakhouri. She was far from suicidal."

"What did you do after leaving the opening?"

"I went for a walk on the High Line."

"Alone?"

"With a friend."

"Name of?"

"Noah Lazeroff. Why is it relevant?"

"It's relationships. It's behavior. It's how we detectives work. We do not solve our cases in a vacuum."

"I want to know who killed Pru and Vance. Why they were killed. And will that person be coming after me next?"

"You're anxious. Several of the members of our squad find yoga helpful along with meditation. Much better than hitting the bottle."

"I'm cracking up and you suggest trendy bromides. I'm not a pretzel. I can't bend to yoga. I need answers."

"We're employing every resource of the NYPD, and you can be sure that the best police investigative department in the country will come up with definitive answers. You can leave now. We'll be keeping your coat."

18

A PHOTO OF NOAH AND Cass filled the front page of The New York Post. The headline blared: HIGH OR LOW-DOWN?

"Cass Cooper and psychologist Noah Lazeroff, who testified in the late Vance Cooper's trial, were seen strolling on the High Line. That same night journalist Cooper discovered the body of former Vogue editor Prudence Duluth .

"Although Ms. Duluth left a farewell suicide note, the NYPD Medical Examiner ruled out suicide because of the knife angle. Ms. Cooper, regarded as a person of interest in the Duluth case, is out on bail, charged with the murder of her ex-husband Vance Cooper. Both Cooper and Duluth were stabbed to death.

"Cooper remains unreachable. According to reliable sources, her relationship with Dr. Lazeroff, known for his work with addicts, could extend back five years to the time of the trial of Vance Cooper for a Ponzi scheme. Lazeroff was instrumental in getting him a lenient five-year sentence. He testified that Cooper was not a criminal, but a gambling addict who could not resist playing with Wall Street millions."

Cass threw down the paper. The doorman buzzed her.

"Please," Cass said. "I'm not talking with journalists or anybody else."

"It's Angelina DeMarco."

"Send her up."

Angelina arrived with a rush of perfume and a gust of fresh, cold air. Wrapped in a red cape with hood, she looked like an oversized Little Red Riding Hood. She hugged Cass, then reached into her shopping bag and pulled out a casserole.

"It's my triple-threat lasagna, loaded with meat and three kinds of cheese, and it's juicy. What's the last time you ate?" Angelina didn't wait for an answer. "I'll put it in the oven." Angelina walked into Cass's kitchen, and returned to the living room.

"What can I get you to drink?" Cass asked.

"How about a glass of wine?" Angelina settled in the chair by the fireplace. She wore a brightly flowered dress, black with enormous red peonies.

"I can do that. In fact, I have a bottle of Zinfandel."

"That's perfect with lasagna. Let's be good to ourselves."

Cass opened the wine, poured, handed a glass to Angelina, and filled a glass with Coke for herself. "Congratulations on your art. Brava!" Cass raised her glass to Angelina.

Angelina's beautiful, dimpled face, framed by chestnut colored curls, glowed. "Thank you, darling. I never expected that kind of reaction. I thought I would be laughed out of town. Pru had made it all possible."

Till then, Cass realized, they were acting as if nothing had happened. Cass eyed the wine glass but reached for the Coke. "I found her. I fainted. The papers leave out that detail. She looked so lovely – in a gold dress –"

"Don't tell me. I saw the dress." Angelina sipped wine. "She bought it for the opening. It cost a fortune. I knew she would never kill herself in that dress. She could not wait to show it off. Of course the police and the newspapers make it look like you stuck a knife in her."

"The media loves a sensational case. They're milking this for all it's worth."

"I occasionally have murderous impulses, as you know," Angelina said. "Anything is possible in this best of all possible worlds. I was worried about Pru. Maybe you know things that I don't know."

"And visa versa." Cass gulped Coke. She could use a glass of wine, or better, a Scotch. "Because I don't know how much you know about Pru."

"About her strange involvement with your late husband, for instance? I wouldn't take it too seriously. The affair was typical of Pru. Somewhere in her struggle to make it to the top, she decided that she would screw any guy she wanted, no introductions necessary. Because men had that attitude and why shouldn't she? She told me that she never experienced any guilt afterwards. Like she had a quickie with a Japanese guy in Central Park. She didn't know his name. She said he had a small penis but lovely skin."

"So this is apropos of --?"

"Of nothing. The Vance stuff was meaningless."

"But maybe it wasn't." Cass swirled the Coke.

Angelina shivered. She made the sign of the cross. "Godspeed, Pru. I hope it didn't hurt." She checked her watch. "The lasagna should be ready."

Angelina floated out of Cass's living room and into her kitchen, a woman inured to playing hostess. Cass got up to follow her, and sat down again. The woman who had come to see Cass was not the artist but the house-wife, Angelina, the shirt ironer and lasagna maker. Cass sniffed Angelina's perfume and now the aroma of lasagna, of tomato, noodles and melted cheese, meat, onions.

Angelina returned with two plates in hand, forks and napkins. She handed a plate to Cass. "It smells delicious." Cass put her fork in and took a bite. "It is delicious. I'll wait a bit before I dive in."

"Eat. Eat," Angelina advised. "You need to keep up your strength. I happen to be Italian, but I'm also a Jewish mother. So what's this about you and the psychologist. What's his name? Noah? You are a fox. You never told us."

"Because I had not met him until Dev's book party. What the papers say is strictly false news."

"Eat, eat. Food always works for me."

Cass spread the napkin on her lap, picked up the plate and found herself devouring the lasagna. Across from her, Angelina had already finished with her portion and was daintily touching the corners of her mouth with a napkin. Cass finished her plate. "Thank you, I needed that."

Angelina picked up the dishes and headed for the kitchen.

"I don't mean for you to do all the work," Cass called out.

Angelina returned. "To me it's not work. I like serving people. It's who I am. So let's get down to business. Tell me why you killed Pru."

"Are you serious?"

"Never more so. You notice I did not bring knives when I served the lasagna. I understand why you needed to kill the great Vance Cooper. But Pru? What had she done to you besides getting it on with your husband a few times. Of course you felt murderous. I understand the impulse. But did you have to act on it?" Angelina was breathing heavily. "Did she say something? Did she do something?"

"Stop." Cass put her hand up. "I did not kill Vance. I did not kill Pru. Where do you get these ideas?"

"It's not me." Angelina moved her glass in an agitated motion. "It's everybody. I read the papers. I talk to people. It's the buzz, the zeitgeist, or whatever you want to call it. You are regarded as most likely suspect, in fact the only suspect."

"If I'm so evil, why did you come here? What makes you think I will not stick a knife in you?"

"I doubt if you would stab me to death in your apartment. And how would you dispose of my body? Sometimes size can be an advantage. You have no reason to kill me."

"How about painting the oversize naked portraits of my ex-husband? Did you consider that I might be turned off by this artistic extravaganza? You owe me an explanation. How did that happen? Don't tell me that you, the Madonna, had an affair with Vance."

"Quite the contrary." Angelina smoothed her hand over the flowered fabric in her lap.

"But you had met Vance."

"Yes."

"Where? At Pru's?"

"No." Angelina looked uncomfortable. She reached for the wine bottle and refilled her glass, took a healthy swallow. "Something you don't know about me. I'm a gambler."

"Since when?"

"Church. It started with church bingo games. Then the Solidarity Group took a trip to Atlantic City, and I was hooked. It's the slots, how I love the slots, the sound, the lights. The first time I hit the jackpot it was Nirvana. You can't imagine that rush, with the bells ringing, the lights flashing, and, on that occasion, barrels of coins spilling out."

"Heady."

'I would look around me at these old chicks glued to their machines and feel pity for them, but I was one of them. I was spending the household money. My father left me some money and I lost that as well. I gambled on line. I kept asking Mario for money. I finally broke down and confessed to him. He pushed me to go to Gambler's Anonymous."

"And?"

"On the night when Mario told me about screwing the skinny blond, I went to my first meeting. I was going out of my mind. Vance was sitting next to me. It was his first Gambler's Anonymous meeting, and as far as I know, his last. He told me he wasn't planning to return. He did not approve of group think. I told him I needed to talk to somebody. In fact I practically begged him to talk to me. We went for coffee. I had coffee and an almond croissant. Okay, two croissants. It's not relevant but rage and sorrow does fuel my appetite.

"I poured it all out, the pathetic confessions of Angelina DeMarco and her unfaithful husband." Angelina paused. One tear formed in her right eye. She brushed it away. "God, but I'm emotional. It still hurts. Even now, with my accepting the bitch as part of our lives."

"And Vance?"

"He offered me his advice," Angelina huffed. "Instead of going to Gamblers Anonymous, I should go to Weight Watchers or Over-Eaters Anonymous. My body was the problem. He said I had a beautiful face. He also said that he would never make love to me because of my size. That over-weight women upset him, but not to take it personally." Angelina kicked her heels up. "Not take it personally?" Her voice rose. "How else should I take it? He made me feel gross and disgusting. I was in such a fragile state and that shattered me.

"In my dark artist's heart, I vowed my revenge. I didn't know who the guy was, only his first name and that he was a Wall Street man. But I figured that maybe someday he would see those paintings. It fired my imagination. You know, life hands you a lemon and you make lemonade."

"How about my feelings?"

"When I paint, I don't consider anyone's feelings. I just do it. After I got to know you, I realized he was your husband." Angelina shrugged. "I won't apologize. I'm not sorry I did the paintings."

"OK, forget the paintings," Cass said. "You were close to Pru. She had this lavish lifestyle. But many of her projects were non-paying, like her involvement in chic charities. Do you know how she survived?"

Angelina licked her lips. "I never asked. I took it for granted that Fazi Fakhouri, the billionaire from Saudi Arabia, helped her out. He keeps an apartment in New York, like a glassed-in floor in this stupendous high-rise. He also has his digs back in Saudi Arabia. Sometimes he would fly Pru over for a weekend."

"She rarely talked about him."

"She couldn't. That was part of the deal. She was not to discuss him with anybody."

"Why the big secrecy?"

"He has a wife in Saudi Arabia and several kids and an extended family. The mysterious Middle East and all that stuff."

"Did you ever meet him?"

"Once. At Pru's apartment. He wasn't bad looking. Black hair graying at the temples. A fine moustache. A bit of a corporation, the expanding tummy, but not hideous. Beautiful gray suit with a silk handkerchief – maroon – in the pocket. Maroon tie. Gold rings. A flashy guy. Sharp."

"You took in all the details."

"I'm an artist. I look. His hands were beautiful, and manicured. She left us alone. She had some important calls to make and went upstairs in the duplex. He came on to me, told me how beautiful I was and offered to fly me over to Saudi Arabia. For a weekend or more. How he would show me a wonderful time strictly out of an Arabian Night's dream. Of course, it would be covert. I would not be permitted to reveal where I had been or that I even knew him. He said that would work better all around, since I was a married lady. I turned him down.

"He was smooth as silk, except when I said 'No'. And then his tone changed. He told me that I should not tell Pru about the invitation, or anyone else. Like we never met. He sounded cold and threatening. I've read about these Arab princes of old who would get bored with a mistress, and throw her off a balcony or lop her head off. I never spoke of him to Pru again, except occasionally to ask, 'And how is Omar Sharif'? And she would say 'Fine.' And that would be that."

"It could have been Fazi," Cass said, "who killed Pru."

"But why?"

"Perhaps she knew too much about him. How he made his billions. Do you know the source of his vast wealth?"

"I have no idea. He certainly would be the proper villain. I can picture him sticking a knife through a woman's heart." Angelina ran her finger around the rim of her wine glass. "Lately Pru had been thick with Jane. They were the same size. Pru had Jane wearing her clothes when they went out. She said Jane would be a perfect high-fashion model, showing off clothes for the mature woman."

"Jane does have that great bone structure, the hollow cheeks."

"The poor man's Katherine Hepburn." Angelina warmed to the subject. "So they were into clothes and men. I walked in on a conversation. Jane was pushing some guy on Pru – and Pru said he would be the last man she would go out with. She told Jane to date this dude instead of her and Jane said, no thank you, he's dangerous. And Pru said 'Too sexy?' and Jane said 'Too insane.'"

"Did Jane come to the opening? I didn't see her."

"She ran in for about five minutes, congratulated me and left." Angelina sighed. "I wish it wasn't you who killed Pru. But can you prove it?"

"No," Cass responded. "Not yet."

19

CASS WALKED ANGELINA TO THE door. "Do me a favor." Angelina pulled up her red hood. "Keep the stuff about Fazi trying to put the moves on me confidential. I don't know why I told you. Maybe I'm trying to prove that men like me. But honestly, he scares me."

"More than me?" Cass mustered a smile.

"You do not scare me." Angelina threw her arms around Cass and hugged her. "I fear for your immortal soul. I'm praying for you. God help."

Angelina climbed aboard the elevator. She had left the shopping bag behind. It held a box filled with three cannoli, the toothsome crème filled Italian pastry, a large container labeled pasta fagioli soup, and a frozen lasagna, plus a short note: "Enjoy. Love, Angelina." Cass put the soup and pastries in the refrigerator and the lasagna in the freezer. Angelina suspected her of killing Pru, but she did not hate her. She was offering her nourishment. Perhaps she was feeding her out of a Roman Catholic imperative. Feed the poor, the crazy and the guilty. Cass hated charity. But Angelina was a friend, and she needed her friends.

The phone rang. Noah Lazeroff.

"I would like to see you. It's important."

Cass opened the door to Noah, all black eyes and tweed jacket. He carried a small bag. He kissed her lightly and followed Cass into her office. "Welcome to my inner sanctum. It's where I burn the midnight and round the clock oil."

"Beautiful." Noah walked around. "I approve. Files. Reference books, pictures taken with the famous and infamous. A messy desk. It's all good."

She sat down in the desk chair and gestured towards the couch. "Just push those books out of the way. In the midst of this nightmare, I'm trying to work on a freelance piece."

"What's the topic?"

"Cures for Cataclysmic Living."

"It sounds ambitious."

"It's about survival in our topsy-turvy world. Whales beach themselves. The US government admits the possibility of UFO's. Some take to addictions, ranging from injecting heroin to pornography, or they meditate around the clock. Do I babble? I'm searching, as you can see – or hear."

Noah reached down into the bag. "Perhaps this will help." He handed her a copy of his just-published *Everything You Will Ever Need to Know About Addiction.* "You did say you wanted to read it."

Cass took the book in her hands. "This is wonderful." She opened it. "And you signed it. Of course I will be tempted to quote but I promise, nothing without attribution."

He leaned back on the couch. "I spent years on that book, writing and rewriting. Writing's hard."

"It's my addiction."

"You enjoy being out of control."

"Yes, yes." Cass was thrilled by the insight. "You do get it. I love it and hate it and can't live without it. I need it, and it can get in the way of my life."

"Tell me more."

"It's my primary intoxication. I'm dealing with so-called reality, but it's another dimension. That's the thing about journalism. You're shaping reality. You're miles away from the real world, like on a daily. You write the piece at a feverish pace and there it is with your byline. Who wants to come down from a high? Journalism breeds alcoholics. Anyway, when I signed on to this profession, I wanted to meet the world."

Noah spread his arms out on the back of the couch. "And now?"

"People are writing about me. Not so nice."

"Even painful," Noah said. "I've seen the distorted stories."

"Can I pick your brain?"

"Please do."

"Tell me about Vance. It still pains me that I missed all those five years in prison. It was a big gap in our relationship. We never had a chance to catch up."

"He was trying to make changes in his life. The people who he screwed with his Ponzi scheme weighed on him. He realized he could never repay them – not in money. Maybe he poured a lot of that into the memoir. He struggled with it. He was an amazingly eclectic human being. It's as if he had been liberated from the world of finance and wanted to learn about everything, including the new experiments happening in LSD."

Cass had been doodling on a pad, realized she was sketching Noah, even as he talked about Vance. She put her pen down and sat up. "That surprises me. Whenever I mentioned psychedelics, he totally turned off the topic. He considered LSD dangerous."

"Like I said, he was making changes in his life. While at Balaban, he tripped."

"Are psychedelics allowed in prison?"

"Of course not. But neither is booze or many other things. Determined prisoners find a way. Vance took the LSD on his own, which is dangerous.

You're supposed to have a guide. Fortunately I was there. It was tough going but I talked him through it."

"Where did he get the LSD?"

"A visitor. A Dr. Marsha Newman. She only came to Balaban once. Visitors often bring gifts. It appears that a tab of LSD was her gift to Vance."

"Another unknown woman. They are coming out of the woodwork, women who were involved with Vance or knew him."

"Does that bother you?"

"This Doctor Newman is one more person for me to put on my suspects list."

"Isn't that a bit extreme. Everyone who spoke with Vance was not out to murder him."

"But it feels that way to me."

Cass felt tired and let down. She couldn't cope. Vance's taking LSD was so totally out of character or was it? Just one more facet of the man she did not know.

"You look terribly unhappy," Noah said. "I'm sorry I told you."

"Don't be sorry. I need to know everything."

"You and I shared a wonderful adventure on the High Line," Noah said. "Now you feel so distant from me. You have put the desk between us. Like a barricade. I'm not going to hurt you. Are you afraid of me?"

"Of course not – it's just – The High Line -- I had a few glasses of wine and lost all my inhibitions. It was not really me."

In the middle of the floor, Cass had placed one of her favorite possessions, a finely woven prayer rug from India in an intricate red and gold design. Now a sunbeam hit the rug, making the colors radiant.

"I like Oriental rugs," Noah said. "That's a beauty." He moved down to sit on the rug and ran his hands over the silky surface.

"What's so important that you had to tell me?"

"You are important. Have you ever made love on a prayer rug?"

"No."

"The woman I met on the High Line is the real you. You are making changes in your life. Don't be afraid to reach out to me. I want to help you."

Cass moved down to join Noah on the rug. Their kisses felt so natural. She pulled some pillows down from the couch. "Discussing my late husband is a strange prelude to lovemaking."

"It's sharing." He gently pulled off her jeans. "Blue silk. You are wicked." He bent down to kiss her. She rolled to her side to help pull off his gray slacks. He slid inside her like a homecoming. Sun beamed golden through the windows. As they moved together, slowly and perfectly in sync, she felt her universe expanding. They climbed mountains, reached for new horizons. They were going there. They were there. They clung to each other. A burning moment of discovery, all happening at three o'clock on a Thursday afternoon.

"From the moment you walked in the door," Cass murmured, "I was hoping this would happen."

When Noah left, he kissed her tenderly goodbye, but did not promise to call. Perhaps this is how adults conduct their emotional lives, Cass told herself. At the moment, she was glad for Noah to leave. She did not have to spend long hours with him in or out of bed, sharing confidences, eating and drinking, diving recklessly into love and potential heartbreak. She would take the hot, measured moments. She was not sure if she was capable of more. Her life was taking new twists and turns, opening new roads that she would follow to their conclusion, no matter where they would take her.

20

CASS SAT IN HER OFFICE chair. She meditated. She drank tea. She then got online and looked up Dr. Marsha Newman, using her special app for finding information about people who wanted to remain private. She achieved zero results in her search. Apparently Dr. Newman preferred to stay beneath the radar. Cass then opened her thick brown directory where she kept the names and contact information of her trusted journalistic resources. She glanced down a page and found her top go-to person.

Ira Grant was "Granny" or "Gran" to fellow journalists. Gran had seen the film The Front Page as a kid and had been smitten by the news game, played old style. He went to work for The National Enquirer, the notorious tabloid, and learned to dig up the dirt. He lived to expose. Like a medieval torturer, he enjoyed flaying his subjects, ripping off their false fronts in print.

If a celebrity refused to see Gran, he would put a "death watch" on that star, the journalist's term for relentlessly following that person to scare up all the details of where the star had been, for how long, how many drinks, every individual he was in contact with, from doorman to superstar. Gran's sources were enormous, reaching into the highest echelons of government and to the lowest street walker.

"Are you keeping good notes?" he growled in response to Cass's call. "It's a book. Not just a book, but a break-out book. Your whole sick, complex murderous story. How can I help?"

"I'm trying to get some background on Dr. Marsha Newman. There's no information on line."

"I will call you back."

An hour later, the phone rang. "No wonder you could not find Dr. Marsha Newman. For many years she went under the name of Miranda Nightingale. Who could forget that name? Wasn't Nightingale the woman who helped send Vance to prison? Who also busted up your marriage?"

"The same." So Miranda had visited Vance at Balaban. Had they continued their relationship after Cass got out of the picture? "Is she somehow involved with LSD?"

"She directs an outfit called the Brainiacs. They are experimenting with what's called the new LSD. They have not officially launched their operation yet."

"Do you have an address?"

"It's outside of Woodstock. Look for an old farm, and keep your eye out for a big, shiny red barn. That is, if you're planning to go there. If you do, be careful. Just remember that Gran loves you."

21

CASS WAS UP AT 7 A.M. She went down to the basement garage and got into the black Jaguar. Settling in, she headed for the George Washington Bridge and the Palisades Parkway. She did not stop for coffee but drove directly to the outskirts of Woodstock where she slowed down and searched, driving down rustic roads. Finally a bright red barn beckoned behind a low stone wall. A large tin "B" hung from an open gate.

She drove in and continued up a road to a small lot where she parked her car. If she walked up a hill, she would reach a farm house, a fanciful Victorian structure with a large front porch, the kind of place you would want your grandmother to own. A swimming pool, emptied for the winter, occupied a space near a tennis court.

Instead Cass turned down the path to the shiny red barn. Bold, colorful graffiti covered one side of the barn, and a sign painted on a large blue door read "Welcome." Cass rang a bell, and was buzzed in. A huge red and gold mural covered one wall. Graffiti covered another wall. The barn appeared to be arranged in a haphazard style of office structure with glass cubicles, scattered tables and chairs. A group of what might have been students, possibly techies, with pale faces and eager expressions, sat in a circle talking in undertones.

A young woman sat at a large blue-painted desk near the front entrance. She greeted Cass with a smile. "Welcome to the Brainiacs. How can I help you?" Her red hair streamed, or rather stringed down. Her freckles were enormous. Earnest brown eyes bulged out from under heavily mascaraed eyelashes. Her checked yellow shirt was opened to the third button, with no hint of a breast in sight. Athletic looking. Maybe a runner. Intense.

Cass would seek common ground. "Are you a student? You remind me of one of my young neighbors in Greenwich Village."

"Greenwich Village. Wow! How exotic. No. I'm from Chicago. I graduated from the University of Chicago last year." She scrunched her mouth up and moved her head to the side as if to examine Cass from a different angle. "Chi's a great city. The windy wonder. But I left."

"And how is that working out for you?"

"Wonderfully. Fabulous. I adore the Brainiacs. I'm thrilled to be an intern here."

"Who wouldn't be?" Cass looked around as if seeking a hint to what the Brainiacs might be. "I am intrigued. Tell me more about the Brainiacs."

"You tell me." The young woman offered Cass a challenging grin as she shuffled papers on her desk, apparently bored, latching on to Cass as a possible temporary source of amusement. "Like what do you think we are?"

Cass looked around at the graffiti-covered walls and the circle of young men and women with the bleary, eager look of graduate students. "It looks like something imaginative and experimental is happening here. The Brainiacs. I love the tag."

The young woman held her hand out to Cass. "Ginger."

"Lovely to meet you, Ginger." Cass shook her hand. "My name is Cassandra."

"Hello, Cassandra. As an intern and beginner, I don't share my views on the Brainiacs. We're in the formative stages and it's like, so fresh and fun and exciting, and like if I were Madame Curie, would I want my assistant who cleans the tubes blabbing?"

"Probably not." Cass nodded her head.

"What else can I do you for?" Ginger's smile now had a tinge of superiority, of the insider pushing out the intruder trying to put her foot in the door. "Or maybe you're lost and just wandered in here by accident. That happens."

"No. I am here to see Marsha Newman."

"Hmmn." Ginger consulted a piece of paper on her desk. "What is your last name?"

"Cooper."

Ginger looked down the list and shook her head. "You don't have an appointment with Doctor Newman. Besides that, she does not see anybody until 4 P.M. or later. And she's way booked up. I doubt if I could make an appointment until maybe four months from now. Of course, if somebody cancelled first, I could put your name on a waiting list."

"I'm afraid that's impossible. I'm sure she would want to see me."

"Why?" Ginger doodled on a yellow pad. "Give me ten reasons. Or at least one." She offered a sly smile.

"I'm a journalist. I'm doing a piece on the Brainiacs and I was told that Doctor Newman would be the prime source for information."

"Oh." Ginger looked startled. "Then why the not-knowing about us act?"

"It's not an act, dear." Cass used the 'dear' to put herself in the senior and knowing role. "I'm a journalist. I wanted a fresh perspective on the Brainiacs. In fact, can I quote you?"

"I would rather you didn't." Ginger leered. "You must realize that we currently are not talking to the press. Listen, the Wall Street Journal and the New York Times both came begging, to say nothing of those icky tabloid types. But like I told you, think of Madame Curie. We're in the experimental stage. Like the Brainiacs is planning a big press party six months from now and we'll have something to tell the world. Wow. Kazow! Do you get it?"

"I get it. Okay, will you do one thing for me?"

"I'll try. If I can."

"Tell Doctor Newman that I want to see her and that it's urgent. I drove up from New York. It's Cass Cooper."

"Cass Cooper." Ginger eyed her with new interest. "I thought you looked familiar. I've been following your case."

"And?"

"You are a murder suspect. In not one but two cases. I prefer the tag 'suspect' to the euphemism 'person of interest'. You practically announced yourself as a suspicious personality by giving me that long first name of Cassandra, rather than your fairly well-known byline, Cass Cooper." Ginger eyed her speculatively and munched on the end of a ball-point pen. She put the pen down. "When you say you're Cass Cooper, do people ever eyeball you and give you grief?"

"Occasionally."

"Murder's not really my thing. I do not read mysteries as a rule. I gave Clinton's first novel The President Is Missing a whirl. He's no Dostoyevsky."

"I found the lady villain a preposterous bore, but the critics loved her."

"Let me try and reach Doctor Newman." She picked up the phone and pushed buttons. She turned away from Cass. After a conspiratorial minute, she turned back to Cass.

"Doctor Newman will see you. But you will have to wait. Like an hour or maybe more. Over there." Ginger gestured towards a group of chairs not far from the receptionist's desk. "There's coffee. Help yourself." Ginger pointed to a table with an urn, milk, sugar and paper cups. "It's not bad. We keep it pretty fresh."

Cass walked over to the reception area. She opted to seat herself in a green chair with a wicker seat. The seating group included an old-fashioned rocker painted a startling hot pink. From every angle, the Brainiacs presented themselves as free and unconventional. Cass poured herself a cup of coffee, and sat down to wait. Despite the new age atmosphere, the Brainiacs had the decency to offer real coffee rather than herbal tea.

She opened her phone and glanced down at the messages. More journalists were in pursuit. She erased their names. She was glad she had escaped to the country, if she could count this an escape. Donaldson had called her. He had called repeatedly about Pru, asking her not to talk to the NYPD without him present. But she had already had it out with Detective Adams. She needed to call Donaldson but this was not the time nor the place.

Joe Blinger, a literary agent who specialized in the sensational, had tried to contact her. She hated his message and his nasally voice. If she did write a book, Blinger would be her last choice for agent.

Cass drank a second cup of coffee. An hour passed without an entrance by the former Miranda Nightingale.

Receptionist Ginger approached. "You have been patient. Unfortunately, Doctor Newman cannot see you today. It's just impossible for her and she sends her regrets." Ginger carried an official looking book in hand. "You can make an appointment, which would bring us to four months from today at 3 P.M. Can I pencil you in?"

"Please do." Cass stood up.

"If you give me your number, I will call you if there's an earlier cancellation."

"I would appreciate that." Cass gave Ginger her number.

"Not a problem. Have a nice day." Ginger smiled in what she appeared to conceive as an empathetic manner. "And good luck with everything, including your trip back to the city. A snow storm has been predicted. So it's good that you're getting on the road now."

"Before I leave, I'm desperate to use the lady's room."

"Sure. It's down at the end there by the right. You can't miss it."

"Is that the only lady's room?"

"Unfortunately, yes. But the lady's room is quite large. We don't have a unisex room but in moments of desperation, I head for the men's room. I always knock first. It's closer." Ginger grinned.

"Thanks for the tip, Ginger."

Cass headed down to the lady's room, which was capacious, as promised. She picked a stall on the end and settled in for Miranda/Marsha to make an entrance. She did not know any woman who could get through several hours without least one visit to the john. She listened, but she was not familiar with Miranda/Marsha's voice. If she opened the door just a crack, she could peer out into the room. Fortunately the john had a lid. She closed it and sat down. She had expected Miranda/Marsha to be curious about her, Cass Cooper. She would want to meet her – to learn how Cass had managed to find her, and why had she come? The two women had never met. How strange and ironic that they might collide for the first time to the sound of flushing toilets in an upstate barn.

She waited and listened to the bits of chatter. It was business as usual. Talk about the weather. A new bargain outlet in a mall near Kingston. Plans for a wedding shower. It took an hour before Miranda/Marsha made her appearance. Cass opened the door a crack and looked out. She had seen pictures of Miranda, a glamorous creature in vivid make-up, dramatic earrings, hair teased, curled, and colored. An arrogant expression on her face.

Marsha presented quite a different picture. Her hair, cut short, was salt and pepper black. Her only makeup was lipstick in a pale shade. Tiny studs in her ears. Large horn-rimmed glasses. A black turtleneck. Black form-fitting slacks that set off her excellent figure. A large wristwatch. Despite the new, subdued Marsha, a certain glamour persisted. She could have been a professor or a movie director.

Cass stepped out of the booth and approached the sink where Marsha washed her hands.

"Marsha. Doctor Newman. Or should I say Miranda? It's Cass Cooper."

LOVERS AND OTHER KILLERS

Marsha turned to direct a hard gaze on Cass, putting her under the microscope, totally evaluating her in about one second. Everything about Marsha bespoke efficiency and action. If she could, she would probably display the wheels turning in her head. Look at me. I am smart.

"Ah, Ginger said you wanted to talk with me. It's just impossible. Maybe in a few months. Of course, I would really like to accommodate you –"

Cass broke in. "I need to see you now. And you need to see me."

"What's the urgency?"

"It's about Vance and LSD and murder."

Marsha did not look happy. "Yes. We should talk. Let's go up to the main house. There's a library where we can have some privacy."

22

CASS FOLLOWED MARSHA AND HER long strides on a wordless walk from the barn to the Victorian farmhouse. Inside, the house had the comfortable look of a well-used dormitory. A place of fraternization and intellectual activity, where an elite group could mingle in the assurance that their fellow members were also smart, while secretly believing that they, of course, were the smartest.

Marsha took an "Occupied" sign hanging from the doorknob of the library, hung it on the outside doorknob, closed the door, gestured to a leather chair, and sat down across from Cass. "We use this library as a private retreat. With so many people around, one needs a place to get away."

The room was a jumble of worn furniture, with books and notebooks scattered about, a bulletin board, and chess and scrabble games set up on small tables. "It feels like a college dorm recreation room."

"We are definitely collegial. We share. I am the director and founder of the Brainiacs, but I do not impose my ideas. I am not dictatorial." Marsha cleared her throat. "I'm amazed that you would seek me out. I thought you would hate me and avoid me."

"To be absolutely candid, in the past I did avoid meeting you. I didn't hate you. I despised you. At this point, we don't have to play games with each other."

Marsha's smile was more of a smirk. "Before I spill my guts, tell me about yourself, Cass. You've been coming off your high horse, caught by the cameras – wrapped around an attractive man, strutting up the High Line, and so soon after Vance's death. Then the murder of your friend Prudence. You found both of the bodies. I'm not sure the publicity about you and the guy is good for your case." She frowned. "Cases."

"Life happens."

"If it would make you more comfortable, we could smoke." Marsha held up a small marijuana pipe in invitation.

"Not for me, but don't let me inhibit you."

Marsha stretched her long legs out in front of her and leaned back into the chair. She reached into a drawer, took out a small metal container, opened it and tamped a few nuggets of cannabis into the pipe, lit it with a match, inhaled deeply, held her breath and exhaled. She rested her head back against the chair, appearing far from the seductress, more like a weary academic who has graded too many papers.

"Meeting you is quite a revelation." Marsha inhaled again, held the smoke, blew it out. "Did Vance ever talk to you about me? Tell you wild tales about my inordinate fascination with him? Also repulsion. His feeling of superiority would occasionally erupt out of him like a cudgel. He would make me feel low and inferior. Basically like a piece of shit. Of course, Vance compartmentalized. He kept all the parts of his complicated life separate. That's how he maintained his sanity. He was difficult but I persisted."

"If you had all these objections to Vance, why the avid pursuit?"

"I liked his voice."

"Voice?"

"Some men's voices turn me on. I dig Sinatra. So what now? More cozy girl talk about the late Vance Cooper."

"You visited him in prison. What was his state of mind when you saw him?"

"Hard to say. I was kind of nervous myself." Marsha inhaled deeply and blew the smoke out into the room. "Isn't that smell delicious. It always reminds me of sex, or the prelude to sex." She closed her eyes, opened them and smiled. "Does that bother you? My sex talk?"

"Would it matter?"

"You can relax, Mrs. Goody Two Shoes. I didn't stand a chance with Vance, not that I didn't try. I went after him. He resisted me. I wore him down, worked on his vulnerabilities." She took another puff. "I was a calculated bitch. I didn't care. I wanted what and who I wanted. Then the big Ponzi scheme scandal and prison. I needed for my own self respect to get back into Vance's good graces after turning him in. I contacted him at Balaban but he refused to see me. I wrote him a short note. I told him about my voyage towards self-discovery. I was desperate to make it up to people I had screwed. Vance agreed to see me.

"We spent about an hour together. We both were trying to change our lives, and that's what we talked about. I told him about The Brainiacs. How I'm involved with experimentation with mind altering drugs. LSD. Psilocybin mushrooms. What we call entheogens, from the Greek word for 'the divine within.' Our goal is to create personal transformation through use of the substances and guidance."

"Why call yourselves the Brainiacs?"

"Although we are seeking psychic enlightenment, we're using our brains to set us on that path. We're eclectic. Meditation, group meetings. If you will recall, several years back Timothy Leary was heavily into experimentation with LSD. Then there were problems. Too many people OD-ing and jumping out windows, taking the wrong stuff with the wrong people. Here we move slowly and everyone is safe and carefully guided. This is one reason why we don't want to talk to the press or publicize what we're doing. We do not want anyone getting ideas, experimenting on their own, and getting into trouble."

"And Vance?'"

"I wanted him to get involved with the Brainiacs when he was released from prison. I thought it would engage his creative energies." She raised her eyebrows and dropped them. Slapped her knee. Puffed on her pipe. "He thought it was a brilliant idea, but he had no desire to be a part of it."

"And what were his objections?"

"He had other plans. But he was interested in LSD on a personal level. He had never tripped and wanted to try it, thought it could bring up some stuff that he could use. So I slipped him a tablet. And that was that." Marsha sat back in the chair, spread her legs and arms wider, like someone trying to float in a pool. She closed her eyes.

"Do you usually recommend people taking LSD on their own?"

"Not at all. But what the hell. I felt like it was a charitable act. A man locked up in prison could use an LSD trip. Like I owed him something." Martha's eyelids hung at half-mast. "He came out of prison. You two met, and whatever he told you did not please you. You stuck the knife in his heart. Now you're sorry and scared and came here and you're trying to figure it out."

"I did not kill Vance," Cass said. "All of that brain food -- the mushrooms and LSD --seems to have screwed up your mind."

"LSD does not affect the brain."

"When did you decide to ditch Miranda Nightingale for Marsha Newman?"

"I was never Miranda except I was. I assumed that name when I tried to shake off lower class non-respectability in Scranton, Pennsylvania. "

"And why the Doctor tag?"

"I have a PhD in psycho analytics. After college, I pursued that at UCLA. But I did not use the degree, not even in defense of my own sanity.

I went on to Wharton for a business degree. I'm quite the whiz at academics, if not personal life. I gave myself a beautiful name. I became Miranda Nightingale. But everything crashed for me. I went through a terrible time including Vance's going to prison. I was shattered with guilt and pain. Who was I anyway? I had no clue. I had a genuine breakdown. I had to crawl back to sanity. I decided to try and be who I was. Marsha's such a flat name compared to Miranda. I am learning to accept it."

"Doesn't the country life oppress you? Do you ever go into the city?"

"Never. I'm like a nun in a convent. I am loathe to leave here and my fellow novitiates. I have not been away for at least two months. It's an inner trip."

"I see."

"Do you? I expected you to be the picture of calm. Instead I see nerves and tamped down hysteria. If you feel trapped, I can open the door."

"Claustrophobia is not my problem. Finding Vance's killer is. I thought it might be you."

23

MARSHA MOVED HER FEET UP and down, as if exercising, and responded with a "Ha," somewhere between a snort and an exclamation. "Really. That's kind of rich, isn't it? Why would I of all people kill Vance? I don't think you really get it, who I am, the kind of driven personality that I am for better or worse. The Brainiacs are what matter to me, not futile romance. I had no motive for killing Vance."

"Suppose he didn't like what you were doing. You paint a glowing picture of the Brainiacs, but what if Vance knew something hidden about your operation. Why the big secret? Why avoid the press? Suppose he threatened to expose you."

"There's nothing to expose. We want to help people fit into society. I'm not talking conformity. I'm talking the productive life. The enriched life. Wider horizons. Creativity." She refilled her pipe, put a match to the cannabis, and inhaled. "I told you I had given up on Vance. That he despised me. But I do believe there was some reconciliation at our last meeting in that prison."

"You didn't feel disgusting and hateful?"

"I harbored the hope that later, perhaps much later when I was a more wonderful person, and Vance had found himself, that we could be new people in a new relationship. That was my dream. I was working towards that. Then he was gone. Forever." Marsha looked stricken.

In the distance, a guitar played, counterpoint to fragmented laughter outside the window. "It's possible to murder someone and regret the action. It's called the crime of passion."

"I do not act on impulse. I am an intellectual. I think things through."

"You went to visit Vance in Balaban to plead your case, to show him what a swell person you had become, and how he could find a new life with you and your Brainiacs. He slammed the door in your face. Everything turned to ashes. You couldn't have him and decided that nobody could have him. You found your way into Donaldson's house. You stabbed Vance and left. Back to the Brainiacs. Such a convenient cover. Then you made a return trip to New York and murdered Pru."

Marsha put down her pipe. Her face darkened. "If I were going to murder another woman, it would not be a superficial, social-climbing twit, the likes of Prudence Duluth. What's my motive?"

"She knew that you killed Vance. She had to be eliminated."

Marsha's face had gone from dark to pale, almost ashen. She looked weary and on the verge of ugly. "This is all so dumb and meaningless. How would I even know Pru?"

"Pru went in for the mind-bending and esoteric. She might have sought out the Brainiacs and dropped LSD. Vance might even have clued her in on the Brainiacs. She visited him in Balaban. Prudence and you could have shared secrets that you both regretted."

"That's a stretch."

"I would like to see your records of people who sought treatment here."

"They are private. Of course we would not reveal their names. There's a doctor/patient confidence."

"You would have to turn them over to the police."

"The police have not approached me."

"How could they find you? You changed your identity."

"The police can find anybody if they really want to." Marsha tapped her pipe into an ashtray, opened her tin vial, popped a couple of buds into the pipe, lit the pipe and inhaled. "Sure you won't smoke, Cass? It makes everything friendlier."

"Thank you, no. I am driving back to New York, and weed does change one's perceptions."

"As we talk, I'm wondering if we might have been friends. Despite your accusations, I do not dislike you. You are not a bore. No, you are definitely skewed, and I appreciate that in a person." Marsha puffed and exhaled. "But no, we would not be friends because I do not like women. I have always preferred the company of men."

"Any special reason?"

"Men don't compete with you. They admire you and bring flowers and buy dinner and make love. Women are always conniving and wanting to steal your guy, and they want to talk endlessly about themselves or nothing. Gets me down."

"You could love a man and kill him."

"You do not give up, do you? You claim to be innocent. You seek another to take your place in Sing Sing. I could arrange for a consultation here. You could drop a mild form of acid with a guide, and it might lead to some new perceptions."

"Thanks but no thanks."

"Figured you wouldn't go for it." In the corner, a clock bonged. Snow flurried past the window. "If you're looking for suspects to hang Vance's murder on, how about Jane Endicott? She called me and said 'Vance screwed me blue.' She did not explain."

"One remark hardly makes her a murder suspect."

"Jane has murky depths beneath the cool librarian façade. Supposedly she's your friend. But what woman is really your friend? She's your friend until she stabs you or somebody else in the back."

"So you're in touch with Jane."

"I avoid her. She called me. I cut her off quite abruptly. She was a part of my old life. I do not party. The idea is anathema to me. For the first time in my life, I'm moving toward serenity."

"I'm amazed that you're still compos mentis after all the smoking." Snow flurried past the window. "I had better get going before the storm hits."

"I'd offer you a room here for the night, but we're completely booked."

Cass stood up. As she turned, she noticed the small painting that hung in the corner, composed of a bright red sky, yellow stars and a purple moon, with a prominent signature in black. "A Fozer," she exclaimed. "Is that a new or old Fozer?"

"I actually could not say. I had not even noticed it before. Almost everything in this house was already on the walls when we took it over."

Cass moved closer to the picture. "I believe it's a new Fozer. The paint is so bright. It could be a kiddy picture."

"Does it matter?" Marsha said peevishly.

"Everything matters."

"Everything matters and nothing matters. There's no need to attempt profundity as you exit. As for the painting, one of the interns could have hung it there. We want the young people to feel that they belong and are making a contribution. I am not prepared to discuss old Fozer or new Fozer with you. Art is not one of my fields of expertise or interest. I have never nor do I plan to pick up a paint brush. I do not do crafts. You might find other Brainiacs stringing beads or throwing pots, but not yours truly. That is not my path. Now I encourage you to take care on the road." Marsha attempted a smile that didn't make it. Her green eyes looked sphinx-like. "The snow's coming down. You don't want to meet with an accident."

Marsha did not walk Cass to the door.

24

Cass stopped at the Woodstock Groceria and bought a large container of coffee. She felt jumpy, nervous. She was over-caffeinating but meeting Marsha had set her on edge. The snow thickened and her wind-shield wipers thwacked. She turned on the radio to hear the weather prognosticators predicting the worst. She should make it back to New York before the serious snow hit.

When a blue car side-swiped her, causing her to spin her wheels and almost go off the road, she was ill prepared. The blue car kept moving. She slowed down and watched it speed away, the driver's license number indecipherable in the falling snow. She could not help but shiver, and wonder if Marsha had pursued her or dispatched a hit man to create an almost-accident. A warning.

Stay away.

Marsha had pointed the finger of suspicion at Jane. Known for her lust for sexual experimentation, Jane also had the reputation for being one of the most rational people on the planet. As for Vance screwing her blue, Vance might have invested money for Jane and lost it. But Jane did not manifest an excessive love of or need for money. She had spent a fortune on doctors for her transition from male to female and never begrudged a penny. Her lifestyle and wardrobe were conservative. Her one indulgence was buying expensive gifts for nieces and nephews. Occasionally she splurged on dinner in a good restaurant.

But Jane had been acting strange lately. She had shown up so briefly for Angelina's gallery opening. She did not contact Cass after Pru's murder. Cass almost spilled coffee as the idea flashed that Jane could have stabbed Pru. She tried to turn away from that chilling thought. Marsha suspected Jane of killing Vance. Had Jane moved beyond voyeurism and dropped a pair of bikini panties, prelude to stabbing Vance to death?

Back in New York, Cass garaged the car and entered her apartment. The phone rang. She ignored it. She needed a hot shower. She undressed and relished the water pouring over her. She dried off with a fluffy towel and pulled on jeans and a sweater.

Outside her window, snow tumbled down, fat flakes ready to transform the city into snow sculpture, to put caps on fire hydrants, turn winter's bare trees into dancing beauties, their graceful white arms swaying in the winter wind. Cass had always loved snow, the indoor warmth it created.

Her nerves were frayed. She could use a brandy. She had earned it. It was medicinal. She turned away from the brandy bottle and brewed a cup of tea.

The TV weather catastrophe criers were having a field day, interrupting regular programming to carry on about the snow, telling viewers to put on their scarves and boots and offering other annoying admonitions, predicting how many inches would fall and where. The phone rang. Donaldson. Cass picked up.

"Where have you been, Cass? You don't respond to my messages. I had blocked out time today to talk with you about Prudence Duluth. When I couldn't reach you, I was afraid something had happened to you. I contacted your doorman. He said that you took off in your car this morning and had not returned."

"I drove up to Woodstock."

"Why?"

"To meet the infamous Miranda Nightingale. She's now going by the tag of Marsha Newman. Doctor Marsha Newman."

"Why seek her out? Suppose something happened to Miranda or Marsha or whoever she is. She could fall down a flight of stairs and claim that you pushed her. She is capable of that kind of action. Nothing would make her happier, I'm sure, than to have you hang for Vance's murder."

"No doubt. But right now she's too busy polishing her halo to make a move. Doctor Newman is a mover and shaker in the Brainaics program."

"Which is?"

"She's experimenting with LSD and other mind-bending substances to help people make changes in their lives.. Transformations. This is the new LSD, doled out with care."

"She was always bad news," Donaldson spluttered. "Don't listen to her pathetic and unreal bullshit."

"She could have killed Vance. So many people could have killed Vance. It could even have been you, my beloved Donaldson."

"Please don't say that, even in jest." Donaldson sounded genuinely wounded. "Just to set the record straight, I talked with Detective Adams, told him where I was that night, in minute detail. We also went over my house plan. I'm working and I'm praying for you."

"A Buddhist prayer?"

"I am a Buddhist *and* an Episcopalian. I maintain a strong bond of fellowship with the members of St. James Church on Madison Avenue."

"Do you think there's such a thing as the murderous personality? For instance, would Macbeth have been a killer without Lady Macbeth to egg him on?"

"If I were William Shakespeare, I could answer that question."

"Is it possible that you gave the killer entrée? Did you ever give the keys to your house to a woman?"

"Now you're interrogating me, Cass. And I find that offensive. No, I did not offer my keys to any woman. The women I invite to my home are those with whom I have a serious relationship. They are few and far between."

"Of course." Cass wondered if his lady friends had as much difficulty sometimes getting through to Donaldson as she did. The boy's boy. The man's man. "I didn't mean to offend."

"I did not mean to bark."

"In your conversations with Vance, did he ever voice fear – like somebody had it in for him?"

Donaldson did not answer immediately. Finally he spoke. "He was afraid of you, Cass. He believed you had it in for him. I did not probe. I felt it was personal business. Maybe I did not want to know."

"Did you tell that to Detective Adams?"

"Of course not. I am your lawyer. I am defending you, Cass. You need to work with me. I am here to save your life. We have not discussed your new embroilment in the death of Prudence Duluth. What did you tell Detective Adams?"

"The facts. That Prudence did not kill herself. She did not even sign the farewell note."

"From now on, do not discuss your case – cases – with anybody. If you are going to talk with any member of the NYPD, I want to be present. Call me. Avoid Miranda Nightingale at all costs. Will you do that?"

"Oh, Donaldson, why am I so wrong?"

"You are not wrong. You are in a difficult, albeit heartbreaking situation. Do not punish yourself. We will get through this somehow. I promise."

"I have complete confidence in you." Cass put her phone down. As she did, a sinking feeling hit her in the gut. She looked at the prayer rug, so recently the backdrop for her love-making with Noah. Could she call it love?

Experimentation? Affection? Need? Passion? Screwing around? Her new lifestyle demanded a new vocabulary, yet to be invented.

She could call Noah, just to say hello and be reassured by his warmth. No. Rules for men and women were changing but not fast enough for women of her age. The man still had the prerogative to make the phone call, to ring the doorbell, to make the pursuit in the ongoing ritual practiced by men and women. The mind games. The body games.

Bugsy Fozer answered on the first ring. "Cass Cooper. How delightful to hear from you."

"I was excited to see an original Fozer hanging in the Brainiacs headquarters," Cass said. "It's smashing – wonderful colors."

"Marsha Newman requested the colors. She left the configuration to me."

"Fascinating. Do you know Marsha well?"

"Ha ha." Fozer broke into an extended giggle. "I could tell you stories, and you, of all people, would be interested. Maybe you would like to come down to my studio. I could give you the tour, and we could exchange pleasantries."

"Give me your address. I'm there."

25

Cass stepped out into the snowstorm. She counted herself lucky to quickly find a taxi to take her to Spring Street in Soho. Arriving at Fozer's building, she rode up on the huge elevator, originally made to transport goods rather than people. The elevator dated back to the days when Soho was a place for manufacture rather than the creation of art. Fozer was waiting for her when she clambered off the elevator.

"Greetings, Cassandra." Fozer welcomed her with a flourished bow. He had dressed for the occasion in a black velvet jacket to accompany his baggy jeans and brocade slippers. A red silk scarf looped several times around his neck completed the ensemble. "Welcome to my humble abode and studio. Now give me that wet coat and I will hang it up to dry. Come in, come in."

Cass had always enjoyed visiting artists' studios with their atmosphere of things being made, of inspiration and originality in action. Fozer's studio was no exception. The room burst with stars, skies, suns, sunsets, moons and more stars in every color of the rainbow. Star pictures hung on the walls, and dried on the floors.

"And which one belongs to me?" Cass asked.

"None," Fozer replied emphatically. "For a special person like yourself, I will create a unique painting that's totally you. I want you to tell me the colors and what's important to you – the elements to be included."

"That's wonderful. But doesn't it interfere with the creative impulse. I mean – wouldn't Van Gogh have been insulted if I asked him to do a painting for me and specified the colors?"

"I cannot speak for Van Gogh, but didn't various people ask him to paint their portraits, and he was happy to comply? Regardless, I am not Van Gogh. If that were the case, I would be mad and brilliant. I am merely Fozer. I am not a good artist. I am not a bad artist. I am an adequate and even occasionally inspired artist."

Fozer led them over to a seating area. Cass sat down in a green leather chair and Fozer settled on a couch covered with colorful scarves and pillows. He picked a notebook up from the table, and a pen. "Now, what do you want in your picture?"

"This is so sudden."

"Spontaneity is key. Don't think. Respond to your impulses."

"I want a black and blue sky. A silver Empire State building. A big beautiful white moon. And stars. Big and small, and every color of the rainbow. I want to be dazzled. In fact, you could include a rainbow."

"Divine." Fozer quickly wrote what Cass had requested. "You are piquing my creativity. About the rainbow, must it be many-hued?"

"Not at all. I leave that to you."

"Excellent. I'm considering a black and white rainbow, special for you, because you are a journalist."

"That's genius. Do all of your pictures reflect the sensibilities of the people you paint them for?"

"Only my favorite people."

"Doctor Marsha Newman?"

"I would not call her a favorite person, but she is certainly significant." Fozer stood up. "Why don't I get us a drink. What's your poison?"

"How about Coke?"

"Excellent. And brandy for me."

"Good choice for a snowy night."

Fozer returned with two amply filled snifters. They wished each other good luck. "May you live forever, and may I never die," said Fozer. They clinked glasses. "Now we can settle down to business. I sensed that you wanted to talk about Marsha Newman, the former Miranda Nightingale."

"Yes."

"I was uncomfortable discussing her on the phone, and curious to know of your involvement. She claims to have hung her Fozer in her inner sanctum. Obviously you were there. Why? Were you considering taking a trip with the Brainiacs – that is, getting the treatment?"

"Honestly, no." Cass took a tiny sip of Coke. "Let's say I had mixed motives. I wanted to meet Marsha – the former Miranda Nightingale – because I believe that she might have been involved in Vance's death, and my mind has not changed. I went up there to meet her for the first time."

"Intriguing," Fozer said. "I will share what I know, but I would appreciate it if you would – what's the expression – keep it off the record."

"Of course."

Fozer sat back. A plump black and white cat had come out and settled on his lap. "This is Aphrodite. Beautiful, isn't she? My feline goddess." Fozer stroked the cat absently as he talked and received a purring response. "Are you a cat person, Cass?"

"Not at all."

"Aphrodite will not bother you. She understands the world. That everyone cannot love her. Marsha is a cat person. She's clever and cunning. But let me fill you in on how that connection came about. I visited Vance in prison. As I told you, it was a low point, my black and blue period. He suggested that

I do the kiddy pictures. He also said I might want to try tripping with the Brainiacs." Fozer swished the brandy and gazed into the glass.

"So the recommendation came straight from Vance. "

"I was ready to try anything to arouse myself from the dreadful funk. One fine spring day I rented a car and drove up to Brainiac headquarters. I spent four enlightening days there. I tripped. Let's say that it had its ups and downs. Marsha was my guide – the person who stays with you during the trip and discusses it with you afterwards. I suppose I should have felt privileged getting the four-star celebrity treatment from the top Brainiac person. Reason for all the attention? I don't know. In many ways, the trip was enlightening. In other ways terrifying." Fozer took a long sip of brandy.

Aphrodite the cat jumped off his lap and disappeared into the star pictures drying on the floor.

"Aphrodite likes the smell of new paint," Fozer said. "I do not object to her occasionally leaving her cat paw print on a picture. I believe it adds to the picture's charm. I enjoy having an artistic collaborator. The kiddies don't mind."

"Why were you frightened?"

"The unreality of the situation scared me to death. Marsha Newman was dishing out her party line to me – all about freedom and independent thinking, and breaking down borders between people and states and countries, men and woman. The works. But I did not believe a word she said. It struck me as an enormous lie. As if she had something else up her sleeve and this Brainiac camp in Woodstock was just a front."

"But why?"

"What gave me that insight? Perhaps it was the acid. But it goes beyond that. I consider myself an intuitive. It's not always a comfortable feeling. Often when I meet a person I sense things about them – more than I want to know. I was born with this – some consider it a gift, or a curse. I know that I blabbed at length about my feeling that Marsha was false while I was tripping

– I remember that she tried to talk me down and out of it. I was babbling. I could not stop. Those words were not in the verbatim transcript they gave me when I left. Somehow they were erased from the record. We did not discuss my feelings in our follow-up talk. I broached my views gently and she did not respond. I proceeded to play dumb. It felt safer.

"She presents herself as the founder of the Brainiacs, and the big cheese. But when I was palavering with Ginger – the receptionist – I heard her answer the phone and say to Marsha, in hushed and awed tones: 'The Leader is on the line and it's urgent.' I do believe there's another person on a higher level than Marsha. An unnamed person in command."

"Who could that be?"

"It could be anybody. It could be the President of the United States."

"Wouldn't that be a shocker?" Cass sipped warm Coke.

"Anything's possible. But Ginger suggested that I clear out swiftly, because for some reason or other Marsha had been asking questions about me. And had I been sniffing around? And could I be trusted to keep what I knew about the Brainiacs under my hat? One signs a waiver when one signs up to trip with the Brainiacs, promising not to disclose anything they learn, until the Brainiacs are ready to go all-out with publicity and reach out to the press."

"Thank you for sharing with me, Fozer."

"I feel better for talking with you. I have not really felt safe since I visited the Brainiacs and mad Marsha."

"Did Marsha tell you what the colors she requested for her picture signified?

"Only the red sky. A new world was coming."

26

CASS LEFT FOZER'S. THE STORM had accelerated. Snow stung her face. Taxi headlights beamed through the white storm, but all cabs were occupied. She struggled towards the subway and descended down to the crowded platform where city dwellers, dressed for the storm in colorful hats, hooded coats and boots, stamped their feet. A busker played a lively tune on a harmonica. A festive feeling filled the air, as if the season's first serious snowfall had hung out a banner that said "Let's celebrate." Cass took the train uptown, exited at 14th Street, and then slogged through the snow to her apartment. She hung her coat up to dry.

She craved a brandy but settled for instant cocoa that she drank in her office. Snow was coming down now in big, fat, beautiful flakes. In Charley Blue's, her favorite watering hole, just a block away, she could sit at the bar and have a quiet Coke. Let the conviviality flow around her while ignoring the booze. She had not been in Charley's for at least a year. She had last met Pru there for a drink. Everything had emotional strings attached. Like she was a balloon wanting to get free and could not. Sad. She did not want to feel sad.

Cass pulled on her boots and coat. She picked up her pocketbook and took the elevator downstairs. "Take care, Mrs. Cooper," doorman Jose admonished. "I hope you're not going far."

"I don't think you'll have to send the St. Bernard dogs after me."

Cass walked into the storm. She was still capable of doing something dumb and necessary. She had been trying so hard to be sane and rational. Now she wanted to kick, to break things. She turned her face up to welcome the snow.

Charlie Blue's had retained its non-upscale atmosphere. Far from a dive bar, it served excellent hamburgers and chili for which it was renowned. It was still a neighborhood place, not a destination bar written up in New York magazine or tourists' guides. Cass opened the door. Most of the tables were full. Miles Davis on tape played in the background.

Cass took her favorite seat at the end of the bar. Harry, the bald, burly bartender who never forgot a name, stood behind the bar. He greeted her with an enormous smile. "Cass." His smile grew wider. "We have missed you. Where've ya been?"

Cass appreciated Harry's pretending not to know about about her present situation.

"Busy, Harry. Really, really busy."

"I'm happy to see you." He winked at her. Before Cass had a chance to order, Harry had placed a double Scotch on the rocks in front of her, with a side of water. She should ask Harry to change the order, but the Scotch tantalized with its smoky aroma. She would drink the Scotch slowly, nurse it. Then she would leave.

"You've got it, Harry. Scotch rocks. Thank you for remembering." Cass picked up the glass. Ice cubes rattled like musical chimes. "Let me pay you now." Cass put her bills down on the bar.

"Put your money away. This is your welcome back drink. We're glad to see you. You've been a stranger too long."

Cass raised her glass to Harry before taking the first sip. How smoothly the Scotch slipped down. She needed to take it slow.

A New York Daily News reporter, Arnold Rand, sat down next to her. His ugly attractive face with its huge nose and oversized mouth had always appealed to her. His laugh crackled. He launched into one of his reporter's anecdotes about an actress who slammed the door in his face. "But at 3 A.M. she fell in love with me." Cass laughed in response to his journalist's war story. The drink she had planned to sip slowly slipped away. When Arnold insisted on buying her a second drink, Cass did not refuse.

In the festive atmosphere engendered by the snowstorm, Cass felt her tensions ease. She had reached that boozy platform of having an edge, the kick up into a sparkling world. It was all so delightful, people coming into the bar, stamping their feet, brushing off snow.

Her glass appeared empty again. She had not been aware of drinking the second – or was it third --Scotch. She had been so absorbed in conversation with a young writer who had sold Christmas trees before the holiday to support his screenwriting ambitions. He had a broad forehead with damp brown curls hanging over it, a serious set to his chin.

What advice did a successful person like herself have for him? "Get some writing credits. Don't lock your self in an attic and play the artiste." Did the kid hear her? He had told her his name but she had forgotten it. Had she paid for the last drink? She motioned to Harry and made a sign asking for the check.

"What's the rush?" Harry put a Scotch in front of her. Cass picked up the drink and turned away from the young writer. She had talked with him enough. Time to assess other possibilities. She had forgotten how much she enjoyed bar talk. Unlike cocktail parties and receptions with their demands for cards being exchanged, bar conversations existed outside everything. In the same breath, you could discuss your favorite dollar store and Aristotle.

She felt a sag in the high, wanted to get back up there. If she opened her mouth, would her words slur? Vance had told her she was an unattractive drunk. Despite his excessive drinking, he disliked her when she drank too much and told her so. Why the double standard? He didn't know, he would say, and pour himself another drink. She put her glass down on the bar. She would leave. She did not move from the barstool.

The young writer was now engaged in a conversation with a young woman with long blond hair. "I am an ac-tor," the young woman said, stressing the two separate syllables in the word "actor," giving them importance. If Cass knew the young writer better, she would warn him off the egomaniacal blond.

She picked up the Scotch glass. Why waste good Johnny Walker Black? How could she get happy? Was she ever happy? No point in getting morose. Nothing worse than a morose drunk. Pathetic. She needed to get up, up.

Like a genie out of a bottle, Noah Lazeroff materialized at her left elbow. Snow drops melted on his black, curly hair. When he smiled at her, his teeth were white and even.

"And what brings you to my favorite bar?" Cass asked.

"I was looking for you. Nice to see you. Nice to celebrate the snow with you. I called but you didn't answer. I didn't leave a message."

"Welcome to Charlie Blue's." Cass raised her glass to him. "I have not been here for a long time. I gave up drinking. I mean serious drinking." She was babbling. She heard herself, but seemed incapable of putting a lid on it. "Do I look drunk?"

"You look merry."

"We were very tired, we were very merry, la la la on the Staten Island ferry. Edna St. Vincent Millay wrote that. You have beautiful teeth."

"I floss."

"Bravo. A man of discipline."

He had moved one inch closer to her. Everybody looked better when she was high. At her worst, she had occasionally fallen into bed with a man she thought an Adonis who turned into a toad. Right after she and Vance split. That had been part of her impetus to give up extreme drinking, as she had tagged the bad habit, loathe to call herself a drunk.

"Are you a flosser?" Noah asked.

"Not a serious flosser."

"What are you serious about?"

"Murder most foul. Or was that Agatha Christie?"

"Are you ready to leave?"

"Are you coming on to me?"

"I'm offering you a supportive arm."

She waved to Harry for another drink. After that came the blur.

27

CASS CAME TO – OR woke up – feeling like she had chewed on glass that made its way into her gut. Brilliant light assaulted her eyeballs. A light blanket covered her. She was fragmented. Powerfully hung-over. Her head ached and felt heavy. She could not lift it without adding to the pounding. Her mouth was dry. She was alone, dressed in bra and panties – at least not naked, one saving grace -- the space next to her in the king-sized bed unoccupied.

If this were a movie thriller, she would find a bloody body in the bed next to her with a knife sticking out of it, her role to be played by a younger Jane Fonda. She pulled the blanket closer around her, pulled herself up and sat on the end of the bed.

The room was neat. Walls painted a pale grey. One huge black and white painting. Enormous window panes looked out on a scene of snow banked on sills, and beyond that the Hudson River. The dazzling light did not brighten her feelings. She would have liked to throw up but that urge did not come.

Noah Lazeroff walked into the room dressed in chinos and a black and green wool sweater. "Come on out into the living room. I made coffee. There's water and aspirin and whatever else you need. Bathroom's over there." He gestured to a door. "Your clothes are on that chair." He handed her a shower cap. "I know you'll want a shower. You'll feel better."

"How was the sex?"

"I slept in the other room."

"Too hideous?"

"It's more fun when you're there."

Cass took a hot shower, combed her hair, and skipped the lipstick. She needed to look bare-faced and ugly. Noah had put coffee, coffee cups, a bottle of aspirin, a large bottle of Coke, another large bottle of water, milk and croissants on the coffee table near two large chairs. Cass sank gratefully into a chair, filled a glass with water, and took two aspirins, followed by a Coke chaser. She filled her coffee cup, added milk, and drank.

"What disgraceful thing did I do?"

"Nothing. But you were in no shape to be out on your own. I brought you here."

"I couldn't walk back to my apartment?"

"I wasn't sure if you could maneuver once you got upstairs."

"What do you want with me anyway, Noah? Why such a nice guy? What are you trying to prove?"

"You interest me."

"I'm not interesting. That's why I write about interesting people. I record their witty quotes and deep thoughts."

Noah refilled her cup. He was close to her now. She smelled him, his skin with its faint odor of lime, like the aftershave that Vance used. The wool of his sweater. She wanted to touch him, to reach out and feel the wool. She still wore Vance's old sweater. Noah's face was close to hers. Her face burned. She had a case of the hangover hots, a collegiate expression from the past popping into her head.

"No," Cass said, as if responding to a proposition. "No. No. No. No."

"Don't write me off so quickly."

"Please stop giving me that probing shrink's look. So I fell off the wagon. Do you blame me?"

"You might need help."

"No AA recommendations, please. I'm not ready for reformation."

"Do you like John Coltrane, the jazz musician?"

"Love Coltrane."

Noah walked to his Bose music player and turned on on Coltrane's album *My Favorite Things*. Coltrane's saxophone rendition of *Every Time We Say Goodbye* spilled out into the room.

"We have tried the park bench and the floor. Let's consider the bed." Noah took Cass's hand and led her to the bedroom. He turned the blinds to create a mellow light. "There are other forms of therapy."

The psychic pain and sick feeling in her gut began to dissipate. Cass feel like she had been let out of jail. Liberated. "What do you call this?" Cass asked. "Tantric sex?"

"I only know that you turn me on."

Afterwards, they lay in bed side by side.

"You talked a lot last night," Noah said.

"What was I blabbing about?"

"Edna St. Vincent Millay. Science fiction. Take me to your leader. Only Vance was the leader and that's why Marsha killed him. She knocked him out with stars. Maybe Vance did it. The red sky. The Brainiacs.."

"I went there. I met Marsha Newman."

"You'll have to tell me all about it – later."

Cass pulled closer to Noah. She sniffed his shoulder. And then she was in his arms again. It was Sunday afternoon. No need to rush away.

Later they watched the sun set together. Noah opened a bottle of wine and ordered in Chinese food. Chicken with black mushrooms, and shrimp in lobster sauce.

"Old favorites," Noah said.

"Old friends are best," Cass answered.

He gave her his blue velour robe to wear.

They ate at his coffee table

"Did I say anything else unusual last night?" Cass forked a black mushroom.

"Something about how Marsha brainwashed Vance but it wasn't Marsha. It was Miranda. And Jane. Jane and Marsha. They killed Vance together."

"Swell." Cass sipped tea. "I remember none of it. You certainly have a good memory."

"I'm a psychotherapist. Remembering is part of my job."

"So dumb to get drunk and babble. So unnecessary, and even dangerous."

"The shit you are in is so deep that I doubt if you even realize it."

"I said Marsha and Jane killed Vance."

"Yes. You did say there were four people in Donaldson's house the night of Vance's murder. You and Dev account for two – but there were two more."

"If I had Vance's book manuscript, I would know more about everything."

"I watched him write that book. It seems almost impossible that he would destroy it . It was his life. Does a man throw away a life?"

"The NYPD turned the house inside out. If it was there, they would have found it if he had hidden it. If it existed." Cass felt her spirits dropping, the sort of feeling that in the past had led her to take a drink to get up. And one drink was never enough. "How is your book doing?"

"Dev says it should be on The New York Times Best Seller list next week."

"That is exciting, and well-deserved.What time is it?"

"8 P.M."

"I need to go."

"What's your hurry?" He sat closer to her. "Do you play Scrabble?"

She was feeling too warm and cozy. She could stick around a few more hours and be lulled into a false sense of security. This was not a call-you-every day relationship. It was not what she trusted. He was so intact, and she was such a mess.

Cass stood up. "How did you know that I once frequented Charley Blue's?"

"From a piece I read about you in the New York Post."

"Oh." Cass headed into the bedroom. She pulled her clothes on, the black turtle-neck sweater and the black jeans. She returned to the living room.

"Why so abrupt?" he asked. "Have I developed a contagious disease?"

"You are wonderful. Maybe too wonderful. I am afraid of you. Of liking you too much."

"There can never be too much feeling."

"I don't hear you pledging undying devotion."

"You will not be happy if you leave now. It's too early to go to sleep, and too late to do any meaningful work. You will be at loose ends. You might even have a drink."

"Possible." Cass pulled on her coat. He turned her around to face him.

"I will miss you." Noah walked her to the elevator and handed her his card. "I'm here when you need me."

The snowfall of the evening before had turned gray and slushy. A passing truck splattered her. She would have to take her coat to be cleaned. Even in a life or death situation, the mundane prevailed.

She walked.

Survive, Cass, survive.

28

Cass took Noah's card out of her pocket and placed it down in the center of her desk. She glanced around at the familiar furniture, books. Stuff. She felt as if she had been away for weeks, months, as if she had returned from a trip abroad. So this was her life. The landscape that she cherished so desperately. Suppose she lost it all. She could survive if she could hang on to her laptop and her sanity.

Cass went to bed and fell asleep almost instantly. She woke up to the phone ringing. Bugsy Fozer was on the line.

"Are you drunk, Fozer?" Cass struggled awake. "It's 2 A.M."

"I finished your painting. You have to see it."

"The paint can't even be even dry."

"Sure it is. It's acrylic paint – dries fast – and glue. Also rhinestones and tin and beads and paper. It's called mixed media. After you left last night, I was all fired up and started working on it. I could not stop. Like I was on this high."

"I will come to your studio tomorrow, see the painting, buy the painting, and carry it away."

"No payment. It's a gift. And not tomorrow. Now."

"I would not get dressed and come downtown now if Picasso was knocking at my door."

"No need to travel. I'm here. I have been waiting for you for hours, drinking coffee in Dunkin' Donuts and sucking up beer in Charlie Blue's. I consider this picture one of my superior efforts. I would even call it inspired. I am across the street. I will wait here. I left the picture with your doorman. After you look at it, you can shout out your opinion to me."

"All this trouble –"

"For you, it's a pleasure. You acknowledge Bugsy Fozer as a human being and artist. Half of these fucks won't even speak to me. When I was riding high they were happy to suck up my booze and use my connections."

"Okay, give me a couple of minutes. I'm coming down."

"I have something else for you. I have an idea about Marsha Newman's leader. Whom that person might be."

"Oh?"

"I was working on your painting, in the throes of creation, when I remembered something. A face. A conversation."

"And?"

"After you look at the picture I will tell you."

"Will the painting give me a clue?"

"That's up to you to decide. Perhaps my idea about the Leader is unimportant to you. You think it's just the mad ravings of Fozer, looking for attention."

"I am interested, although barely awake." Cass threw off the blanket. She pushed her feet into slippers and moved towards the hall closet. "I'm sure that your theory is relevant. I'm just not sure how. You do have a vivid imagination, Fozer."

"Now come downstairs and gaze at your new work of art. I am standing across the street. Give me your reaction to the picture. Then I will cross the street and talk to you about life, and the leader. And then I will leave."

Cass threw her coat on over her nightgown and buzzed for the elevator. The doorman retrieved the painting for her from the storage space off the lobby.

Cass gazed at her painting, "Cass Cooper's New York." The letters were emblazoned at the top of a black and white rainbow, next to an Empire State Building cut out of tin, glittering with rhinestone windows. A cartoon man in a purple suit sky-dived off of the Empire State. Acrobats cartwheeled at the subway entrance. The sky, black and blue squares, backed a newsprint moon. Stars tumbled across the sky in a riot of color. Fozer had signed his name in magenta sparkles with a bold script.

Cass stepped outside and held the painting up to Fozer, who stood directly across the street. "Magnificent," she called out. "It's your masterpiece, Fozer, your Mona Lisa."

A smile lit up his face. He put a foot out to cross the street. The blue car came out of nowhere. It knocked him down and sped up the street. As the doorman called 911, Cass ran across the street to Fozer, who lay limply in the cold slush. Ignoring the dark snow, she sat down on the curb and cradled his head in her lap. "It's a perfect painting," Cass said.

Fozer's eyes were half open. "Loved making it," he mumbled, and then in a whisper, "That's the fun. The Leader. I talk too much…"

Bugsy Fozer closed his eyes for the last time.

Cass was talking to the police when Detective Adams arrived on the scene.

He wore old-man galoshes, and a heavy, belted raincoat. He had dark circles under his eyes. His voice sounded even more weary than usual.

"Did you see that accident?" he asked Cass.

"It happened so fast. It was a small blue car. I did not see a license plate. For some reason, I'm not surprised to see you here, Adams. What's your interest in Fozer?"

"Fozer contacted us. He had some insider's information about Jane Endicott that he wanted to share with the NYPD. He asked me to meet him tonight. He was anxious and wanted to get it off his chest. You see what happened." Adams shifted in his galoshes. "The mysterious Jane has disappeared."

"Since when is Jane mysterious?"

"She looks like the innocent librarian, the happy trans. In truth, she is a dangerous person."

29

Cass's nightgown dripped slush against her legs. She pulled her coat tighter around her. Adams rocked on his feet as he stared down at Cass. "Let's go up to your apartment and talk."

She and Adams sat in her living room across from each other. She still wore the coat over her nightgown. She needed its warmth.

"By the way, I wouldn't make it a habit to hang around Village bars. It does not do much for your case to be carousing in Charley Blue's."

"I don't understand Jane as a dangerous person. Dangerous how?"

"You probably have some knowledge of her interest in sex in all its manifestations."

"She likes sex. So?"

"For the past ten years, Jane has been running a service that finds companions of any sex desired for both men and women. She deals with wealthy, powerful people, and manages to find these people through connections. She is known for the quality of her escorts. Her prostitutes are well-educated, classy. She pays well. Her operation is named 'Call Jane.'"

"This is surprising, but not completely despicable."

"Jane promises discretion but she has not always kept that promise," Adams continued. "In fact, she threatened one important party with revealing his unusual sexual proclivities, a person in a position where this particular information could destroy him. He had to pay her to keep quiet. Big bucks. He did it, and has continued to pay."

"That is criminal – I can't believe Jane of all people –"

"That is the least of it. Jane has been branching out lately into a sex-trafficking operation that deals with underage kids, boys and girls."

"Is that proven or is it speculation?"

"We are following leads. Of course she is using all sorts of devices to hide what she's really doing – disguising it as a social club operation – working beyond the USA borders. Your late ex-husband Vance knew Jane. He – how shall we put it – socialized with her. The late Vance Cooper was not exactly a Boy Scout. We could not help but wonder if she talked with him and then feared that he knew too much. And this is where we're at. As I said, Jane has disappeared. Have you talked with her lately?"

"No. Not since two days after Vance's murder. Where did Bugsy Fozer fit into the picture?"

"Like I said, he contacted us."

"He did not mention being acquainted with Jane."

"Why would he?"

"A blue car side-swiped me on a ride down from Woodstock a few days ago. It could have been the same blue car that ran down Fozer." Something stirred in Cass's gut. "I don't get it."

"What's to get?" Adams responded.

"Jane's amorality, for starters. And why was she going after the big bucks? She was thrifty to the point of being frugal."

"That was a good front. The conservative research librarian."

"Why did she need all the money? What did she do with it?"

Adams shifted his weight, spreading his muscular thighs as if to expand his influence. "We don't know. She has a bank account. Something like $75,000 at Chase Manhattan. Accrued over the years in small amounts. She has no investments that we can discern."

"Perhaps she's helping needy transsexual people achieve their dreams."

"Millions of dollars?"

"Millions?"

"So her clients claim. Several cooperated with the NYPD and told us what they had paid her and for how long. On the one hand she's a modest librarian. On the other hand she's this powerful wheeler-dealer."

"Could Jane have a family that she supports? She never discussed her life as John."

"We investigated. John Endicott was briefly married. It was an amicable divorce. They had no children. The ex encouraged him to become her true self, the happy trans."

"Please do not refer to Jane as the happy trans," Cass said. "She made the transition. She's a woman."

"I appreciate your sensitivities." Adams stood up and rocked in his galoshes. "Please respect mine. A trans is a trans. To make the case that this type of individual is dull normal is off the mark. A trans is exotic and perhaps does not always think or act as you or I might. Perhaps their values are different, their approach to sex and right and wrong. It's like all of you sob-sisters are begging men to cut it off. It was so much easier before, with just men and women and not all the in-between sexes and sensitivity. Do you have anything else to share with me?"

"Nothing. Except for my disillusion and heartbreak that a woman I considered a friend is so sick and depraved. If it's true."

Adams buckled his coat belt. "Let me know if you hear from her."

Cass walked the detective to the door.

Jane was now the Wicked Witch. She was bad and a sex operator and blackmailer and a nightmarish sex trafficker. It's as if Jane was living out some kind of a desperate dream, so in love with sex that she wanted to wallow in it in any form possible. To sell it. To punish people with it. To wring money out of them for desiring something illicit. Most horrible – to destroy children. To live the life of not one person but two people or three people. Man to woman to Super Pimp.

Cass met Jane when she did a piece on her struggle to transition from man to woman. Jane had refused to discuss her family or background. "I am the black sheep," Jane had said. "I rarely see my sisters. I send gifts to their kids. My mother Abigail survives in a retirement community right here in Manhattan. I don't visit because I am not welcome. She loved her son John. She doesn't want to know Jane."

Cass began calling the long list of retirement facilities, more aware with each call of the enormous amount of rooms with walkers and crutches, the piss-smelling hallways, the shouts in the night, of the reality of old age and helplessness. Underneath New York's glitter and neon flowed rivers of pain. On the twenty-fifth call, Cass found her. Abigail Endicott was a resident of the Mary Manning Walsh Home, one of Manhattan's top-rated and prestigious retirement residences on the upper East Side.

Visitors were welcome daily.

30

CASS ADDED A STRING OF pearls and small pearl earrings to her ensemble. She considered this her lady's suit, a pale blue that evoked flowers in country gardens. She reserved the expensive blue suit for news interviews with prestigious ladies. Life demanded costumes and masks. Only rarely did one have the opportunity to take off the mask. She had been tempted to lower the mask with Noah. She wanted to tear away at all the layers, if only she could. If she could trust him. If she could trust herself. If she really knew. She screwed in the other pearl earring, substituted a pink lipstick for her usual red and she was ready for her visit with Abigail Endicott.

Cass announced herself at the reception desk of the Mary Manning Walsh Home as a friend of Jane Endicott. The pert blond receptionist turned her away with a patient smile. "I am sorry, but Mrs. Endicott does not know a Jane Endicott. She has left strict orders that she refuses to see Jane Endicott and anyone associated with her."

"How about a friend of John Endicott?" Cass replied. "Would she be more acceptable to Abigail?"

The receptionist brightened. "You will find Abigail in room 816. Elevator's on the right."

On the eighth floor Cass passed a large, sunlit area. Well- dressed occupants of wheelchairs gazed at TV. Others sat quietly by, their hair nicely coiffed, ready for visitors, for a party, for life to happen. In this up-scale environment, no smell of urine or antiseptic conveyed the message of old age and hopelessness. There would be bingo games, parties, sing-alongs to help pass the hours.

Cass found Abigail in a large corner room, seated in a wheelchair gazing at an old movie on TV, The Sweet Smell of Success. Her white hair was arranged in a perfect pageboy, and she wore an elegant flowered robe in pastel hues. She could have been an aging movie star. A plump uniformed aide sat in a chair nearby. The aide stood up as Cass entered the room.

"I am Camille, Mrs. Endicott's assistant." White teeth glowed in her brown, dimpled face. "And you are a friend of John's."

"A good friend."

"Come in." She turned to Abigail. "Mrs. Endicott. You have a visitor, a friend of John's."

Now Abigail turned to take in Cass. "Aren't you the pretty one," she commented. "John always did go for the lookers. Last I heard he was still married. Are you the competition?"

"Just a friend. Cass Cooper." Cass presented the box of Godiva chocolates that she had brought. "It's dark chocolate. That's supposed to be good for you. Absolutely healthy. I wanted to drop by and say hello."

"Thank you for the chocolates, dear. I do enjoy them. Of course Camille rations me, doesn't want me to have a sugar fit."

"I didn't mean to interrupt the movie. It's one of my favorites."

"Mine as well. Not a problem. I have seen it many times and will see it again. It reminds me of my youth in New York, when the city was alive with nightclubs and glamour and vice. It was real. It was gritty. It had an edge. Sit down. Tell me about John."

"He's well. At least I think he is."

"He never comes to see me. He looks after me, pays for me to stay in this place. It's not bad here. I have Camille. I should not complain. I am in no shape to be on my own, which I would prefer. Married five times and here I am, all alone by the telephone. Maybe John has the right idea. Stick with one's spouse, even if she is a bitch."

Camille brought Cass a chair and she sat down near Abigail who continued talking. "Occasionally Henry, one of my ex-husbands, drops in. Always a Henry, never a Hank. I do not turn him away. He's a dear man, and still has all his marbles. Tell me about John. How is the darling boy?"

"I was hoping that you could tell me." As Abigail talked, Cass gazed around the room, a repository of photographs, large and small. "I thought he might have been in touch with you."

"Oh, no. He never comes here. That hurts, but I blame it on her. The wife. She's selfish. Doesn't want to share him. Does John enjoy his work?".

"Absolutely," Cass responded.

"He's a natural-born leader," Abigail said. "Just like his father, who was brilliant at business. John planned to follow in his footsteps. He was president of his high school class. He never joined anything where they didn't elect him the head. That's my boy John. See the pictures." She wheeled closer to the wall filled with framed photographs. "There's John in his track suit. And with his fellow class officers in high school. That's John in the middle. And at Boston College. Once again class president. He went through a spiritual phase there. I thought he might even be considering the priesthood. Instead he married." Mrs. Endicott sniffed.

"Do you ever see his wife?"

"Never, never, never. Won't allow her near me." Abigail turned to Camille. "How about one of those chocolates for our guest? I wouldn't mind one myself. The wife is a bad influence on John."

"In what way?"

"She's a weirdo. Has odd ideas, such as occasionally dressing up in each other's clothes – playing around with sexual identity. Bizarre enough on its own and downright offensive if they invite you for Sunday dinner." Abigail rolled away from the wall of pictures. "I suppose they find it amusing. If they ask you for Sunday dinner, inquire if there's a dress code before you accept."

"What's her appeal? Is she beautiful?"

"Far from it," Abigail said emphatically. "John claims she's brilliant. A genius, he calls her. I say she's a witch."

Camille opened the candy box and held it out. Abigail picked one chocolate and took dainty bites. "Chocolate's a no-no for me. But it's fun to cheat. Help yourself to a chocolate, dear. You too, Camille."

"Has John been in touch at all lately?" Cass asked.

"If so, I have not been aware." Abigail took another small bite of chocolate. "Ask Camille. She's in charge."

Camille shook her head "no."

Camille leaned over and whispered in Cass's ear. "Jane checks in with me every week to see if her mother needs anything. But I have not heard from her this week."

"Now what are you two buzzing about?" Abigail broke into their conversation. "Let me in on it."

"I was just talking with Camille about John's new career. He's become a research librarian."

"Why, that's absurd," Abigail laughed. "You must be joking. John was never interested in being a librarian. He's CEO material. He's a man of action." She looked pensive. "I miss John, that's the truth, but when I was around that couple, I felt left out. They have a special rapport. They were not with me. They were on some other planet."

"Tough to be the third party -- the also," Cass commiserated.

"The also. Yes. You put it so well. Sometimes I thought they could have been brother and sister, like twins. They seemed so close. They share a special kind of mental telepathy, John claims. One can be miles away from the other and know what the other feels or thinks," Abigail smirked. "I call it nonsense. At least it saves on the phone bills."

"I would love to see what this special couple looks like. Is there a picture of them?" Cass gestured to the wall.

"I have removed those photos of them together. I do not care to look at her face, which is nothing to write home about. Now you my dear are stunning – not candy-box pretty, but smart-looking. But what can I do? If I suggested to John that he consider having more than a friendship with you, you can be sure he would laugh that away. Whatever I suggest to John, he will do the opposite."

"I value John's friendship," Cass said. "As you pointed out, he is still married, so it's best not to dream of romance." Cass stood up. "It was such a pleasure to meet you, Abigail. I hope that I can stop by again."

"Please do, dear. Please do. Thank you for coming. You are always welcome here. And if you see John, please give him my love and a big kiss, and perhaps you will bring him with you next time."

"I will definitely try. Can Camille walk me to the elevator?"

"Of course," Abigail replied. "It's the only polite thing to do."

In the hallway, Cass turned to Camille. "Abigail's lucky to have you, Camille."

"We have become good friends." Camille dimpled.

"Would you possibly have a picture of Jane – when he was John – with his wife?"

Camille winked at Cass. "Let me get it from my locker." She hurried off, returned quickly, reached into her pocket and handed Cass a snapshot. "That's Jane when he was John, and the wife. Abigail threw away all the other pictures. You might want to give it to Jane, if you're in touch with her."

Cass took the snapshot. "I have not seen or talked with Jane for a week. I thought she might have dropped by."

"Never. She looks after her mother. But Abigail will have nothing to do with her. It's a tragic situation. For her, Jane simply does not exist. Jane stays in touch with me."

"If Jane calls you, please ask her to get in touch with Cass. Thank you for your help, Camille. I will try to stop by and visit Abigail again. We seem to share the same taste in movies."

On the elevator, Cass looked at the snapshot Camille had given her.

Love lit up the bride's pale, thin face, framed in white lace. She gazed up adoringly at John Endicott, a slender, darkly handsome man. The wicked wife was unmistakably a young Marsha Newman on her wedding day.

Cass called Detective Adams. "Anything new on Jane Endicott?"

"There seems to be an epidemic of hit and run drivers who find their mark. Jane's in Bellevue Hospital. It was not a blue car, but a black sedan that knocked her down on West 34th Street while trying to hail a cab. She was on her way to Kennedy airport. She had a ticket to Zurich, Switzerland in her bag. Zurich, as you might know, is the country's banking center. She was apparently trying to escape justice – realizing that the law was catching up with her."

"Can I see her?"

"She's in critical shape. Absolutely no visitors allowed."

Cass cabbed to Bellevue Hospital. She affected a confident look as she walked through the hustle-bustle of the hospital. She congratulated herself on reaching the correct staircase. She had done a piece on Bellevue, and as such had gained access to routes around the hospital as well as a now-expired press pass.

A young cop stood outside the door to Jane's room. She flashed the press pass. "Detective Adams gave me the go-ahead to visit Ms. Endicott," Cass said. "I am the surrogate. Ms. Endicott does not have a family, and I have been appointed to speak for her if she cannot speak in her behalf."

The officer gave her the once-over.

"I promise not to stay long."

"Go ahead. But five minutes max."

Slender Jane looked lost in the welter of tubes and paraphernalia that surrounded her. There was a bandage on her head. Her face was a black and blue mess. Cass walked to the edge of the bed. Jane breathed with an effort. Her eyes were closed. One hand was outside the covers. Cass took her hand and held it. "Jane." She spoke softly. "It's me, Cass. Can you hear me? We need to talk. Fast. There's a cop outside the door and in five minutes he will throw me out." Jane stared back expressionless.

Cass needed to add leverage. "Sorry to hit you hard when you're lying in a hospital bed in intensive care feeling like shit. But here are the grim facts. The cops are on to your illicit sex operation, trafficking in underage kids. I believe you confided in Vance – you told me how you told him everything. He disapproved – threatened to turn you in. 'Vance screwed me blue,' you told Marsha."

Jane pulled her hand out of Cass's. Her eyes looked pained. She turned her head away.

"Did Marsha work with you? The two of you moving in on Vance for the kill? Husband and wife. It's all damned incestuous – fun and games for all – but I am left holding the bag. I am the murder suspect. I am the scapegoat, a role that does not appeal."

Jane turned her head back and looked helplessly at her. She was biting her lip.

"You know who killed Vance. Was it you?"

Jane seemed to be trying to open her mouth, to move her lips, but it wasn't happening. Jane's eyes fluttered. She raised her hand slowly. She held it against her cheek, then raised an index finger, pointed at herself. Tears filled Jane's eyes. Her face distorted, as if in terrible pain. Her eyes grew enormous.

She tried to lift her head. She fell back. Her eyes closed. The monitor on the side of the bed moved swiftly in a jerky green line. Lights flashed and bells rang. A nurse rushed into the room followed by a doctor, and another nurse.

Cass did not wait. She hurried out of the room, down the stairs, and out of the hospital.

31

OUTSIDE BELLEVUE CASS JUMPED INTO the first cab she saw, driven by a turbaned elder with a gray beard. At 3 P.M., the White Horse Tavern on Hudson Street in the Village proved dark and redolent of beer. Once considered the ultra Bohemian bar where poet Dylan Thomas drank himself to death on a visit to New York, the White Horse somehow retained vestiges of boozy poetic rage.

Cass found a seat at the bar and ordered a double Johnny Walker Black Scotch on the rocks. "And a large glass of water, please." She tried to make the request sound as if she was ordering tea with lemon on the side. Who was she kidding? Certainly not herself or the bartender, who poured her a hefty double Scotch.

Cass had crashed in on Jane, in defiance of Detective Adams. Had her visit precipitated a heart attack? Had she killed Jane?

She picked the glass up and put it down.

She opened her cell phone and called Detective Adams, who did not try to hide his anger. "You seem to take my admonitions to stay away from Bellevue as a signal to jump in," he rasped.

"Is she breathing?"

"Barely." Adams cleared his throat. "I have left strict orders not to let anyone in, you in particular. We want her alive. We need to know what she knows."

Adams hung up. She eyed the fresh tumbler of Scotch, ice cubes afloat in amber liquid. "There's nothing in the booze," a reformer had once told her. But for her, booze held escape, freedom, and access to her own subconscious. It pulled her away from reality. It offered a high. Like writing when it went well. And sex. Good sex. Great sex. There was also bad sex. Not many people talked about that. How awful sex could be.

Her phone rang. It was Donaldson's housekeeper, Millicent.

"Forgive me, Mrs. Cooper, but I've been a wreck since it happened." Her voice shook. "Mr. Frye is in Lenox Hill Hospital. He was attacked in his study last night. I just came from the hospital. He has two black eyes, a broken arm, and I don't know what else." Millicent ran on. "Mr. Frye is trying to make light, but I worry for him. The man who attacked him tore through his desk and files, a horrible mess. The police told me not to touch anything."

"Can I call him?" Cass asked.

"Of course," Millicent said. "I know he would be glad to hear from you."

Donaldson answered the phone immediately. "Don't worry. I'm fine. I should be leaving the hospital this afternoon. There's no concussion. I arrived home late and found this masked bum. He tried to kill me. He had torn my study apart. I assume he was searching for Vance's manuscript. Or he could have been seeking evidence about one of my other cases."

"What can I do for you?"

"Nothing. I'm happy to be alive. What you can do is stay out of trouble."

Cass left the Scotch untouched, drank the water, paid for the drink and left the White Horse.

Walking up the street, she called Dev. "The search goes on," she told Dev, recounting Donaldson's attack and his wrecked library. "I thought you would want to know. But Donaldson's okay."

"Thank God for that. I live in hope that someday we will see that manuscript. One bright spot is that Noah's book is climbing up the Best Sellers List – this week it moves from eighth to seventh."

"That is exciting news."

"Noah spent seven years working on that book. He did not let me down. He made the deadline, and we made the publication date. He's a good man. Smart. Gifted. Reliable. He's been married three times, but don't hold that against him."

32

CASS HAD NO PROBLEM FINDING the number of Call Jane. It was listed on a modest website with a photo of the New York skyline in the background. She made the call on a cell phone she used strictly for reportage when she did not want to reveal her identity.

A woman answered the phone. She had a musical voice, a mellifluous contralto. She sounded like the receptionist in an upscale spa or hotel. "How can I help you?" Cass wasn't sure how to play it. What had often worked for her before, revealing directly how she felt and what she wanted, might be the best mode of action. She pitched her own voice to sound seductive and charming.

"I'm a forty-something woman, considered extremely attractive by my peers. In the past, I worked as an advertising executive and copywriter." Cass paused. She actually had done that job for several months. "I have been successful. Married. Divorced. Traveled. Currently I need work."

"Yes?" The woman drawled.

"I'm no longer interested in a conventional position. I like men, and I enjoy going to good restaurants and meeting people on an upscale level, what I consider my level. If I could be paid for it, even better."

"In other words, you enjoy being sociable." The woman's voice did not drop. She sounded almost amused.

"Absolutely. I do enjoy being sociable."

"But do you discriminate? Are you only sociable with certain people on a certain level?"

"Not at all. One of my greatest pleasure is mixing with all kinds of people."

"And you are open to do all the social niceties?"

"Absolutely. I do everything," Cass blurted.

"We do have a social service for diplomats and other important people. Mainly those who are away from home and would appreciate an attractive companion to help show them New York. Does this sort of work interest you?"

"Very much so. But how is the pay?"

"Excellent, if you meet our standards. This would be a try-out on both sides. If you like it, and we like you, you would be called back and the pay could go up. We had a mature escort who did well. Unfortunately we lost her a couple of weeks ago. We have not found a replacement. Like you, she was an older, sophisticated woman."

"I see," Cass said. "And she was sociable."

"Extremely sociable. She loved the work and was not ashamed to admit it. I must tell you in advance that if you have any inhibitions about being paid to be, shall we call it charming, you should not put your foot into these waters."

"I pride myself on being a swimmer who enjoys going out to the depths."

"There are other prerequisites for the job. You need a good wardrobe. I mean a total wardrobe including lingerie because one never knows, and one does like to be prepared if, for instance, one's slip shows."

"Of course. I'm into Bergdorf Goodman."

"And what are your measurements?"

"36. 28. 36."

"A voluptuary would appreciate you."

"I hope."

"We're extremely discriminating in whom we hire. We have a reputation and want to maintain our standards. You will have to come in for an interview before we can actually consider hiring you."

"Of course."

"How about 3 P.M. this afternoon. Ask for Lydia."

Call Jane's offices dazzled. They were in a super-modern glass structure in the fashionable new section on the West Side of New York, Hudson Yards, overlooking both the Hudson River and the city skyline. Cass took the elevator up to the 30th floor, and walked into an all-white room with one black and white abstract painting on the wall and a vase of yellow tulips on the receptionist's desk. An elegant young woman with long black hair and bangs, wearing a white dress, sat at the receptionist's desk. There was no computer in evidence.

On the large coffee table next to a white leather couch, up-to-date copies of Vanity Fair, Vogue and Harper's Bazaar beckoned with their glossy covers. Cass had a difficult time equating these surroundings with Jane Endicott, the research librarian who had read all of Proust's Swann's Way and reveled in scholarly esoterica. She had expected Call Jane to be in an unmarked office in an older building, like something out of a noir film. On the contrary, Call Jane was completely public. Downstairs, the building directory simply stated Call Jane Inc.

"I have an appointment with Lydia," Cass said.

"And your name?"

"Melina Xanthis," Cass responded, using her middle and her maiden names.

"Please take a seat. Can I get you anything? Water? Coffee?"

"No. Thank you."

Cass sat down on the white leather couch. She had taken extra efforts with her make-up, extended the eyelashes, piled on the mascara. She wore her best black suit from Bloomingdale's Designer Floor, a Dior that she had bought ten years ago —almost vintage – but it worked. Her heels were four inches, showing off what she knew were good legs. Dressing up and getting out had somehow boosted her confidence. Suppose she was recognized. Her picture had been all over the papers.

A tall black woman in a long silk purple ensemble came out to greet her. She was a stunner with high cheekbones, and looked herself like a high-fashion model. She wore pearl earrings, and two strands of lustrous golden-hued pearls at her throat. Short maroon boots on her feet. She extended a long, cool hand to Cass. "I'm Lydia. I am happy to meet you. Please follow me, and let's talk."

Lydia's office, like the reception area, all in white, offered the perfect setting for Lydia's own beauty. She did not waste any time in getting down to the essentials. "Tell me more about yourself, Melina. But first, I would like to note your resemblance to Cass Cooper, the woman now suspected of murdering her husband, and of being instrumental in the death of Prudence Duluth."

"Of course there's a family resemblance. Cass Cooper is my first cousin and growing up people often mistook us for twins when they saw us together. But we have not been close for years. Of course, blood is thicker than water as they say, and I am sorry to see Cass get herself into the soup like this."

"Have you talked with her lately? "

"No. I thought about calling her to express my sympathy over her losing her husband, but actually he was an ex-husband."

"From what you know of her, do you consider her capable of murder?" Lydia folded her elegant hands with the black nail polish in front of her on the white desk.

"I believe we are all capable of extreme violence if pushed hard enough," Cass replied.

"Tell me some more about yourself. What are your interests, other than sociability?"

"I like films, theater – in fact I love the theater – the Philharmonic and the classics, jazz, ballet, crossword puzzles, Scrabble, reading, poetry and travel."

"Do you prefer a particular type of man?"

"Probably your more exotic. For some reason, I am drawn to men from the Middle East. Most women would do anything to get away from the Arab man with his reputation for misogyny."

"Interesting." Lydia opened a small index box and pulled out a card. "I think I have something for you. We will give you a try-out." She handed Cass the card with a name and address on it. "Please be there at eight tonight. Dress for dinner. If there is any problem, do not hesitate to call me. Understand that we will be contacting the gentleman afterwards to learn if you had a pleasant evening together. We hope you will live up to Call Jane's standards."

"I will do my best."

"And a suggestion. This gentleman likes open-toed shoes."

"I happen to have a pair of open-toed shoes with five-inch heels. Jimmy Choo's. Red."

"Perfect. Jane, our founder, appreciates elegance."

"How is Jane? Just before coming here, I heard that she was in an accident."

"Disturbing news." Lydia folded her slender hands with the long, elegant fingers. "Her condition continues to be critical, I am told, but Jane is a survivor."

"And if God forbid something does happen to her, will Call Jane go on?"

"Of course. Although a few days ago she was talking about getting out of this business, about selling it. She even suggested to me that I might be interested in buying it from her." Lydia smiled for the first time. "Of course I'm not in a financial position to afford that."

"Did she say why she was considering selling?"

"No, but she does want the person who takes it over to enjoy and appreciate the business. She also said she might not sell. She was just testing the waters. She's invested a big part of her finances and know-how in Call Jane. She would miss it."

"I'm sure."

Lydia picked up a letter opener with a sharp point, looked at it and put it down. "Enjoy tonight. I think the man you are going to meet is somebody quite special."

33

CASS DECIDED AGAINST STOCKINGS. HER toe nails sparkled with red nail polish and peeked out of shoes with five-inch heels. The shoes pinched her feet, but she could suffer for one night. She wore her second- favorite cocktail dress, a black silk V-necked design with flouncy sleeves, lady-like but alluring. She added diamond earrings.

A tiny jeweled bag held a lipstick, comb, and mad money with which to escape. She would not carry any identifying cards. She doused herself with Chanel No. 5 perfume. The downstairs buzzer rang. A private car had been scheduled to pick her up and bring her to her "Call Jane" date.

The driver in the blue cap courteously opened the door for Cass. He drove her to Park Avenue and New York's highest and most expensive residence tower. Cass, who followed real estate with the same avidity that she read film reviews, knew that a penthouse on the 95th floor cost $95 million. A bullet-fast elevator driven by a uniformed operator whisked her up to the 95th floor.

She did not have to ring the bell. A dark, slender gentleman in tails and white gloves opened the door for her. "Good evening, Ms. Xanthis," he said. "Can I take your coat? Mr. Fakhouri is waiting to greet you."

Fazi Fakhouri stood up as Cass entered the room, an incredible space with a fantasy view of New York. Through enormous glass panes, the city unreeled its lights, skyscrapers, bridges, a view that took the eye up, out and beyond the city. Inside, the room vibrated with bright colors, brocades, gold and silver ornaments. They could have been inside a palace or a prince's tent.

Fakhouri took her hand, leaned over to gently kiss her fingers and gestured to a brocaded couch. After Cass sat down, he sat down next to her but kept a respectful distance. "Please call me Fazi. And I will call you Melina."

Fazi had a round face, framed by well-cut, longish black hair. He wore a dark grey perfectly tailored suit that covered a bulging but not offensive stomach, a navy blue shirt, and a brilliant red and blue tie. A red handkerchief. Gold rings. A gold necklace.. A fine moustache. A small beard. Plump cheeks. Black eyes. Heavy straight black eyebrows. He looked like an Arab billionaire should look. The only thing needed to complete the picture would be the traditional red and white checked ghutra held on his head by a black cord.

"No ghutra?" Cass had been reading up on Saudi Arabian customs.

"I only wear it at home and on formal diplomatic occasions. The original purpose was to keep the sun off of one's head, and it is useful." His dark eyes moved to Cass's toes. He smiled. "It is a pleasure to meet you."

"And you, Fazi." Cass crossed her legs. "What a magnificent apartment."

"I have grown fond of it." He poured liquid out of a carafc into two small glasses. "An aperitif?"

Cass nodded her head. "Please."

"This apartment was not my first choice." He handed a glass to Cass and raised his glass to her. "My first choice was the Dakota, the famous building where John Lennon lived. I fell in love with its charm and architecture. But the waiting list for an apartment was too long. I am afraid that the musician Sting and a few other stars outranked me. Of course I love your USA pop culture." He had a mild accent.

"What are your favorite amusements?"

"Broadway shows. Las Vegas. I fancy Mozart as well, and have season tickets to the Philharmonic."

"You are eclectic." Cass raised her glass to Fazi. "Drambuie. I personally do not indulge but I enjoy a whiff of the delicious aroma. I thought drinking was forbidden in Saudi Arabia."

"Indeed," Fazi nodded. "One caught indulging in liquor could receive five hundred lashes. But I, the youngest son, was rarely punished, certainly not with lashes. I studied abroad in Oxford, and went on to earn a Master's Degree at the Harvard Business School. Such delightful years."

"And you returned to Saudi Arabia."

"To my brothers, sisters, mother, father and large extended family. I returned to follow the customs. And there I do not drink. Away from home, I will occasionally take a sip of this or that. But I have never gotten into the alcohol culture." His black eyebrows drew together. "Life offers so many other delights. Do you not think?" He proffered a small smile.

"I agree completely," Cass said. "The USA sometimes sounds like a country beset with alcoholics. I believe we give people a false impression."

"Indeed. Alcoholism, drugs and politics. That's America, according to the media." He leaned back and unbuttoned the suit jacket. "No wonder you Americans keep building jails and rehab centers. Who could take the stress?" He laughed, a rich, booming sound that stopped abruptly. His full, sensual mouth twitched. "I hope you don't mind that we will be dining in."

"Not at all."

"I lost a dear friend recently. A woman."

"I am sorry."

"I asked if a woman about her age could visit me." Fazi sat back, his head against a green velvet pillow. "And that is you. You are beautiful. And alone."

"A widow," Cass said.

"You resemble the woman suspected of murdering her husband, the late Vance Cooper."

"We are first cousins. As youngsters, we were often taken as twins."

A waiter came into the room with a large tray. He placed the various contents on a table at the end of the room near the window. The table had already been set with gold plates and crystal goblets.

"I believe we are ready to dine." Fazi stood. He took Cass's arm to walk her across the floor, and held her chair for her before sitting down himself to a superb dinner of exquisite caviar and blinis, beef tenderloins perfectly sauced, and small asparagus.

"Utterly delicious," Cass commented.

"I have an excellent chef. I like to dine lightly at dinner, so as not to interfere with the rest of the evening."

"Of course." By the time they hit dessert, vanilla gelato with super-fresh sweet raspberries, and a swirl of real whipped cream topped by a few slivered almonds, Cass wondered what else the night might hold. Would she be capable of going through with it? Perhaps she could cool his ardor with a subject guaranteed to squelch sexual desire.

"Tell me, Fazi, what do you think of the furor over Gordon Ramsdell losing the election for governor? I was sure that the liberals had it in the bag. Afterwards Ramsdell said his financial support had fallen through. How about that? Should money be necessary to sell a worthy candidate?"

"In your democracy of consumerism, money rules. You buy and sell everything, including government. It intrigues me, and disturbs me. For years, American pop culture has led the world. Now the same holds true in politics. The right wing dominates in the USA, and conservatives conquer the globe."

"That should make you happy. Doesn't that go along with the traditional Saudi Arabian point of view?"

"True. But I personally like to consider all sides of political issues." He dabbed at his mouth with a large damask napkin. "Shall we take coffee by the fire."

"Lovely."

Cass sat down on a low couch and this time Fazi sat close to her. His cell phone rang. He answered it. She expected to hear a barrage of Arabic but he spoke in English. "Sunday. In a week? Send me the details and directions. Yes. Discretion. Please."

He smiled at Cass and turned off his phone. The waiter ceremoniously placed small cups of espresso with slices of lemon peel in front of them, along with a plate of filigreed cookies. Sensuous Arab music came on.

Cass felt a change of mood. She could plead indigestion and leave. No. She had to see it through.

"Why don't you remove your shoes?" Fazi asked. "You would be more comfortable."

"Thank you for the invitation." Cass slowly pulled off the shoes and placed her feet on the velvety rug.

"Beautiful." Fazi gazed at her feet. "What is that color on your toes?"

"I believe it's called Spanish Melon." She dug her feet into the rug.

"Charming." Fazi sat back, closed his eyes, and began to hum to the music. He smiled. "And now, can we try a little game?"

"If you will tell me the rules."

"There are no rules. It should be spontaneous, for your enjoyment as well as mine." Fazi then unbuckled his belt and smiled. "You have not played the game before?"

"Consider me a complete novice at this particular game."

"It's easier than chess. Can I teach you?"

"I can't wait."

Fazi unzipped his fly, and brought his now engorged penis out. "And now, if you could play with my organ with your toes, that would give me great pleasure. " For one split second, Cass considered refusing. Then she raised her toes for the task at hand.

She closed her eyes and remembered the high school necking party when a classmate with a blond crewcut had made a similar request. What had she done then? "But that's not part of the game," she had said, leaving her virginal toes protected by their yellow socks. Her girlfriend Mitzi had complied with her toenails painted Passion Pink. You necked with one boy and then moved on to the next. Kissing styles varied. She and her girlfriends had assigned tags to the boys. Liver Lips. Hair Tonic. Were they mean girls?

"There, there. Ah, harder, yes, ah ah. Let us not hurry, but relish the moment. Both feet, oh yes, oh oh. Now. There. Harder. Aaaaaaah. Aaaaaah." He whipped out his handkerchief as his orgasm erupted. "Oh yes. Delightful. Yes." He sat back with a sigh. His dark eyes glowed. "Your turn is next, my dear."

"Might I use the rest room first?" she smiled.

"Of course."

Cass began to put her shoes on.

"Please," Fazi said. "Leave them off. For your own pleasure, as well as mine. It is good for the soul to put our feet on the earth, or in this case the rug, which also contains miracles of God."

34

IN THE BATHROOM, A SPLENDOR of marble and solid gold fixtures, Cass eyed herself in the mirror. She looked the same, despite playing the whore, a role she perhaps had slipped into too easily. Or should she tag herself a semi-whore who had volunteered to play a supporting role in the sexual drama of Fazi Fakhouri. The experience proved surprising and unsettling.

She refreshed her lipstick. She had suspected Fazi of murdering Pru, and yet he seemed genuinely heart-broken when he referred to the "dear friend" he had lost. Money appeared operative in this confused mess, and he was the billionaire. And there was the Call Jane connection. Somehow, Fazi was involved. Cass felt like she was chasing a story and getting warm. But she could not yet identify the major player, or center of the piece, despite her dogged pursuit of breadcrumbs through the snow.

Leaving the bathroom, she passed a table that held an elegant gold and white phone, and a white leather phone directory. Even Saudi Arabian billionaires needed to keep track of phone numbers. As oud music played in the background, Cass opened the book and went directly to the D's. There was Prudence Duluth. He had actually scribbled a star next to her name. Jane Endicott and her home phone number. Cass moved on to the N's. She quietly turned a number of pages before finding the name Marsha Newman.

A piece of torn paper stuck out of the phone book, crisp and newly inked. Cass grabbed it, crumpled it in her hand and shoved it in her pocketbook.

Fazi's voice boomed. Cold. Angry. "That book is private." He closed the book for her. "What are you looking for?"

Cass attempted to make light but knew she was doing a bad job of it. "It's a terrible habit of mine. Like some people look in medicine chests. I'm intrigued by phone books. Forgive me. It's just that I find you such a fascinating person. I could not help but wonder what other amazing people you know."

"You are a bad liar, Cass Cooper." His straight eyebrows drew together. "You have abused my hospitality. Why did you come here?"

"It's about Prudence. She was fond of you."

"She was also fond of your late husband. But that did not justify your sticking a knife through her heart."

"I did not kill Pru. She was a friend."

"Until something went wrong. Until she confessed her love of Vance Cooper." Fazi took Cass's elbow and led her back into the living room. "Sit. We have played enough games. I knew it was you as soon as you walked into the room. The story about the cousin's identity did not wash. I am a diplomat and part of my extensive schooling includes studying and identifying faces."

"Why didn't you call my bluff earlier?"

"I wanted to see how far you would go. But I think we have gone far enough. I will not push you into my bed. Then you would cry rape and probably be justified, but that kind of experience would give me no pleasure."

"I see."

"Do you see? I wonder. You American women. It's to laugh, but this situation is not amusing. What do you want?"

Cass was aware of her bare feet on plush carpet with Fazi's dark face looming over her. She felt undressed. "I would like to put my shoes back on."

She walked back into the dining area. Fazi followed her. He sat down across from her as she pulled on her shoes.

"I am waiting," he said.

"I thought Pru might have confided in you. Told you things, like people she feared. Or things she knew which would make it necessary to eliminate her. Or was it a crime of passion? Although it appeared terribly dispassionate. Cold."

"You found her body."

"Yes."

"I assumed immediately that you killed her, and fabricated that ridiculous confession that she had killed Vance Cooper – and then the false suicide note. Absurd. Prudence was in love with life. You are a journalist. Perhaps you had better leave fiction alone. That is not your talent."

"I did not write the note. I did not kill Pru. I resent your accusation." Cass stood up.

"Sit down, Mrs. Cooper." Fazi's voice boomed. "I am not ready for you to leave. And you would have a difficult time departing without my help. I employ a full-time bodyguard. The waiters and even the chef are trained to work in my behalf should there be – how shall I put it – a problem."

Cass sat down. She had come without even pepper-spray or mace to use in her defense. "Let us reason together, Fazi. There's no reason to create an international incident. Call Jane knows I'm here. They would not want me to be harmed."

"I have no inclination to injure you. But if it came down to that, whom would Call Jane side with, the billionaire client or the intrusive journalist? As for Prudence, I can't be involved in this sordid mess. I have a position to maintain. That woman deserved to live. It pains me to see beauty perish. *You* suspect *me* of murdering Prudence? How totally ridiculous. It would be laughable if it were not so sad."

"Absolutely not. It never occurred to me."

"You lie. You read news stories about the brutality of Arab men and their misogynist attitudes. I am not a brute. I am a sensualist. I love women."

"Prudence did not discuss you. She was extremely discreet. I heard that you treated her well. Possibly lavishly."

"Did I support her? No. I helped her."

"How did you meet? Call Jane?"

"We met at a cocktail party at the Saudi consulate. I was struck by her loveliness and her style."

"And you met Jane through Pru?"

"Yes. The twins."

"Twins?"

"Occasionally they dressed alike for my amusement."

"How well do you know Jane?"

"Not well."

"She, too, has met with an accident."

"So I heard. Pity. I rather like her. She's smart. She's not afraid to cash in on life's realities including the universal sex drive. This is the one thing that all we animals have in common. She will play the sex game to the hilt and convention be damned. She wants to try everything. I wager that if there was a third sex, she would morph into that."

"Don't you think she's missing something?"

"And what would that be?"

"The gentler emotions. Love."

"You are quite the sentimentalist. I know nothing of Jane's deeper feelings. And, by the way, I do not object to whores, a nasty expression with the connotation of life in the gutter. I prefer to call them courtesans. They are great ladies. Even street walkers have their merits, on occasion."

"Pru must have known her killer. There was no struggle. It's as if he leaned over for a kiss and struck a knife through her heart."

"This hurts me. Here." Fazi placed his hand over his heart. "Imagining that scene."

"What do you know, Fazi? What can you tell me?"

"I know nothing. I am more in the dark than you. I ask myself if Pru's murder in some way threatens or involves me. The police tell me nothing. I want to know. I need to know. You found her. Are there any other important details that have been omitted from the news stories?"

"It was all in the news. Except for the white rose."

"White rose?"

"One white rose in a vase. There was a similar rose in the room when I found Vance murdered."

"A white rose." Fazi's face darkened. "That's all? That's all you can tell me?"

"Yes." Cass found herself regaining some semblance of control. She had not blown it completely. "What will you tell Lydia at Call Jane about tonight? "

"I will tell her that the experience was unsatisfactory."

Without asking, the butler reappeared with Cass's coat and helped her on with it.

"My driver will take you home," Fazi said.

"I would prefer to take a taxi."

"As you wish."

In the taxi, Cass permitted herself to look at the crumpled piece of paper grabbed from Fazi's phone book. It read "Woodstock meeting. M.N."

35

FAZI'S RAW NEED MASKED BY barely civilized niceties had disturbed Cass, but her foray had been worthwhile. She had wanted to study Fazi close up. Mission accomplished. He could have killed Pru. Initially so charming and warm, he had turned hard and cold, looked like a killer, his face dark and menacing. He was connected to Marsha, who was connected to Jane, corrupt powerhouse, who had been connected to Pru, and they had all been connected to Vance.

If this were a huge web, who was the spider in charge? "The Leader," as designated by the late Bugsy Fozer? If Fozer had started out as an artist manqué, maturity had deepened his talent. She considered the collage he had done for her as a small masterpiece. It captured the essence of her New York. Perhaps maturity had also deepened his powers as an intuitive, a person who can sense what lies beyond the obvious.

Cass spent a restless night. At 8 A.M. the phone's ringing jolted her awake.

Mario sounded panicked. "Angelina is missing. She's been gone for two days. Have you seen her?"

"No." Pru had been murdered. Jane was barely alive. And now Angelina, reliable earth mother, was missing. Cass felt her stomach turn over. "I haven't talked with Angelina since shortly after Pru's death."

"I'm a cop who can't find his own wife."

"Have you contacted your kids?"

"Of course. I called all the family connections, upsetting everyone, because they have not been in touch with Ang for the last few days, and she has always been the family rock. Keeping everyone together. I also talked to her agent and to the gallery. They are looking for her. The gallery sold a couple of her pictures and wanted to get in touch."

"Could you have done something to upset Angelina?"

"I spent a night with Dorrie."

"I thought that was against the rules."

"Rules are meant to be broken."

"Let me call you back."

Cass called Noah.

Cloaked in grey fog, Atlantic City presented a bleak sight on a winter morning. Noah, Cass and Mario searched for Angelina in the city's hotel casinos. Bally's. Caesar's. The Golden Nugget. The Showboat. By 2 P.M. they had reached the Borgata, Atlantic City's top-rated hotel and a favorite of high-rolling gamblers.

They found Angelina ensconced in front of the Texas Tea machine, wearing jeans and a colorful Mexican jacket. Her bag on the seat next to her reserved that slot machine, Jungle Fever, as hers to play as well.

Mario rushed up to Angelina. "Angie. Thank God. We've been looking all over for you."

Angelina glanced at Mario, then away from him, her eyes moving back to the screen of the slot machine in front of her. "I like to be alone when I play. I need to concentrate."

Mario put his hands gently on Angelina's shoulders. "Are you on a roll, Ang?"

"I'm in the zone." Angelina kept pushing buttons. "That's where I want to be. You and the bitch don't exist."

"You ran away from me." Mario kneaded her shoulders.

"I couldn't take it. I love you. I can't live this way. It's me or her or nothing." Angelina did not turn. "We made a deal when I agreed to this so-called open marriage, but then you run off and stay with the bitch."

"That was a mistake, Ang. I'm sorry. Can't you tear yourself away from that damned machine?"

"Can you dump what's her name?" Angelina did not turn to face Mario but looked straight ahead. In front of her, oil wells gushed on the Texas Tea screen.

"Ang, Ang, we're killing each other. You're breaking my heart. Suppose I said I would never see her again. Suppose you said you would never put another dollar in a slot machine. Where would that take us?"

"To happiness," Angelina said.

"Does that exist? In this world?"

"We could try." Angelina turned to face Mario.

"Cash out. Let's go home."

"How did you find me?"

Mario gestured to Cass and Noah, who stood a few machines away. "Noah is a psychologist. He works with addicts. He suggested that we come here."

"So you think I'm a case?"

Mario put his arms around Angelina. "You're not a case. You are my wife and I love you. I was desperate to find you."

Angelina picked up her bag and walked over to Cass and Noah. Cass introduced her to Noah. "You have a great face," Angelina said. "I would like to paint you. I see you with a black beard with a few grey streaks. Naked, of course, like maybe in the David pose – you know, the famous statue by Michelangelo in Florence."

"I am flattered."

"Not at all."

"Do you ever paint people with their clothes on?"

"I did when I started out. But that did not excite me. I wondered why I wasn't inspired. Then I did my first naked picture. I was angry with Mario. I put myself in bed with a man. I didn't know the man. But I loved creating the painting and looking at it. To paint, I need to be turned on, to really get into it, to forget everything. I paint naked sexy people. That's me. That's my voice. I don't need you to pose. I have a good memory for faces, but a photograph would be nice." Angelina took out her iphone and snapped.

"Can I see the painting when it's done?"

"You will be the first."

"Did you break the bank, Angelina?" Cass asked.

"That's not why I play. It's just to play, and keep playing. Anyway, I broke the bank art-wise, courtesy of the late Vance Cooper. Somebody bought the solo portrait of Vance. Guess what they paid?"

"I have no idea.".

"The gallery owner kept pushing the buyer and got him or her up to half a million because the individual wanted that particular painting that badly. Five hundred thousand dollars for my painting."

"Who bought it?"

"The buyer insists on being anonymous. The picture was picked up by a private driver and taken to an unknown address. The person who bought it paid with a certified check from J.P. Morgan that can't be traced. They appear to have a special interest in the late Vance Cooper."

Mario and Angelina headed back to New York.

"Are you in a hurry?" Noah asked Cass. "How about a walk on the boardwalk?"

"That would fit my mood perfectly."

They left the Borgata and hit the boardwalk. On that grey winter day, people were out walking, breathing in the ocean air.

"It feels wonderful," Cass said. "I needed this."

"Happy to get away from the slots?"

"I'm attracted to the slots. The jingle jangle turns me on. And there's that bounce up when you win. I could get hooked."

"Wouldn't the slots builders love to hear you. It's a multi-billion dollar enterprise with experts working around the clock dreaming up better ways to part the slots addict from his dollars. It's not just little old ladies. Everyone plays the slots. It's the biggest casino game in the USA. People actually try to beat the slots."

"How?"

"Crazy ways. Using magnets. Formulating theories, such as the machine near the door will always pay off better because that's the 'come on' machine used to lure customers in."

"Do any of these beat-the-machine methods work?"

"Until the companies catch on."

They stopped in front of a window filled with boxes of salt water taffy, souvenirs, and antique Atlantic City postcards. Atlantic City felt like an oasis of tranquility, games, and phantasy, removed from urban trauma and murder.

"Thank you for today, Noah. You really rode to the rescue."

Wind ruffled Noah's dark hair, heightened his good looks. "I'm glad I could help. How is everything going for you?"

"Confused, as to be expected." Cass had no desire to unload her angst on Noah. "Tell me about yourself. We're always talking about me. I really don't know who you are, except that you are brilliant and I am madly attracted to you."

"What would you like to know?"

Cass looked up at Noah. "Everything."

He tucked her arm in his and they continued walking.

"It's a private history that I share with few people."

"I promise not to take notes."

As they walked, the wind and the churning ocean buoyed them along. "My father was a mail carrier, a strong man who resentfully trudged the sidewalks of Brooklyn," Noah began. "He was a frustrated artist. In his off hours he painted, drank and created family drama, including beating my mother. She didn't know how to fight back. In one of his drunken brawls he smashed her head. She never recovered. He hung himself. Apparently he loved her. I was fourteen years old. I went to live with an aunt.

"At sixteen I was considered a juvenile offender. I drank. I would not go to school. I brawled with a cop. They locked me up in a youth prison upstate. It was a vicious hellhole that turned kids into criminals, if they were not sufficiently bent. I married my counselor. She was twenty-five. They let me out of Tryon Residential Center in her charge. This intelligent woman saw my potential. She introduced me to books and psychology. The marriage lasted less than a year.

"After we split, I set out to find myself. I experimented with drugs and at twenty, I married my great love. We were together for five years. She died. She overdosed. She was a cocaine addict. That's how we met. At a meeting of C.A. – Cocaine Anonymous. You're told not to get involved with anyone from a meeting at least until a year after joining, but as soon as I saw her that was it. We got together that night. We did cocaine. We never went to another meeting. Our five years together were glorious and terrible. Terrifying. I did not know from one minute to the next how or where I would find her.

"I was no saint. I loved that blow. I was into injecting it. She moved on to heroin. Her death shocked me into some kind of reality. It finally occurred that I was killing myself and I had this enormous guilt that I had killed her. I gave up everything. Cold turkey. Columbia University gave me a scholarship and I began studying with the same intensity that I had given to cocaine." Noah pulled Cass closer to his side as they strode down the boardwalk. "Getting tired of my monologue?"

"Not a bit. Please continue."

"Columbia helped me. Learning, achieving and being a member of that community. But that's when I started tripping. Experimenting with my own psyche. I'm not sure how many LSD trips I took. Finally I stopped. That phase of my life was over. I craved stability. I married again."

"And who was your bride?"

"The best friend of my great love. She had no interest in drugs. Her greatest indulgence was a glass of wine. She reminded me of her but she was not her. We divorced."

They stopped to watch the waves rolling in, the grey roiling, the white-caps. Noah turned to Cass and took her two hands in his. "I lied to you before. I had told you I had never been married. But I never lied to you about my feelings, did I?"

"What's your view on the institution of marriage now?"

"I plan never to get married again. I want you to know that. I also want to tell you that I care about you. You are important to me. As for marriage, I envy people who really have it together, who achieve that true marriage of body and soul. But I do not believe that person will ever be me."

"I don't know if I'm capable of that kind of love anymore." Cass watched two seagulls searching for a beach snack, beaks down towards the boardwalk. If only she could mourn Vance, have a catharsis of grieving. But after the initial pain of discovering him, her heart had frozen over. Pru's revealing their affair fell on her like ice cubes. The orgies with Jane and the then-Miranda Nightingale pierced what was left of her heart. "My feelings about Vance have not been resolved and perhaps might never be. But being on the boardwalk with you, this feels good. I like making love with you. Like you are my secret lover – all raffish and sexy." Cass knew that her nose was red and eyes stung from water spray. Her hair was flying wild.

"I have an idea. There's an old-fashioned hotel right on the boardwalk. They serve a delicious lunch of fish and chips. And they rent rooms out by the afternoon."

"I just realized how hungry I am."

Noah might be a liar – call him a fantasist – but he was also a lover and a charmer. Cass could not resist charm. At this juncture in her life, he seemed almost heaven-sent.

36

CASS RETURNED FROM ATLANTIC CITY at midnight, sated with sea breezes and sensuality. At this point, happiness was beyond her, but the day that began so bleakly had ended on a positive note. She and Noah had moved beyond sex to something real, to a situation of trust. For a few hours, she had indulged in a blissful escape.

Doorman Jose handed her an envelope, jolting her back to reality. "Kevin the mail carrier wanted to make sure this got in your hands. It's been traveling." Torn at the corner, an official stamp indicated that it had gone back to the post office for "insufficient postage."

She grasped the well-traveled envelope with trembling fingers. It was addressed in Vance's bold, distinctive handwriting. Holding it like a precious object, she felt a small bulge in the envelope. Cass took the envelope upstairs, threw her coat off, carefully slit open the envelope, reached inside, and pulled out a lipstick. Vance had remembered. More than once he had commented on her idiosyncrasy of always wearing lipstick, her "coat of armor," as he called it. She swiveled open the lipstick, a vibrant red, touched it to her lips, then closed it.

She reached back into the envelope, pulled out a one-page letter, unfolded it, and ran her hand over the paper's surface. A message in a bottle, hand-written and mailed before Vance left Balaban. She put her head down and sniffed the paper, as if to inhale Vance. Noah's masculine aroma still lingered in her nostrils.

She began to read.

My dearest Cass, I miss you and bizarre as it sounds think nostalgically of some of our worst moments – at least they were original. We weren't always nice, but I never liked nice. I'm enclosing a small gift. Please take care of it and think of me. I wanted to give you something, but diamonds and pearls were not available.

You won't take my phone calls and we are divorced, but I still feel that we are husband and wife. Adam and Eve. A primitive equation. I want to see you when I leave Balaban in two days and live in hope that we can be together again.

Initially I experienced true despair, but believe I have seen the light, or at least glimpsed it. I've struggled with gambling. You know a true gambler can bet on anything, even what time the sun will set. But I need to kick it if I am to survive, and I want desperately to live. I want to simplify. Get all the unessential crap out of my life.

Noah Lazeroff has been a big help to me. He has been a life-saver on many fronts.

While here I actually wrote a memoir (therapy?!) – a tell-all confessional. Once I started, it obsessed me. Memories flooded back. Various views that mostly I had kept to myself. About love. Sex. Desires of all kinds. Cravings. Thrills. Hurt. Pain. People. When finished, I destroyed it. Don't ask. Someday I will tell you all about it.

I'm in touch with Dev. And Donaldson. Unfortunate about Donaldson's Alicia falling in love with a neighbor at their Vermont ski lodge, a woman named Betsy who taught Alicia how to make the cookies that Donaldson craved. Irony. Donaldson seems to be doing okay. He's discovered Buddhism and spends an occasional weekend at an upstate monastery.

I've had lots of visitors -- the good, the bad and the ugly. I'm not complaining.

Take care, my love. Until we meet – Vance.

Cass slept with the letter under her pillow.

She got up late, and that afternoon headed for a favorite haunt of herself and Vance, the Pont Verte on East 50th Street, an excellent French restaurant with a cozy, sophisticated bar that attracted intellectuals, people in the advertising and book industries, and talkers. She stepped off a gray, cracked cement sidewalk and walked three steps down. Lace curtains at the window. The atmosphere was lush with faint aromas of wine and possibly a stew bubbling in the kitchen. The lunch crowd had left, and the restaurant had a pleasant, relaxed atmosphere.

The owner/chef Rudolph, a striking man with a large head topped by a mop of salt and pepper hair, sympathetic brown eyes, a large nose, and a wide full mouth ever ready to smile, greeted her. He poured a tall glass of Coke with ice and lime. "Don't worry, Mrs. Cooper. If you did kill him, I would not blame you." He winked at Cass. "I miss Mr. Cooper – he was one of my favorite people. A true gentleman. He was not perfect but –" Rudolph shrugged.

"I thought he might have stopped by here that afternoon when he got out of Balaban."

"I would have been delighted to see him." Rudolph stood behind the bar with his arms crossed. Rudolph's wide, flexible mouth turned down. He reached out to rub a spot off of the counter. His French accent, light but distinctive, colored his conversation with an undeniable elegance, intoning rich crusty French bread and walks by the Seine. Rudolph shook his head. "But no, he was not here."

"I was sure he would crave his favorite chicken with walnut dish that you created and only you make."

"No, Mrs. Cooper." He shrugged his shoulders again. Neither of them spoke. And then Rudolph leaned across the bar to take Cass's hand . "May I extend my sympathy."

"Thank you, Rudolph. So many seem to be of the opinion that I hated Vance."

"Perhaps they are brainwashed by a bourgeois construct. Love should be like in the movies. A long romantic comedy. No. Love is passion, and desire, and joy, and bitterness, and blood spilled – love does not fly out the window because of mistakes." He stopped abruptly, then -- "It's war, Mrs. Cooper, but worth the battle."

"Is it, Rudolph?" She sipped Coke.

"My wife and I have been fighting for twenty-five years. I adore her."

Cass eyed the array of bottles behind the bar. A bottle of Crème de Cassis sat so alluringly between a bottle of Crème de Menthe and a bottle of Greek Metaxas, a delicious Greek brandy that had given her the worst headache of a lifetime. Creme de Cassis was Vance's special liqueur. Rudolph kept it on hand only for him. It was rarely ordered by others.

"A refill on the Coke, perhaps?" Rudolph asked.

"Please. By the way, I see a bottle of Vance's favorite – Crème de Cassis. Did you get it anticipating his return?"

"No, oh, no." Rudolph looked uncomfortable. "I keep it on hand. The company waged a big advertising campaign and it's become quite popular."

Cass put on her glasses and took a closer look at the bottle. The initials V.C. were distinctly written on a small label attached to the bottle. Rudolph tagged bottles for special customers.

Was Rudolph, ever the discreet gentleman, keeping Vance's visit to the Pont Verte a secret from her? He looked so anxious when she asked him about Vance's Crème de Cassis. Why the concern? Had Vance brought somebody with him to the restaurant? Or was Rudolph just playing it safe, unwilling to get involved with anything that screamed of police and scandal. He had been so gracious. He did not know how to act any differently.

"If you tell me that Vance was here with a woman, I will not be hurt."

"But why do you trouble yourself? Now?"

"It's not for sentimental reasons," Cass blurted. "I'm trying to piece together everything that was Vance's life from when he left Balaban until I saw him. It's important. Have you talked to the police?"

"Of course not." Rudolph picked up a glass, polished it and put it down. "Why would I? In this profession, one must be discreet. I have seen people act their lives out at this small bar. It is like that saying about Las Vegas – what happens in the Pont Verte stays in the Pont Verte."

"I see his initials on the Crème de Cassis bottle, and several drinks have been consumed. Please, Rudolph, I'm fighting for my life."

Rudolph's moustache twitched. "He came here with a woman. She was doing some serious drinking. Mr. Cooper was quite sober. Their conversation was heated."

"Did you hear any of it?"

Rudolph sighed. "She said 'Somebody's getting in my way.' Then she laughed and whispered in his ear. He appeared stunned. He knocked his glass over. I poured him another drink. She went to the lady's room. He left abruptly. When she emerged from the lady's room she cast her eyes around for him. I told her that he had gone."

"Did you recognize the woman?" Cass asked.

Rudolph shrugged. "I have no clue to her identity. I can guarantee only one thing for certain, that she consumed four martinis, with two olives apiece. She wore a big hat and dark glasses. If I saw her again, I would not recognize her."

Cass left the Pont Verte and walked down Third Avenue, getting in stride with the after-work crowd pushing their way to belly-up-to-the-bar, to rendezvous, to shop, to get home to the apartment, take off the work mufti, pour a drink, sit down in front of the TV, and perhaps plan a different future. New Yorkers lived with the dream. Writing novel after novel that might never be published, or it could be the big breakthrough. Working as an accountant but doing stand-up at night. Cutting hair while saving money to open a hotel in Greece.

Cass called Donaldson. "Did you talk with Vance the afternoon before the murder, after he checked in with you?"

"Not really. We exchanged a few words and I was on my way to the airport."

"He went out to the Pont Verte and met with a woman. It could have been Jane or Marsha Newman or Pru or anybody. She told him something which he found disturbing. I thought he might have told you."

"In our phone call that night he said nothing. That was Vance. If something bothered him, he would keep it to himself. Are the police aware of this?"

"Not to my knowledge. Rudolph, who owns the Pont Verte, has not talked to the police."

"Let me follow up on this with Rudolph. I will contact Detective Adams if this could work in your behalf. I'm glad you're catching on, Cass, communicating with me. This could be nothing, but it could be important. Tell me everything. As for yourself, I don't believe that your contacting Detective Adams on this matter would further your cause. It could make you sound like the jealous ex-wife."

"True."

"How are you otherwise, Cass?"

"Never better." She had no desire to share her news about Vance's letter with Donaldson. It was private, hers and hers alone. "Wonderful."

"I appreciate your humor. We need to sit down for lunch and talk, really talk. I will call you tomorrow."

The Third Avenue traffic had built to a crescendo. Beeps. Whistles. Shouts. Cass closed her phone. In the next instant, it rang. It was Lydia of Call Jane.

"Melina, or should I say Cass." Lydia spoke crisply. "I'm dismayed that you lied about your identity. This is not only unacceptable but dangerous. Fazi Fakhouri gave you a zero rating and has severed his relationship with Call Jane. Mr. Fakhouri claims he's going away, and will be spending more time in Saudi Arabia, but we suspect that he's trying to put a good face on an excruciating experience. We will not be contacting you again."

Before Cass could respond, Lydia hung up.

Fazi *was* going away, but not to Saudi Arabia. He was headed for Woodstock and M.N..

That was another nugget of information Cass would keep to herself.

37

"Mrs. Cooper." Ginger greeted Cass with a grin, both shy and aggressive. "How nice to see you. You're still out?"

Ginger was back at her seat in the receptionist's desk in the big barn with its colorful walls filled with graffiti and art. She wore a silver-spangled T-shirt with jeans, and earrings that featured tiny skulls. Her hair had been pulled up in a top-knot. Even in its unwashed state, her hair was beautiful, a rich auburn red. Today her pale face accentuated the freckles.

"And where would I be?"

"There's that oldie -- 'Stone walls do not a prison make nor iron bars a cage' – indicating that a free spirit can remain so. I thought you might have been convicted, sentenced and locked up."

"It does not happen that fast. Even for a trial, one has to wait on line. It's called getting on the docket. As the population expands, lines continue to grow longer."

"Pity, isn't it?" Ginger tapped her pencil on her desk. "I'd say 'That's life' but it isn't life really, is it?"

"I hope not. I always prepare before going on a line. I have a Kindle or book or something to think about to stave off the madness."

"Smart. So what can I do for you?"

"I have come for the Brainiac experience. I do believe that I would make a perfect subject. And I am in need of spiritual uplift."

"Oh." Ginger sucked her breath in and drew herself up straighter. "That's a beautiful idea, but absolutely impossible. I mean like we're turning people away and you need an appointment at least six months in advance now. And recommendations. The Brainiacs are extremely selective."

"You would not put just any head on the block."

"Ha ha. Funny."

Although the chair was not offered, Cass sat down in the seat next to Ginger's desk. "I do not have six months to wait. My case could come up before then. I could be unjustly convicted and sent away to prison. I am offering the Brainiacs an unusual subject. Who knows what they might learn from me?"

Ginger lowered her voice. "Personally, I like you. You seem to have a good aura." She lowered her voice even further. "But you are on our shit list. That's a nasty term but a real one, and people whom our director Dr. Newman finds undesirable land on it. The last time you came here you hid in the lady's room and waited for Dr. Newman. I was held responsible for that, although I directed you to the lady's room in good faith."

"I hope this did not lead to serious trouble for you."

"I was reprimanded. But Dr. Newman is a fair person. I told her that you charmed your way past me, and she understood. She constantly reminds us that we're dealing with the human element. Always. That the rules can stretch and bend."

"I think that she would want me to be part of this experiment," Cass said. "I certainly don't think she would want you to turn me away without consulting her."

"I don't know." Ginger's voice sounded strangled. "I just don't know." As Ginger twisted her mouth and tapped her pencil on the desk, the decision was taken out of her hands. Marsha strolled up to the desk, slinky in black jeans, her short hair smartly coifed.

"Cass. This is a surprise. How can we help you?" She extended a strong, cold hand and shook Cass's hand.

"I'm here for the Brainiac experience. The whole thing."

"You're serious?"

"Completely."

"I can't offer you any guarantees. I mean – it could be unpleasant."

"I am aware."

"It would require a few days stay. There's usually at least one day of preparation. A day for the Brainiac trip. And a day for the all-important follow-up session."

"I'm ready for that."

"We have a waiting list that's six months long."

"As I told Ginger, I do not have time to wait, or to waste."

"I don't like pressure, Cass."

"I'm a murder suspect. It should make me even more desirable as a Brainiac subject. You can study me. Put me under the microscope. Write a paper about me. I'm offering you fresh material. Myself." Cass had purposely not worn make-up. She wanted to look pale and troubled.

Marsha boldly gave her the up and down. "You are right. You have no time to kill. Your trial could come up. You will probably get life, because New York State no longer allows execution. Occasionally my compassion wins over my rationality. Then let's do it. Welcome to the Brainiacs. Wait here. I will make the arrangements for you."

Ginger led her to a comfortable chair. "Help yourself to coffee. It could be a while. There are also books and magazines." She gestured to the coffee table heaped with books and magazines.

Cass poured herself a coffee, added milk and sugar, and sat down. Her eyes moved around the room. Once again, a group filled a circle of chairs, talking seriously in undertones.

The walls were filled with art, an enormous variety of the good, the bad, the garish, the charming, the execrable. Somehow grouped together the paintings worked. One painting held a place of importance. Prominently displayed hung the enormous, naked portrait of the late Vance Cooper.

38

GINGER INSISTED ON CARRYING CASS's overnight bag and laptop for her, and filling her in as they worked their way through the Victorian main house and up to the attic.

"This is actually a prized room," Ginger said. "You have your own bathroom and lots of privacy up here, and you can really dig into your experience. You know, like digest it. Integrate it into the totality of your life."

"Sounds like you have done the Brainiac thing."

"Oh, no." Ginger frowned. "Not yet. Dr. Newman says I'm not ready for it. I came here with the hope of becoming a guide. The person who takes the others, like you, through the experience." Ginger grinned. "Dr. Newman says I must do this preliminary work first. Then I can take the trip and ultimately guide others. I suppose it's something like being a monk in training, or I don't know. Maybe I'm just babbling. It can get to you." Ginger broke into a sunny smile. "I am going to be your special person while you're here."

"Don't you have to stay at the receptionist's desk and greet people?"

"On and off. When you are doing your thing, swallowing that gorgeous magic mushroom or LSD, and going on the great journey, I will be at the desk. But I will join you at those other times and, so to speak, show you the ropes." Ginger gestured with her hand. "Do you find this satisfactory?"

Cass gazed around the room. It had an old-fashioned feeling about it, wall-paper with a cornflower blue pattern, a rudimentary desk that could have belonged to a high school kid, with its scratched surface. A book shelf. A single bed covered by a thin beige cotton spread in an Indian pattern. Scatter rugs. A reading lamp.

"I'm sure it will be perfect." She walked to the window and glanced down. She had a view of the grounds of the Brainiacs.

"I'm so glad you said that," Ginger said. "This is actually the best room, but it's not always appreciated. The blue flowers on the wallpaper gave one gentleman a bad after-glow you might call it. Like they started talking to him. This actually turned into an excellent experience for him when he discussed it with Otto, his guide. Like that's the deal. You go with the flow. You take it all in and see where it takes you."

"How can you know, Ginger, if you've never done it?"

"Believe me, I do know. I have been the go-to person for at least fifty visitors to The Brainiacs. Dr.Newman says I'm almost ready myself. I'm looking forward to it." She walked over to a maple dresser with knobs. "You can put your stuff in here. If you want. Or wash your face or do whatever. Then you can meet me downstairs in twenty minutes. We will go for coffee and I will show you all the preliminaries. Hey, relax. I can see that you're tensing up. You're going to love this. I mean it's life-changing. And God knows, you of all people need that."

Ginger picked up Cass's laptop in the black carry and slung it over her shoulder. "I'm going to take this and put it under lock and key."

"My laptop?" Cass felt a mild panic. "I need it. I never go anyplace without it. I made the mistake of taking a trip to Japan and leaving it behind and it's as if I was missing my best friend."

"That's the problem," Ginger said. "In its own way it's an artificial kind of spiritual experience. You will be having the real thing and the laptop can interfere."

"Please."

"It's the big no-no here. You have a choice. If you want to have the Brainiac experience, you must live without the laptop for three days. It's up to you." Ginger turned one hand to the right. "Keep the laptop. No Brainiac." She turned another hand to the left. "Live without the laptop for three days. Have the experience of a lifetime."

"Okay. Take it."

"See you in twenty minutes." Ginger grinned. She swung away from her with Cass's laptop over her shoulder.

Cass emptied her bag. At least she had a notebook, and her Kindle for reading. Even without the laptop, she was not totally cut off from the world. Her cell phone was in her pocketbook.

Ginger waited for her at the bottom of the stairs. "You are punctual. I like that. And you look refreshed. You have put on lipstick. With your dark hair and everything that red looks great on you. I myself stick to no lipstick or pale."

"A bright pink would be stunning with that gorgeous hair of yours."

"Good idea. I love beauty tips. I'm so out of it here, appearance-wise."

"What's our next move?"

"There are a few preliminaries," Ginger said. "Come. We'll go to the cafeteria where we can sit and I'll go through everything." Ginger was now carrying a large manila envelope. They walked to the barn and Ginger led her to the back of a large room with tables and a counter bar.

Ginger got coffee for them, and they sat at a table by the window. She took a form out of the manila envelope. "You will have to fill this out. It's like a bio form and maybe you think it's a crock, but not really. Because let's say you have an experience and afterwards talk to your guide, and you and the guide can't figure it out and this bio could help."

"But you're not my guide?"

"Oh, no, no, no. Absolutely not." Ginger shook her head vehemently. "I'm just here to show you the ropes. Don't you love that expression. Show you the ropes. It's like really ancient from old sailing ships. Did you ever sail?

I tried, and couldn't learn how to operate the ropes and ended up cooking for everyone. I preferred it to running around on the deck and getting beaned in the noggin by a rope."

"Indeed."

"You are an unusual case, because as a rule a candidate for the Brainiacs works up to the experience, comes maybe a week ahead of time. But you are being given the classy express treatment. After you fill out the form, I'll introduce you to your guide. His name is Otto, like he was the one who helped the guy with the talking flowers. Otto is a sweetheart. Definitely. So do the form, and then meet Otto, and you will have the experience probably tomorrow."

"Good," Cass said. "The sooner, the better."

"Nervous? People do get anxious, and sometimes back out. But relax. It's going to be good. Although I don't understand exactly why you came and what you want to get out of it."

"What do you mean?"

"Most people come with a purpose. They're depressed. Or they have cancer. Or they have a terrible addiction like heroin that they're trying to beat. Something. A purpose. You mentioned 'spiritual uplift.' That strikes me as the motive of a bored suburbanite. I expected better of you. I mean you're supposed to be a writer – at least a journalist."

"My late husband tripped. I'm trying to share an experience with him."

"That's utterly cool. So impossible. I adore it."

"I'm also looking for a killer. Although an individual confessed to me in a strange fashion -- I harbor doubts about that person as killer."

"Fascinating. You caught a vibe. Anything else?"

"I'm in the world, but under suspicion for murder. Mentally, emotionally and spiritually I could be a prisoner in a cell. I would like to break free."

"That's utterly primitive and speaks to the existential condition of being alive. Dr. Newman loves a purpose. Several purposes are even better than one. And she will be thrilled with yours. They are so urgent and meaningful."

39

TUCKED AWAY IN HER SECRET lab, Marsha tried to forget about Cass Cooper. She needed to think. Damn. If only she had somebody she could count on, but as far as she was concerned, the so-called Leader was evolving into a loser. A dangerous loser. She had trusted The Leader so completely. Now? Falling apart. Almost dysfunctional.

She could have turned Cass away and risked her writing an article about the Brainiacs, which would not be the worst thing that ever happened. In fact, it could be great public relations and further reinforce the false front. Cass would present the Brainiacs as a big scoop while she actually knew nothing.

But unless she had Cass wrong, she would not be done with them. She would return to snoop and pry and meddle. Better to send her on the psychic journey, which could be mind-blowing and wonderful for Cass. She hoped not. She preferred to see Cass laid low.

She donned the rubber coat, goggles and gloves she used for protection in the lab. She would not let Cass interfere with her concentration on the formula. She worked alone. Because the idea for the formula was known only to herself and a few special people. As she worked, she played music. She was particularly partial to Frank Sinatra. His voice made her vagina vibrate, still a good feeling despite being the new virgin, as she called herself to herself.

After a lifetime of playing the free spirit, she had put sex behind her and seized on a totally different life with the Brainiacs. She had loved the Brainiacs with their vast potential to change lives, until she turned against them. Until she got even closer to the Leader. The Leader made her feel needed, essential, a super-woman with a genius IQ who could change the world. She then realized how out of sync the Brainiacs were. It's the Brains who mattered.

Her magic formula would enable the Brains to build a new world order of law and order and white supremacy. Not exactly like Adolph Hitler's Fascism. The Brains would not eliminate Jews, but would seek them out and enlist them because they were white, brilliant and creative. The Brains would rule with extraordinary mind control, build bigger prisons, erect walls at borders. Brains would do everything the opposite of the Brainiacs, who believed in total freedom of the mind. The Brains would practice brainwashing in a thrilling fashion.

Marsha was finished with the Brainiacs and all their trendy bullshit. Of course, they provided the perfect front, and they did amuse her. But she had done all the Brainiac free-spirit stuff, done it intensely, and now it was over. Because where had it gotten her? Nowhere. Including with Magic, her black lover. A jazz musician, he had proved hateful, despite being a tiger in the sack. She had taken up with Magic as an antidote to Vance Cooper, the totally white should-be lover – he had never moved beyond sex with her -- who corrupted her soul.

She had trusted Vance. He had trusted her. Mistakes on both their parts. That last meeting in Balaban Prison had been a killer. The new Vance Elliott Cooper. Damned. Vance reformed. He still had that sexy look. She wanted desperately to get close to him and told him about the Brains, a huge mistake, couldn't stop opening her big mouth. She told Vance too much. At least she had not revealed the Leader to Vance, stopped short of putting her own life in jeopardy. Forget about Vance. Maybe Miranda needed him, like Miranda needed her lover Magic, but not Marsha.

She had reveled in Magic, his ebony skin, his music. How they made love. Super-hot. Smoked grass together. Sometimes they would get naked and smoke and he would play his saxophone right into her cunt. It drove her crazy. And made several other women insane as well. "I have too much love in me," Magic had told her. "Too much for just one woman. I love you and I love them." That would not work. Marsha needed to be Number One. The One and Only. Her lovers could not treat her like she was disposable, a piece of shit, something to flush down the toilet.

She had loved Jane as John back in the day. They had married as kids. Two exceptional minds. John was great in bed and fun later as Jane at those orgies. The Brainiacs and their creative approach to life had intrigued Jane. Until Jane became a different person with her Brains obsession. Putting the pressure on Marsha to develop the formula at warp-speed. Screw Jane. It was she, Marsha, who mattered.

Marsha turned back to her test tubes. She had spent the last year working on the formula to the exclusion of everything else. She could not remember when she had made love with a man, and she had no plans to be lured into anything like an affair in the near or distant future.

Her phone rang. It was Ginger.

"She's filling out the forms. Then I'll introduce her to Otto."

"Good. Any problems?"

"No. She seems kind of anxious, but she wants to go through with it. She stated her main purpose, which I find so intriguing."

"Which is?"

"She's looking for a killer. She thinks that getting in touch with her subconscious and other realms will help her."

"That's absurd." Marsha pulled off the eye goggles and threw them down. "I'm tempted to opt her out of the program."

"She's going through an existential crisis. Since becoming a murder suspect, she feels like she's in prison, isolated from the world."

"Oh, shades of Jean Paul Sartre and No Exit. What a pretentious bitch."

"It's a personal thing." Ginger sounded utterly complacent. "I mean, like she's desperate. Like you know people used to go to the oracle in ancient Greece. And she would predict for them. I think it's kind of like that."

"You are a fanciful young woman. Where did you pick all this stuff up?"

"At the University of Chicago. And Bard."

"Try and keep your feet on the ground."

"Definitely. And you have another call. I'm back at the switchboard."

"I'm busy. Who's calling?"

"A psychologist. You might want to talk with him. He's well-known."

"I don't have time. Make my apologies, please."

"It's Noah Lazeroff. He's a star, at least in his profession."

"Put him on." She would talk to him for two minutes, and turn him off.

"Hello, Dr. Lazeroff. This is Dr. Newman. How can I help you?"

"I'm a psychologist who specializes in the research and study of addiction. I would like to know more about the Brainiacs and their work with addicts."

Noah Lazeroff 's voice took Marsha by surprise with its masculinity, underlying hint of humor, and vibe. As much as she tried to deny it, she felt a definite tingling in her now almost-revirginized crotch. She had always been a sucker for men's voices, which tickled her erogenous zones where a hand might not. Was this a perversion, or a sensual plus? In bed, a great voice could drive her insane, like Magic, who had a husky voice that drove her to ecstasy. Magic. Spell that trouble. She needed to keep her head about her. Forget Magic and sex and everything. Her crotch was dripping.

"Unfortunately I do not have a minute to spare. Perhaps six months from now –"

"But I'm in your neighborhood. How about lunch in Woodstock? Don't you occasionally need to take a break?"

"Let me look at my schedule." Perhaps if she got away for an hour or two, that might give her space and allow her to think. Take her away from everything including Cass Cooper, new Queen of the Nuisances.

"Are you the psychologist who runs the addiction program at Balaban Prison?"

"The same."

"This interests me."

"It appears that we have things in common – a lot to talk about. How about 1:30 at the Bear Café?"

"Beautiful. I look forward to meeting you."

Cass slogged along answering the questions on the form which included everything from her favorite childhood game to a brief description of her last nightmare. She considered packing the form with lies, but where would that get her? She was genuinely interested in the Brainiac experience. This was not the time to fake it. She might actually learn something. Or she could screw her head up for good. Although these new experimenters with psychedelics rarely mentioned bad trips, Cass did not doubt that all things were possible.

She took a break from the form. Ginger's denial that there was a Leader had only deepened her curiosity. Fazi was meeting with Marsha this weekend. It could be Fazi. It could be a political figure or the head of a corporation. Perhaps the Brainiacs were not all purity and goodness, working to help mankind liberate themselves, but a corporate enterprise. Suppose there was a master plan to establish Brainiac branches not only around the country but around the world. It's the kind of enterprise that a big business brain such as Marsha was capable of dreaming up. It would not mean that the Brainiacs were exactly bad, merely sullied. Big business and LSD did not appear to be complementary.

Cass gazed around at other future trippers bending earnestly over their forms, struggling to give meaningful and intelligent answers. Middle-aged. Respectable. Smart.

She missed Noah. It seemed like weeks since they were together in Atlantic City, but it was only two days ago. She took her phone out and called her New York number to see if there were any messages. He had not called, even though the Atlantic City experience had changed their relationship. They were no longer testing each other out. They were lovers. There was a new closeness between them. She could call him. She dialed his number. There was no answer. She decided not to leave a message. How revolting. Still playing games, like a teenager. Does it ever stop?

Nobody knew that she was in Woodstock. She had not told Donaldson. He was the last person she would tell. He was so adamantly opposed to her coming here. She had not informed Detective Adams of the NYPD. Was she doing something illegal? Suddenly she felt uncomfortable, like a kid who's run away from home.

She called Angelina.

"I'm in Woodstock at the Brainiacs. I expect to be here for a few days."

"I think you're crazy," Angelina said. "Why make yourself crazier? And should you be out of town? On TV crime shows, the suspect is usually told not to leave town."

"I could be breaking the rules. But what else is new? I found your portrait of Vance. It's prominently displayed on the wall in the main building. In fact, it is the center of attention."

"So this Marsha – the big trouble-maker who was in love with Vance – she paid half a million for his portrait?"

"So it appears. I can't imagine another reason for the portrait to be here. Unless there's a wealthy art lover who is somehow associated with the Brainiacs."

"To fork out all that dough the buyer needed an emotional connection to the portrait or to Vance. Apparently this Miranda or Marsha or whoever she is really loved him. Even if she did kill him. That's a possibility. That's quite the romantic gesture. Knifing somebody in the heart , then forking out half a million for his portrait in the buff. Some might consider it more perverse than romantic. If I were you, I would be very careful around her. Also, I realize you are a widow in mourning. We Italians wear black forever. But this Noah man you were with in Atlantic City is really adorable. Is he married?"

"Divorced."

"Nice. A good man is hard to find."

40

Marsha pulled on her body-hugging black jumpsuit. She paired it with the $1000 Thierry Mugler leather belt bought in Paris when living the Miranda high life. She applied a second coat of mascara to bring out the green in her eyes. She felt herself morphing back into Miranda. Squelch Miranda. The last thing she wanted was interest in a guy.

She had no time for the hot pursuit. The burning desire. The itch that followed her around the clock. She had always thought that sexual desire disappeared after age forty. Her own mother let her hair go gray and her hips grow wide. Was Mom still getting it on with Dad then in her own quiet way? The thought of the two of them copulating titillated Marsha.

Often when she met someone for the first time, or even observed an individual from afar, she considered how that person would look in the sack, what they might be capable of. She prided herself on being able to pick a winner.

Her mouth looked full and red and juicy with the new lipstick. She looked hot. She had no intention of even liking Noah Lazeroff who despite his voice would probably be a big creep. But she wanted him to like her, to go back to NYC and Yale and all of those places where he was fighting the good fight to cure sickies of their addictions and sing her praises. Boost her image and that of the Brainiacs, the perfect front.

She took the Brainiac station wagon and drove to The Bear Café on Tinker Creek by the Sawkill River, a rustic, romantic spot. She immediately picked him out of the crowd, the handsome guy with the black eyebrows and blacker eyes. He had a real nose and chin. He shook her hand in greeting, then pulled her chair out for her.

"Dr. Lazeroff." She could not stop herself from smiling.

"Dr. Newman. I've been studying the menu while I waited and settled on the steak in green peppercorn sauce, medium rare, with French fries. Why don't you get the same? That way we won't be envying what the other one is having."

"Perfect. You think of everything."

"A confession. I ordered our lunch in advance to save time. You impressed me with your tight schedule."

He had curly black hair, graying at the temples. Stunning. Her kind of guy. Handsome. Brilliant. He looked like he knew how to do it and she already pictured him in bed. With her. She wanted to be on top, to ride him. A huge, huge mistake. She had been so smart and so ascetic for over a year now. Keep things professional.

"You're the addiction expert. We have been working with addicts. In fact, it's one of our most promising and exciting areas of discovery."

"I want to know more. I think the only way to learn is to have the experience myself. To trip."

"That's a bold idea."

The food arrived.

"And I would want you as my guide."

"Oh?"

"Have you had the Brainiac experience yourself lately?"

"No. I have not." She took a bite of the steak with green peppercorn sauce. Divine. Sometimes she missed those heady expense account lunches. Food at the Brainiacs was so basic. She kept it that way. Healthy. But there were few frills with the exception of the cookies that she could not live without.

"Why don't you trip with me. Not together, of course. Suppose you were my guide, and I was your guide?"

"What makes you think you could be a guide?"

"Because of all my training, and my own constant exploration of the psyche and what drives people. I have talked many people through many psychic trips without the use of any artificial stimuli." He sliced at the steak. "I went through a period of taking LSD on my own. I thought LSD could give me some answers."

"Did it?"

"Tripping made me feel connected to the universe. I was less alone. Perhaps there was a God."

"You saw God."

"Not a big bearded guy in the sky. I experienced God."

"Did you hear him? Did he talk to you?"

"No. But I was playing Bach at the time. I suppose Bach's music is as close to hearing God as we humans get."

"I get Bach. Totally. Yes." Marsha chewed thoughtfully. "He is the perfect musician. He's the greatest, also Big Daddy. Also mysterious. I have never experienced God while tripping. Perhaps I should play Bach." She quickly ran her tongue over her teeth to clear away a random fleck of steak. She let her mouth remain open for one additional second, her pink tongue resting there. He was looking at her.

"I would be happy to help you program your trip with music in advance. Certainly you must play Bach. Any other favorites?"

"Vivaldi. John Coltrane."

"I like your choices."

She had managed to get her tongue back in her mouth. She had the impulse to lick him. A few flicks behind the right ear for starters, and then move on. She was sure he had a beautiful cock. She imagined running her tongue up, down and around his cock. She liked the word cock. Penis was a bore. She would make his cock rock hard. She would let him come in her mouth, a pleasure she had granted only a privileged few of her lovers. Vance had turned her down when she offered him that delight. He did not explain.

"This steak is divine," Marsha said. "I have practically given up meat, but occasionally some red meat doesn't hurt." She glanced at him and felt her face turn a bright red. She wriggled in her seat. Sometimes it was better to just open your mouth and say it. "Do you think it's possible to have an orgasm over a steak?"

"You are amazing, Dr. Newman." He broke into a hearty laugh, a real masculine laugh. "That's beautiful."

"We try."

"What do you think of my idea? Of tripping with each other as guides."

"It's unusual."

"That's why it's good."

"How long will you be in Woodstock?"

"It depends on you."

"If we did this experiment, it would take at least four days. You would go first, with the follow-up the second day. And I would go the third day. With a fourth day to follow up. Even this is abbreviating the experience. You have to fill out a form. There's no room for you to stay at the Brainiacs. We are completely full. You will have to find a room in town."

"That should not be a problem."

Marsha opened her capacious pocketbook and handed Noah the form. "Fill this out, please, and bring it with you tomorrow morning. When you arrive, go to the barn and the receptionist will point you the way. I suggest 10 A.M."

"Great," Noah said.

Marsha ate every bit of steak, and the French fries. "I had not realized how hungry I was."

She did not want to let this man out of her sight, nor did she want to bring him to Brainiac headquarters overnight. She would keep him to herself. She would next meet him in New York, certainly a better place to carry on a love affair than in the spotlight of the Brainiacs. Without realizing it, she was licking her lips.

"How about dessert?" Noah asked.

"I will have the cheesecake, thank you. After you are settled in tonight, call and let me know where you are staying. And if you have any questions about tomorrow, remember, you will go first."

"I'll be jumping off the high board."

She reached across and took his strong hand. Despite this powerful urge to go to bed with Noah Lazeroff, professional ethics prevailed. Part of her truly believed in and loved the Brainiacs, despite her change of allegiance. "Do you feel that you can trust me? That you will be safe with me? If not, I can find another guide for you."

"I trust you. It's important to me that you will be my guide. May I ask the same question of you. Are you willing to have me as your guide?"

"This will be a new experience for both of us. Yes. I do. I want you to show me the way." If only he could actually show her the way out of the mess that she was in. She seemed to climb deeper and deeper into the pit. Perhaps this man would prove the hero who could reach down and save her life and her soul.

41

C ASS CONTINUED SLOGGING AWAY AT the bio form. Ginger put coffee and three chocolate chip cookies down in front of her. "Hey, it's pretty fascinating, isn't it. You bring up stuff you didn't even know you remembered. You might get addicted to the cookies. They bake them fresh, none of your Pepperidge Farm stuff, although theirs aren't bad."

Cass dropped her pen and stretched her fingers. "Is there any particular reason why one fills the form out by hand, not on the computer."

"It's more authentic." Ginger nodded. "Plus you might be lucky enough to have your handwriting analyzed by Ezra, a graphologist who is also a guide. He read my handwriting and told me all kinds of interesting things about myself."

"I love your enthusiasm, Ginger."

"I try." Ginger flashed Cass a bright smile. "I have made my commitment to the Brainiacs and do my utmost to live up to them. Like suppose I were a cynical bitch who questioned every little thing. It would be like going into the nunnery and just constantly voicing doubt. Like what's the true purpose of the rosary? To keep your hands busy so you won't masturbate? That kind of thinking's just plain heretical. Some things you need to accept on faith."

"I question everything. I consider it my responsibility as a journalist."

"So what do you live by? What's your credo? Your guide for life?"

"Probably the movies."

"Like what movie?"

"Old movies are best. Casablanca and The Maltese Falcon. A Place in the Sun. Singin' in the Rain. Lines and bits inform me. When in trouble, I will refer to a film. At this second, I could reference Psycho and that strange house where Anthony Perkins lived with his mother."

"I saw Psycho – it's sheer Hitchcock genius, the shower scene and Perkins was such a put-on, but how could it relate to the Brainiacs?"

"The Brainiacs go after things lurking in the attic – only the attic's the psyche. And there's the Victorian house and the stashed mother."

"So who does the mother represent? Dr. Newman?"

"The mother could be Dr. Newman. She works behind the scenes. The Psycho mother also operates off-stage. She's the powerful force behind everything. She forbids him to have relationships with women, and he must murder."

"You are a sketch. I'll be back. When you finish the form, I will bring it to Otto. You will meet him, and after that it's dinner, and the night's practically shot at that point, because we don't watch TV here."

"What do you do?"

"Talk. Read. Play games. Chess. Scrabble. Or write. I keep a diary. Don't you hate that term 'journaling'? What a crock. Later." Ginger bounced away.

Cass was so absorbed in filling out the form that she had not been aware of Marsha's arriving and sitting down across from her.

"It's quite demanding, isn't it?" Lights had been turned on in the room, including one on the table that shone on Marsha's face, offering Cass the opportunity to get a close-up look at her. She had bold, strong features, green almond-shaped eyes accentuated by eyeliner and mascara, and a pointed nose that detracted from the symmetry of her face.

"Did you have a hand in creating the questionnaire, Marsha?"

"I'm involved in everything here."

"When I leave, can I have a copy of the questionnaire to take with me?"

"Of course. We give each individual who takes part in the Brainiac experience a complete package when they leave. That includes a copy of the questionnaire, plus a transcript of the discussion they will have with their guide after the experience." Marsha sat back. "How do you feel about all of this?"

"I'm not sure. I'm beginning to have something of a Shangri-La feeling, removed from the world. Being here reminds me of that novel by Thomas Mann. The Magic Mountain. That involved a sanitarium for recovering TB sufferers, but it really was other-worldly and about the mystic experience."

"You're catching on." Marsha actually smiled.

"When will I meet my fellow travelers, others who are taking the Brainiac trip?"

"You won't. Of course you might encounter them at dinner, but we discourage talking and interaction between Brainiac travelers. Because it sullies the experience, and can become competitive. My trip sucked, but yours was thrilling. Why? Or how was your guide and what did he say etcetera. This brings the level of the experience down to common gossip. Life in the USA is constantly being dumbed down. We would like to elevate it. I will leave you now to your work."

Marsha sauntered away, doing her seductive swivel. Although claiming to be a lay nun, her manner continued to be office erotic. Apparently she was inured to a mode of behavior practiced over many years. Cass could imagine Marsha as a teenager, standing in front of the mirror and affecting the posture and attitude of a movie heroine. A film noir personality would have been her role model. Barbara Stanwyck or Ida Lupino.

Cass returned to her questionnaire, and dotted the last "i". She could use a breath of fresh air to clear her head. She put on her jacket to walk outside. She strolled around the barn, then stood inside an alcove and took deep breaths. She instantly recognized Marsha's voice. She must be talking on her cell phone on the other side of the alcove.

"But must the big meeting be this weekend? There are too many people here including Cass Cooper. I could not turn her away. I know her. If I refused her, she would only be snooping and prying. That's her style. She will trip with Otto as her guide. After that, she will be forbidden to return because that's the house rule. I just created that rule, like I make up everything.

"You will take care of her? Is that wise? Do we want to arouse the scrutiny of the NYPD? You are the Leader but sometimes I wonder. Let's face it. Without my genius there would be no Brains. There would be no formula. Yes, it was your idea. So what do you want, a Hershey?"

Martha roared in a hilarious laugh that trickled away, her voice angry now. "No, I have not discovered some hot guy as you put it, and I resent your implication that I am any less serious than you. And frankly it would be none of your business if I had a tryst – don't you love that word – tryst appears to have gone out of fashion. Do I interrogate you about your affairs?

"The formula? It is complete, except for a few final touches. I did have the opportunity to test it. I went to a homeless shelter in Kingston and found two volunteers whom I offered a hundred dollars each to test out the formula. They took it and it worked. One volunteer was an out- of- work kid, a recent college graduate, a young man with artistic yearnings. The other was a sixty-year old woman who had crashed after her husband left her.

"Both emerged from the Brain experience none the worse for it. In fact, I would say they were improved. The young man planned to look for a job in a right-wing political campaign. The Brain trip might have saved the woman's life, which was not my intent. She kept saying that how did she ever marry her husband in the first place. He was a lefty and a supporter of Bernie Sanders and a communist.

"Do everything in your power to postpone the meeting until next weekend."

Cass pulled back into the shadows. She watched Marsha walk away. Marsha stopped to light a cigarette, inhale, and blow smoke towards the trees. Cass would feel safer inside, although she no longer felt safe. She could leave, get in her car, drive back to New York. Talk to Detective Adams. Exactly what would she tell him? That her own life was on the line? She had come this far. She could not back down.

Cass returned to the warmth of the barn. Ginger was seated at the reception desk. "I was going to come and find you." Ginger turned over her post to a plump young woman with short black hair. Ginger took Cass's questionnaire and leafed quickly through it. "Good. It looks like you did a thorough job. Now I am going to introduce you to your guide, the amazing Otto."

She led Cass to a staircase and as they walked up, Cass sucked in an aroma familiar from childhood when she would spend two weeks every summer with her family visiting an uncle who owned a farm on Long Island. She remembered the loft with its smell of hay.

"I smell hay," she said.

"Yes. Doesn't that tickle you?" Ginger responded. "Isn't that warm and delicious? It smelled of hay when Dr. Newman bought the place, and so when it started to fade she had the hay smell piped in. It's for real, taken from actual hay. It's just not our hay."

"Doesn't that contradict the tenet of the Brainiacs to have everything authentic?"

"Not really." Ginger swung her hair, now gathered in a ponytail. "Because the Brainiacs embrace sensory experience, including smell. Dr. Newman considers aromas important and says that they can be important triggers while tripping."

They had reached the top of the stairs. On either side of the room there were large, glassed- in, over-sized cubicles. Some of the cubicles had shades or other coverings over the glass, including posters and drawings. They walked up to the second cubicle on the left. Ginger pulled on a bell that hung by the door.

A slender man came to the door.

"Otto, I would like to introduce Cass Cooper. Cass, this is the famous Otto."

"No hyperbole, please, Ginger dearest. Welcome, Cass. I am so happy to meet you. Put all of your apprehensions behind you. We are going to be wonderful friends. I feel it and if I feel it, it's real."

42

OTTTO USHERED CASS INTO HIS cubicle, which smelled faintly of incense as well as hay. He wore a black shirt and pants, a colorful painted tie, and a brocade vest. He sported a fine moustache and a neatly trimmed beard. Two small gold earrings. His short brown boots were polished to a high gloss. The total effect was dapper Bohemian.

He took the questionnaire from Cass, riffled quickly through it, and without reading it placed it in the center of his large white desk. "If we need this, we will refer to it." He smiled at Cass. "I would rather read you, the person. You have so many colors in you."

"Really?" Cass voiced her surprise. "I don't think of myself as a colorful person."

"What is your self-image?"

"Smart. Attractive rather than beautiful. I'm a person that people like a lot, or not at all."

"And the people who don't like you?"

"I want everyone to like me. Of course, that's impossible." Otto's cubicle had no paintings or pictures. Instead, there were large squares of color. Red. Pink. Yellow. Blue. Green. Purple. And smaller squares. "You like colors."

"I cannot live without them. Tell me what you're thinking."

"Being at the Brainiacs is like going through the carnival fun house with its distorted mirrors. Reality seems to be bending."

"And what is the most unreal to you?"

"The rules, for starters. Not having access to my laptop. I also find it strange that Brainiac trippers are discouraged from speaking with each other. I consider myself something of a free spirit. I would like to reach out to others. I doubt if I could tolerate it for more than a week. But I am entertained by living for a few days in a different kind of society. It's an escape from freedom."

"The Brainiacs are dedicated to freedom. The discipline – or rules as you put it – is to help lead to the best possible Brainiac experience. Why don't we go for a walk. We can get some fresh air, and get to know each other." He pulled on a jacket and took Cass's arm. They walked outside into a winter landscape of bare trees and crisp air.

"Do I call you Otto, or Doctor Otto?" Cass asked.

"Otto, please. I do not enjoy playing doctor, although I am a PhD psychiatrist and occasionally even do the Freud number, with patients on the couch. This is frowned upon now, with all the new emphasis on drugs. I do not believe in drugs. I do believe in the poetry of the psyche. Freud was the great poet. And Jung. Their brilliance."

"But the Brainiacs use drugs."

"We do not consider LSD and psilocybin mushrooms and their forms and compounds as drugs. They are substances. Just like broccoli or an orange is a substance. They are aids to the soul, helping to open one up to universals."

Otto led them down a path lined by trees, now denuded of leaves. A dog barked in the distance. As they walked down the gravel path, Otto hummed a Viennese waltz. "I'm Austrian," he said. "Or could you tell, as I talked about my allegiance to Freud?"

Cass shivered in the cold. "If you're a Freudian, how does the Brainiac experience fit into the scheme? Freudians spend years with people in analysis.

I thought that was the beauty of the process. The slow accretion of insights. But this experience, according to what I have learned, amounts to a day spent on a psychic journey, followed by a day of retrospection on what happened."

"But one can spend years afterwards contemplating the psychic journey one has taken," Otto responded, his voice aquiver with enthusiasm. "On a trip you can go around the world. You can go back through centuries to the dawn of creation! You can leap into the universe! But you absolutely will not know until you take the trip. Are you are ready for it?"

At that moment Cass faced the fact that she was going through with it. She had come here to track down a killer. The entire Brainiac compound including ingenuous Ginger could be corrupt. Marsha Newman, the woman who broke up her marriage and almost destroyed her life, could be a psychopathic killer. The Brainiacs could be a legitimate scientific organization. Or a community of madmen. And who were the Brains? Ready or not, she could not leave now, despite all the alarms going off which told her to run.

"Could we sit down here?" Cass motioned to a green park bench.

"Of course." Otto sat down next to her. "Does my humming bother you?"

"Since you ask, yes. I feel like it takes you away from me and puts you into your own world."

"I do this as a test. If you had said that you found it delightful, I would know you were lying. That you were going to be difficult, and perhaps unable to open yourself to self-discovery. That you avoided truths."

"Suppose I said at this moment that I felt like running away."

"I would believe you."

"Tell me, Otto, how long have you known Marsha?"

"For most of her lifetime." He pulled himself closer to Cass. "I was her analyst."

"As Marsha Newman? Or Miranda Nightingale?"

"Both. Do you hold that against her? That she became a new person with a different name and identity?"

"I don't admire her for it. It strikes me as, to put it mildly, disingenuous."

"Doesn't every individual have the right to re-create themselves as they see fit. Artists and actors do that constantly, changing their names, assuming new identities."

"That's part of developing a talent and reinforcing an image as an artist."

"Wasn't Marsha entitled to be Miranda Nightingale, rather than a poor Jewish girl from Scranton, Pa.? A brilliant young woman with beautiful eyes and a bad nose. She had her nose changed. It made a difference for her."

"Why did she pick a pointed nose? It's not terribly attractive."

"That was the plastic surgeon's choice. She accepted it. She is something of a stoic. She could have gone back for another operation, but felt that it was her fate. She later threw over the Miranda identity and resumed her life as Marsha. Do you detest her?"

"Why should I?"

"She broke up your marriage."

"I blame myself as much as her. How did you get involved with Marsha and the Brainiacs?"

"I had another career along with that of a head shrinker, an expression I detest. We are not out to shrink heads, but to expand them. I became a politician, the mayor of a small city in Arizona, and deeply committed to liberal causes. Marsha contacted me at the start of her Brainiac enterprise. When I told her about my goal, to make the world a wonderful place ruled by progressive, liberal ideas and people, she suggested that I join the Brainiacs. When my term as mayor was up, I came here. I did not see this as ending my political involvement, but as furthering it."

"How?"

"I would use Brainiac power to get behind certain politicians, or at least one that I supported for office as Governor in another state, Gordon

Ramsdell. He's brilliant. Honest. Charismatic. Original. Persuasive. He opposed a right-winger with a powerful machine and big bucks behind him. Marsha promised to give Ramsdell all the support he needed including money and a promotional campaign. She had learned a lot in her days as a business woman."

"But Ramsdell lost the election."

"Marsha did her best. I live in hope, as does Ramsdell. He has promised to run again."

"You admire Marsha."

"I respect her. And it's rewarding work, meeting individuals like yourself."

"Why do I interest you?"

"All the colors. You are suspected of killing your husband. And a friend. That's dark, very dark. I want to lead you to the light."

In the distance, a bell clanged.

"Dinner time. Let's walk back." Otto took Cass by the arm and they turned and walked down the path. As he held her arm, Cass asked herself if she found that comforting, or were there too many people trying to get too close to her.

They passed a small house, set off by itself with a white-stone lined walk leading up to it. Parked behind the house Cass glimpsed a small blue car with a dented fender. She took a deep breath, and continued down the path with Otto.

43

Despite her anxieties, Cass dug into the stuffed tomato and pepper she took from the buffet. The big dining room in the barn was full, with diners gathered at small tables with their red plates. A bushy-haired kid in corduroys played at a piano in the corner, alternating popular melodies with Chopin.

Cass sat at a table with Ginger and Otto. The conversation focused primarily on the food, reminding Cass of dormitory chats. "The stuffed tomatoes and peppers are delicious," said Ginger. "But it's like the menu's stuttering. I mean like three nights in a row of stuffed peppers and tomatoes."

"It's about time to make a foray into town and treat ourselves." Otto put his fork down. "Woodstock has some excellent restaurants." He lowered his voice. "Dr. Newman believes everyone should stay in the compound. She does not approve of leaving because she says it sullies the concentration and atmosphere. But I saw her today at the Bear."

"Oooh!" Ginger perked up. "What were you doing there?"

"You know me and my walks. I had taken a hike and decided to stop there for coffee and a pastry. She looked stunning, in full make-up and black, and she was lunching with an attractive man. I didn't want her to see me but that was not a problem. She was so absorbed in this man that a bomb could have gone off and I doubt if she would have responded."

"Wow. That's the dish." Ginger cut open a pepper and filled her fork. "She vows that she's sworn off men. But perhaps she's given that up. Like coming off a Lenten fast."

"Astute," Otto responded. "I have known Dr. Newman for many years. Let us not spread this around. It's just between us. But she had the look that I recall from years past of the predator about to pounce."

"Oooh," Ginger said. "You mean in days gone by that she was out to seduce you."

"Not me exactly, Ginger dear. Although occasionally, in one of her more enthusiastic erotic periods, it was in the air. I discouraged it because I do not believe in sloppy and dangerous patient/doctor liaisons."

"You're such a purist, Otto." Ginger sighed. "I have deep admiration for you." She giggled. "So who was the guy? Did you recognize him?"

His voice dropped. "I don't want to name names if I'm wrong. But I do believe I recognized him."

"Tell. Oh, do tell," Ginger urged.

"Dr. Noah Lazeroff. The addiction pioneer."

"Shut the door," Ginger squealed. "He gave a lecture at Bard. I thought he was divine. Are you sure it was he?"

"Positive." Otto ate a piece of charred tomato skin. "I met Dr. Lazeroff at Yale. I was fascinated by his work with addicts. I had gone to New Haven specifically to meet him."

"Did Lazeroff appear interested in Dr. Newman?" Ginger asked.

"He was not pushing her away." Otto paused. "Something was happening. She was also eating red meat and doing it with gusto. A steak. She had given that up along with men. She could be at a turning point in her life."

"Fascinating." Ginger touched her mouth with a large paper napkin. "Do you think it's for the better? She's been kind of up tight lately."

"Hard to tell," Otto said. "Dr. Newman is not a predictable person. But I do sense something major about to take place in her life. A change. Definitely. My friend the waitress overheard Lazeroff tell her he'd call her as soon as he booked his hotel room."

"Wow. That is hot. Dr. Newman and Lazeroff. She once had a reputation as a man-eater, but claims she's finished with that. Looks like she changed her mind. Maybe Lazeroff will get involved with the Brainiacs. We could use an attractive guy here. Somebody cool like you, Otto," Ginger said.

"You are too kind, Ginger. Cass, do you know Dr. Lazeroff? Wasn't he the one who came forth in your husband's defense during his trial for the Ponzi scheme?"

"Yes. He said that Vance was not a criminal. He was addicted to gambling."

"And you have met Lazeroff," Otto said.

"Yes."

"Isn't he the coolest? What did you think of him?" Ginger grinned.

"I haven't formed an opinion," Cass responded.

"Now how about dessert, Cass?" Otto offered. "The chef makes amazing brownies. And there's ice-cream. I am personally fond of a brownie topped by a scoop of vanilla ice-cream. How does that sound to you?"

"Thank you, but not tonight." Cass felt sick, as if she had stepped into a nightmare parallel universe where Miranda/ Marsha would forever steal her lovers. She had trusted Noah, blabbed to him about Miranda/Marsha while sober and while drunk. He could have been involved with Marsha all along, picking Cass's brain, letting Marsha know what Cass knew.

Cass wondered if there was a term for emotional nausea. Because she felt like she was throwing up inside. She had given herself, body and soul to Noah, an admitted liar. Why had she trusted him? He was incredibly slick. He made her believe him. He could be a psychopath wearing the mask of good doctor.

Noah could be one of those vile and promiscuous men who hear about another woman, perhaps spot her in person, or see a picture and find it imperative to meet that woman. To seduce her. If a current girlfriend points the way, that makes the conquest even more enjoyable. Perhaps Noah had been turned on by the difficult and alluring Marsha as portrayed by Cass. The idea of Noah's using her, Cass, to chase after Marsha struck Cass as revolting and despicable.

Cass had the urge to get into her car and drive away from the Brainiacs.

"Cass, my dear," Otto said. "You appear a million miles away. Please come back and join our little party."

"Sorry, Otto. I was just having a mild panic attack – wondering if I had turned off the gas before leaving the apartment." She mustered a smile.

"Is there anyone you can contact to check?"

"Of course. I will call the building's superintendent. He is a gem and always comes to the rescue."

"Will you join me and Ginger in a game of Scrabble?"

"Thank you. But I want to do some private meditating before tomorrow's Brainiac trip."

"Good thinking," said Otto. "Please meet me at 10 A.M. in my office and we will make the journey. Sleep well, dear. Do not worry about anything. If there are bumps in the road, I will be there to help you over them."

Back in her attic room, Cass found a large yellow pad on the desk with a note from Ginger. Ginger had scrawled in green ink "This is for you in case you want to scribble. See you tomorrow. Breakfast starts at 7 A.M. in the barn. Pleasant dreams."

Cass walked over to the window. The room felt stuffy, but she was not able to open the window. It appeared stuck. Tomorrow she would ask Ginger to go to work on the problem. Moonlight shone down on the Brainiac compound. The barn, the trees with their naked branches, created a picture in black, white and silver.

Heads close together, Ginger and Otto strolled down a path away from the barn together.

Cass took her cell phone out of her bag. She called Noah. She would confront him. What would she say? He did not answer. She did not leave a message. Had he found a hotel room in Woodstock and been joined there by Marsha? She tried to put the image out of her head. Were they plotting against her? Could Noah be the Leader? He had the right profile for the job. An experimental psychologist. A brilliant liar.

She needed to know more. Locating the private number of politician Gordon Ramsdell took some effort. She missed the trusty laptop with its larger screen, but finally hit on the number via Twitter.

Cass dialed Gordon Ramsdell's number.

44

GORDON RAMSDELL'S IMAGE POPPED UP on Cass's I-Phone. The face, with a burgeoning beard and uncombed hair, could have belonged to an urban derelict or a rock star. Scruffy. Unkempt. "Ramsdell here." The voice was deep, his tone annoyed.

"This is Cass Cooper, Gordon."

"The journalist?" He put a bottle to his lips, took a swallow and put it down. "I'm not giving interviews."

"I don't want an interview. I just want to talk."

"Blah blah blah. Yadda yadda. You news people come on with that line and you're secretly recording every word. Then I see the big headlines and I don't need them. I'm not in office, and I have no intention of running again."

"I met a friend of yours, Otto. He said you had not given up the good fight."

"I lied to Otto. I did that to get him out of my hair. I do not intend to run. I believe I have been caught in the wheels of a conspiracy and it's bigger than both of us. That includes you, Mrs. Cooper suspected of killing your husband. Correction. Ex-husband. Perhaps you are the sweet innocent running through the daisies, only to be caught up in the conspiracy big-time."

"It's possible."

"Possible? Possible?" His voice rose. "It's more than possible. It's probable. You can count on it. You have been victimized. So why the ladylike response? Why don't you go after the bastards who framed you?"

"Maybe I'm not sure who they are."

"That's a crock. What are you doing at the Brainiacs anyway?"

"Seeking insights into murder. Tomorrow I am going to trip with Otto. I hope to get some ideas."

"The trip will not give you any fresh insights into murder. When you travel to India, you thrill to the Taj Majal. The real marble. The actual thing. But that beautiful experience will not tell you how many people suffered to build the monument."

"I wept when I visited the Taj Majal. I felt the love."

"You're good. You could be the killer yourself but you come off like a deeply sensitive lady. That could work for you on the stand, if you come up for trial. With that kind of line you *should* take the stand. Get the jury on your side."

"Thanks for the advice. Do you still practice criminal law?"

"That's part of my past, before I became a politician. Maybe I should go to India and live there and become a Sikh. Wear an orange turban. This fucking USA is getting me down. And the Southwest. *Fagetaboutit.* This area's overrun with weirdoes and super-conservatives. Like the guy who beat me at the polls. Otto and this Dr. Newman had pledged all kinds of support for me and it turned out to be the opposite. Like the other side did exactly what they had pledged to do for me. Totally uncanny and revolting."

"You blame Otto and Dr. Newman for your losing the election."

"Maybe you didn't hear me the first time. It's a conspiracy. They have launched a program to take over the country. I was a part of that. I felt that they were experimenting with me, using me as the guinea pig."

"I don't understand."

"Maybe you don't want to understand. Furthermore, I would think twice about tripping with Otto tomorrow. He's a two-faced bastard and God knows what path he will take you down. Have you considered that you, too, could be a pawn in the conspiracy?"

"I have not."

"They are fascists. Remember Adolph Hitler? The former paper hanger? He looked like a nice guy, didn't he. Remember him?"

"I saw all the movies."

"You are one funny lady. In the movies, the Nazis always had the best uniforms. They looked good. Otherwise it would be impossible to look at them for five minutes because their philosophy was so disgusting. Just like the Fuehrer, Otto is an Austrian, from Vienna. Oh, sure he gives you all that stuff about the poetry of Freud. I trusted him. And look where it landed me." Ramsdell took another sip from the bottle.

"What are you drinking?"

"You don't approve?"

"I do not stand in judgment."

"It's bourbon. Good stuff. I take it straight from the bottle."

"Tell me about you and Otto. Tell me what happened."

"After I tell you, you might want to cancel your Brainiac trip tomorrow."

"That's why I called you. I had my suspicions. They took away my laptop."

"You are a journalist. They do not want you taking too many notes, observing too keenly what the hell is going on. Haven't you noticed the fascists on the march all around you?"

"My horizon has been limited to Otto's office and the dining room."

"With the brownies and the ice-cream. Been there. Done that. It's to lull you into a somnolent state so you won't know what the hell's happening. It's a front. Like in that movie Rosemary's Baby. Remember all the sweet talk and even John Cassavetes the husband was in on it."

"You're talking my language, Gordon, the movies."

"I love the movies. I should make a movie, the story of my life. It will be a dark comedy, because I'm not egotistical enough to claim that my pathetic life is a tragedy."

"Tell me what happened. You and Otto and Dr. Newman."

"It's like this. It was a sunny day in a small town in the Southwest when I met Otto. He was the mayor of the town. Then he put politics behind him and joined up with this group of super-intelligentsia, the Brainiacs. He called me. He had read about my running for governor. He liked my ideas. He wanted to get behind me, and give me the support of the Brainiacs. They were experimenting with LSD and other compounds of psychedelics, magic mushrooms and the like, in pursuit of a new utopia of the mind. Seeking freedom. This is my basic philosophy. Freedom for all. Dr. Marsha Newman, head of the Brainiacs, wanted to back me. I came East and took the trip with Otto as my guide."

"How was it?"

"Strange. Beautiful. I discovered new worlds. Otto earned my trust." Ramsdell's voice choked. "I am a man of deep emotions. I am a spiritual man. They had grabbed me. How could I not trust them after they had shown me a magnificent universe. I took the LSD and loved mankind even more than I had done before, if that is possible.

"Otto and Dr. Newman promised me financial support to help me run for office. They outlined a magnificent campaign including a special phone program. A team of people would work the telephones in depth. The phone outreach would connect to every person in the state, with each conversation tailor-made for the potential voter. It would not be an annoying record that people turned off. They would enlist college students and also like-minded Brainiac veterans for this. A young woman, Ginger, would be in charge."

"Ginger."

"Another con-artist. She acts naive. She's far from it. She is one cynical pro. The phone campaign did not materialize. Or it did but it was minimal. Far from reaching everyone in the state, it was almost non-existent. Whenever I inquired I was told "We're working on it' and 'It's hard to find good people for a volunteer program.' " Gordon took another swallow of bourbon. "It never happened. But my opposition had exactly the phone campaign that was promised me. He also had a big infusion of money from a mysterious source in the East. He had the big PR campaign painting him as a wonderful person, rather than the true Nazi that he is. He won. I lost."

"Did you confront Otto?"

"Yes. He said that the loser always tries to blame somebody else -- the campaign manager, or the bad weather on election day. He completely dismissed my conviction that they had gone to work for my opponent."

"Do you have any proof?"

"Only the bottle that I'm sucking on now. Only the feeling deep in my gut that I have been had. They experimented on me. They want to take over America. Then the world. There will be no escape from them." The would-be governor attempted to take another slug of bourbon. "This bottle is empty. It's what we drinkers refer to as a dead soldier."

"How about the money? Who put up the major bucks to mount your political campaign for governor? Was it the Brainiacs? Did Dr. Marsha Newman dig deep?"

"Not at all. Newman's totally self-absorbed, barely got involved after her initial enthusiasm. A friend of Newman's stepped up to the plate, Jane Endicott. She was turned on by the Brainiacs and ready to change the world, starting with me. She used her own private source of income to back my campaign. That actually happened."

"Tell me more."

"I would rather not discuss Jane Endicott on the phone."

"Why?"

"Because I value my life. Because Jane Endicott is contemptible. Jane and her weirdo and revolting schemes."

"Call Jane?"

"Call Jane is admirable -- helps people get their rocks off. I call that good deeds. It's Endicott's other operation I call sicko. She calls it freedom. I call it perversion. If I went along with her, she would dump more millions into my campaign. I told her to take a hike." Before Cass could ask a question, he went on. "I don't want to discuss it. Let's just say it's contemptible and involved underage teenagers and sex trafficking big-time."

"Jane has been in a serious accident. Hit and run driver. She's in Bellevue Hospital. She might not make it." Cass paused. Could she trust Gordon? She plunged ahead. "I have been hearing talk of a Leader, the person that Marsha reports to – the ultimate head of the Brainiacs. Could it be Jane?"

"Possible. Marsha is dismissive of Jane. But that could be a cover-up. Jane's bad. She has made enemies. Of course they are all snakes."

"Did you hear anything about psychologist Noah Lazeroff's involvement with the Brainiacs?"

"Otto suggested that I work with Lazeroff on my so-called drinking problem. As you can see, I did not follow up on his suggestion ."

"Did Otto have a personal connection to Lazeroff?"

"Otto's relationship with him appeared to be more than superficial.."

"Do you believe Lazeroff could be seriously involved with the Brainiacs?"

"Definitely. He fits the profile. Brilliant. Experimental. Unethical. He went out on a large limb to get your ex-husband a light prison sentence, after the man lost millions for innocent investors. Lazeroff has a need to show off. To make a name. Justice be damned. Noah Lazeroff could definitely be one of them."

"Do you know anything else about the Leader?"

"That's a subject I cannot discuss. My life is vile but I continue to value it. If I were you, Cass Cooper, I would watch my step. In fact, I would pack my bag and run."

45

OUTSIDE CASS'S WINDOW BLACK TREE branches edged in white snow glowed in the moonlight. Nature's perfection, so at odds with humanity's imperfection. How badly she had misjudged Noah. He had played her like a violin, winning over her trust, pretending concern about her well-being. How she had savored the smell of the old hotel in Atlantic City, redolent with memories of other lovers. The taste of kisses. Of flesh. Of feeling. She had only experienced that kind of sex with one other man, Vance.

Noah must be a genius of an actor. Or one of those promiscuous men who can make love to a variety of women. The woman did not matter. Sex was an appetite, and he reveled in staging a performance.

At 2 A.M. a full moon beamed down at Cass. She turned off the light and finally fell asleep. At 7 A.M. her cell phone's ringing jarred her awake.

"Cass? Donaldson. Sorry to call so early, but I'm going to be tied up all morning, I want to invite you to lunch. How about Mylos? It's a Greek restaurant with outstanding seafood."

"Sorry , Donaldson, I can't make it today."

"How about tomorrow? There are a few points I want to go over with you."

"Can we make it next week?"

"Is anything wrong? God knows but you've been under a terrible strain."

Cass wanted to weep and cry out to Donaldson that she had slipped into a nightmare. "I'm absolutely fine. I appreciate your concern."

"Where are you? You have a distant sound."

"Perhaps because I'm half awake. I'm in Woodstock. I signed on for the Brainiac experience. I know it's going to be life-changing."

"You're actually going to put yourself in Marsha's hands? God knows what kind of LSD she will be slipping you. You don't need this black magic bullshit. You don't know what you're getting yourself in for."

"I'm a journalist, Donaldson. I seek the far-out."

"Please get out of there. Now."

"I can't. Stop worrying. I'll be dining out on this experience for years to come."

Cass indulged in a long hot shower, took pains with her makeup, and dressed for the occasion in a black cashmere sweater and jeans. She wore small gold hoop earrings gifted to her by Vance. With her puffy jacket she would be well cocooned for her 10 A.M. meeting with Otto.

She would have time to stroll around the barn and seek out other Brainiac trippers before breakfast, happily defying Marsha's dictum against Brainiac subjects socializing. She had packed a number of business cards in her wallet before leaving New York for just this occasion.

A knock at the door. Cass opened the door. Ginger grinned at her. "Hi. I thought you might enjoy some company at breakfast." Ginger had arranged her hair in a top knot tied with a purple scarf, and wore a bright pink lipstick.

"I did not expect you to pick me up for breakfast. Why don't I meet you in the dining room at eight?"

"That's an hour away. What will you do till then?"

"I will take a walk."

"Great. I'll come with you."

"Please don't let me monopolize your time. I'm sure you have things to do, confidences to share with other young people."

"But I enjoy your company. Anyway, it's my job. I'm supposed to show you the ropes. Remember? You should not be left alone pre-trip." Ginger's grin widened "I am supposed to stick with you like glue."

"Why?"

"To be supportive. Some people get anxious. They even try to chicken out. Anyway, it's part of the Brainiac philosophy."

Cass grabbed her jacket and pocketbook and joined Ginger in the hall. "What's the rest of the Brainiac philosophy?"

"Communicate." Ginger reached for the handle of Cass's bag. "You don't have to take your pocketbook with you. It's perfectly safe in your room."

Cass pulled the bag back. "Please, Ginger. I'm a city girl. I once had my pocketbook stolen while shopping in Saks. I put it down, looked away for two seconds, and it was gone. Since that time I make sure that I keep my eye on the bag."

"It's a compulsion. I understand. But the Brainiacs stand for freedom from that kind of hangup. Pocketbooks! Suppose we compromise. You put the important stuff that you want to take in your pockets and leave the pocketbook behind." Ginger looked pleased with her idea. "I'll bet that jacket has more than one pocket. You can take your wallet and phone and even squeeze in a comb and lipstick if that's important to you. I notice that you are never without lipstick."

Cass moved the vital items into her jacket pockets. "This is how I carried stuff when I was fifteen years old."

"It's a better way to travel," Ginger said. "Pocketbooks are usually overloaded and bad for your back." Ginger took Cass's pocketbook and locked it inside the room. "Now we're ready to go."

Ginger first took Cass to the large, clean kitchen with stainless-steel counters. "Trippers who wish to do so can help out in the kitchen. Peeling vegetables and the like. It's not an imperative but it's an activity that many people seem to enjoy. Particularly if they are having an attack of nerves. Now, where would you like to go next? You choose."

"Is there a Brainiac art gallery?"

"Of course. At least that's what we call it." Ginger and Cass walked to the Art Gallery, the two huge walls in the barn covered with paintings. Vance's portrait remained the most prominent picture on view.

"He looks like an interesting man," Ginger commented.

"That's my late ex-husband," Cass said.

"I know. Would you like to sit down on that couch and contemplate the painting?"

"No. Let's keep moving."

"Does it bother you?" Ginger asked. "I mean did he pose for it?"

"The artist had met Vance once. After their encounter, she made a sketch that she used for the painting. He never posed for her."

"It looks quite realistic to me, the body, that is. Of course there is such a thing as artistic license. Like she could have borrowed another person's body. Yet the head and the body seem to belong together. They project a special kind of energy. She's a powerful painter." Ginger gazed at the picture. "And the painting went for a huge price. Like half a million."

"I assume that Dr. Newman bought the painting. She must have an enormous private income."

"Oh, no." Ginger shook her head vigorously. "I'm not sure about her income. But she definitely did not buy the painting."

"How do you know?" Cass asked.

"I asked her and she told me. An anonymous donor bought it, and asked for it to be hung here. She also told me the price that individual paid for the painting."

"Are you sure Dr. Newman does not know the identity of the buyer?"

"I would not swear that on a stack of Bibles. She did act a tad squirmy when I raised the subject. I surmise that it was a Brainiac tripper – at least that's what Dr. Newman suggests. Who knows if the buyer even knew the late Vance Cooper. Maybe they just liked the painting."

"Since we're both in the dark, let's drop the subject for now. This is my big day to trip, and I would like to get an early start with Otto. Can he join us for breakfast?"

"Oh, no. He never sees his guide subjects before their meeting on trip day. He is adamant about that."Ginger turned an earnest face to Cass. "Don't look so crestfallen. He wants this to be a special experience for you. Joining you for breakfast first will already bring it into the mundane. And Otto dresses for the occasion. He will wear a robe made of fabric woven by Tibetan monks. He will burn a special incense. You'll see."

"If you say so."

A gong sounded.

"Now let's have breakfast. I think we're going to get lucky today. I noticed the cooks mixing up an egg and milk mixture for French toast."

Ginger was on her second helping of French toast when Cass raised the subject of Gordon Ramsdell losing his run for Governor. "I was told that the Brainiacs worked on his campaign." Cass sprinkled cinnamon on her French toast. "Were you involved?"

"Yes. In fact Dr. Newman made me chairman of the phone campaign. I thought that was a fabulous billion dollar idea. My team would call every single person eligible to vote in the state, and pitch them on Ramsdell. An individual pitch, not something pre-recorded which is so boring when a message is left on your phone."

"How did it work out?"

"Not good. I had volunteers, but every time we got going, Dr. Newman would pull us away to do something else. Then she put a restriction on how many volunteers I could gather because she said they were overloading the system, even though they were unpaid. They also contributed the use of their cell phones so that did not cost Ramsdell or the Brainiacs squat. It just didn't work out. I felt like a huge failure. Dr. Newman told me that I had done my best. That's all that was expected of me."

"Ramsdell must have felt let down."

"He was outraged. He told me that I personally was responsible for his losing the election. I was crushed. I am not over it yet. Otto says that he's a sore loser. That Ramsdell lost by a narrow margin and that if he drank less he could have won the election. He showed up at a few rallies stoned out of his gourd. Like give me a break. Still, it hurts. I hate to lose at anything."

The time had come to meet Otto. He awaited them in his glass cube, which he had transformed with brocade draperies and dim lighting. There was a low couch with a round table next to it, and two comfortable chairs.

A brass bowl and two candles sat in the center of the table, and the heady smell of incense filled the air.

Otto wore a long, textured black silk robe. He had arranged his hair in a pigtail that went down his back. Intricate gold and jade earrings, and leather sandals completed his ensemble.

He put his two hands together and briefly bowed to Cass. "*Namaste.* That is the Hindi greeting for welcome. It derives from ancient Sanskrit. *The best in me greets the best in you.* Please come in."

Cass responded with a bow, her hands together. "I am happy to see you, Otto."

Otto put his hands on Cass's shoulders and kissed her on both cheeks. "Today is going to be special and important."

Cass stood back from Otto. "Meeting you has meant so much to me." Cass paused. "This trip matters. I expect it to be life-changing. But I have an important request. I would like to put the trip off for a week."

"Don't disappoint me. Do not disappoint yourself."

Ginger looked alarmed. "I didn't expect you of all people to be chicken-shit."

"I'm not backing down,' Cass said. "I am eager and committed. But I need more time. The transition from New York was too abrupt. I need to prepare further for this important journey. If I were going to Mongolia, for instance, I would want to read about the country first and at least learn a few words of the language."

According to Martha's conversation, she was pushing to postpone the big meeting to next weekend. Cass would then see the Leader and the cast of characters. During the week ahead she could discreetly find about more about Ramsdell's conspiracy theory.

"And I have some questions about the actual process."

"Ask away." Otto lit one of the candles.

"Did you personally prepare the LSD I will be taking?"

"I am the only one who touches it," Otto said. "I am giving you a mild beginner's dose. You could call it starter's LSD. It rests in that silver cup." Otto picked up the cup and held it up to Cass so that she could examine the small white cube resting at the bottom. He then put the silver cup down on the small table that held flowers and candles.

"Amazing," Cass said. "That tiny cube contains the universe."

"No, my dear." Otto nodded sagely. "It is we who contain the universe. Sophocles wrote 'Wonderful are the world's wonders, but none more wonderful than man.' That's from Antigone, the great tragedy. Antigone gave up her own life to honor her dead brother and give him a proper burial. How tragic to lose one own's life over somebody who has departed." Otto looked somber despite his colorful regalia.

"I hope you're not drawing parallels," Cass said. "I don't plan to lose my life. My ex-husband was murdered. I am trying to save my life." Cass put her cold hands in the pockets of her puffy jacket. "Tell me – if I concentrate on a question before I take the LSD, is it possible that I will receive an answer?"

Otto crossed his arms on his chest. "My dear woman, you cannot interrogate the universe. An LSD trip offers a variety of magic, but what occurs cannot be predicted. That remains a great and beautiful mystery. I will be here to help. I can guide you through awesome possibilities, and I do not use the word awesome lightly."

"That's encouraging."

"Perhaps it would benefit you to put off the trip for a week. Let me check and see if next week will be free for you to make the psychic journey." Otto picked up his phone.

Marsha burst through the door. "Not so fast. Cass. In that huge welter of paper, you signed a contract saying exactly where and when you were going through with the Brainiac experience. This is not a trip to Disneyland. This is your time and you must keep your appointment for what I personally view as a sacred rite."

"I appreciate that, Marsha. But in one week, I will be better prepared, and it will be even more meaningful to me."

"I have already made an exception for you, Cass. I squeezed you in although the Brainiacs were totally booked. Plus I gave you Otto, our top guide. And Ginger. This is a professional operation and I can do no more for you except insist that you do it now. Believe me, this is for your own good and you would regret it deeply and forever if you did not take the trip as planned. Regardless, the gates are locked. Unless you know how to climb over stone walls and barbed wire, there's no way out."

"But that's absurd."

Cass moved towards the door but Marsha blocked the way, suddenly appearing bigger, taller, her green eyes aglow like hard marbles. "There are two guards outside the door. I keep them here to help out when people have problems."

"I don't like to be forced to do anything."

"You asked for it," Marsha said. "You begged for it."

Marsha held up a small yellow tablet and a golden goblet filled with water. "You won't regret it. This LSD is the purest. Now take it, while I watch you."

"Otto has prepared my LSD. I would prefer to take his."

"Another time. This time, it's from me." Marsha held the pill and the golden goblet out to Cass. "I insist."

Cass had no place to run. Ginger, Otto and Marsha had formed a flank by the door.

She put the pill on her tongue, sipped from the golden goblet, and swallowed.

Marsha and Ginger disappeared, leaving her alone with Otto.

46

OTTO CLOSED THE DOOR AND turned a lock. "We don't want any more inter-ference today," he said solemnly. "Come." He led Cass over to the couch. "Lie down, please."

He put a pair of earphones on her head, and handed her an eye mask. "Let yourself go. Give in to the experience and wherever it will take you. Remember that I am here. If you don't like the music, I can change it. If you are thirsty or want to get up and walk, let me know. If something disturbs you, tell me. Be aware always that you are part of the great universe, and you are loved."

To the sound of the Beatles singing Yellow Submarine, Cass began the trip. She traveled up into the Milky Way, an incredible dazzle of a universe, and saw the earth below. She reached out to hug the earth, a beautiful green and blue ball. Then she herself fragmented into splashes of paint, colorful blobs, like she was pieces of a huge work of art. She came back together again. She was five years old.

She met her great-grandmother Calliope, a sweet lady in a kerchief and apron with only one tooth. "Kookla-mou," her great-granny said to her in Greek. "My doll." She was going to offer to buy her great-grandmother false teeth, but then she was gone. Cass sat up and took the eye mask off. She walked to a mirror that Otto had placed in the corner and saw her own image. She was a million years old, her hair white, her face skeletal. She looked back at the mirror. She was an infant.

She lay back down on the couch. She was swimming in the Aegean, near her house on the Greek island of Lemnos. A black and white dog swam with her and tugged at her hair. He pulled her to shore. Safety. But no. She was in Donaldson's bedroom finding Vance's body with the knife in his heart. Mud sullied the green velour bedspread. She pushed away a gold earring that dropped to the floor, outraged with jealousy that another woman had been there.

She pulled the knife out of Vance and stabbed him again, filled with jealousy and rage, screaming as she stabbed him "No! No!"

The dog pulled her away. She was back in the Aegean, being dragged towards shore. Vance was waiting for her, standing on the beach, naked and beautiful. He stretched his arms out towards her. He could not reach her. A Bach piano sonata played, music of exquisite, infinite sorrow. "Vance. Vance." She held her arms out. Vance wept. "I cannot hold you. Because I am dead and you are alive." He pulled back, receded with the dog who had pulled her to shore at his side. "Don't go." she sobbed. "Don't go." She could not stop sobbing. She pulled off the eye mask. She wanted to go back inside that world and this time she would reach out to Vance and he would embrace her.

Otto sat next to her.

"I cannot live without him," Cass sobbed.

"It is a catharsis," Otto said.

"I love him." Her voice choked.

"You will be well. You will be better."

"Don't feed me that pablum. I want to go back to him. I'll spend my life on LSD and live inside that reality with Vance."

"You cannot."

"Don't tell me what I can do. You and Marsha fed me the damned LSD. So don't try to trick me again."

"You are still on the journey. Lie down. Close your eyes. I will be here next to you."

Cass lay down. She saw colors in the sky, an intense sunrise. Then a rainbow. But no Vance. She heard Otto's voice.

"How are you, Cass?"

She sat up. "I would like to go to my room, and then get in my car and drive home."

"You need to rest for a while. Then we can talk more."

"I don't want to talk. I want Vance." The sobs started again, wracking her body. "He was there. So close. I reached out but we could not touch. That was the most heart-breaking experience of my life, courtesy of the Brainiacs. Why did I come here?"

Otto handed her tissues.

Ginger arrived.

"What are you doing here?" Cass asked.

"I'm going to walk you back to your room."

"I can walk on my own. I prefer that."

"But I'm your walker. Every tripper has a walker. It's part of the deal."

Ginger and Otto moved to either side of her. They accompanied her back to her room.

Otto handed her a pill and a glass of water. "Take this. You need to sleep."

Cass took the pill. She did not trust pills. But she was desperate to escape from the overwhelming sorrow that flooded every molecule of her being.

She woke up to a moonlit scene. Her face was damp from tears. She checked her watch. 5 A.M. The Brainiac compound would be coming to life. She pulled herself up and sat down in the room's one chair by the desk. She was desperate to talk to somebody familiar, a person from what she considered the real world. The Brainiacs were removed from reality, and her trip was a totally different reality. But it was real. As intensely as she would try and deny it, the trip did not feel like a dream.

There were so many realities, Cass realized. But she only wanted the one where she and Vance were together. The LSD trip had done that. She, who had been reluctant to grieve, had faced the fact of how desperately she loved Vance. She would forever love him. She had not wanted to do that. The divorce. His death. Now the love. Head-on. She had questioned his love for her. Now she realized that was not the most important thing. She loved him. In her face. She hurt in every molecule of her body.

She lay down on the bed and wept. If only daylight would emerge. She would stop crying. She would get in her car and drive away. Marsha was full of devious schemes, and she was loaded with determination. Why had she insisted that Cass take the Brainiac trip? To make her suffer? To use her in whatever her big experiment was. How about the conspiracy that Ramsdell talked about? Was that for real? The story no longer mattered. The big scoop. Nothing mattered. Only Vance. She would leave the Brainiacs. She would go to another place, find another guide, a compassionate guru, and take LSD again and find Vance. She would live on LSD.

Cass needed to get away from the Brainiacs. She ran her finger over the grooves on the desk. Somebody had carved a heart with initials in the center. VC and MN. Vance Cooper and Marsha Newman?

Cass felt sick. Queasy. What was Marsha's game? She needed to talk with a human being close to her. She could not call Noah. Who? Angelina. She would understand a 5 A.M. call. She went through the pockets of her jacket but her phone and her wallet were gone. Perhaps Ginger had put them back in her pocketbook. The pocketbook was empty. She went through the desk drawers. They were empty.

She went to the door, but it was locked. She banged on the door and shouted. She screamed and banged and shouted. There was no response. She moved over to the window and watched the sun come up like a golden ball. If she were still tripping, she would have hugged that ball.

She had no desire to do anything except be with Vance. She would take LSD and find him. They would be together . But that was insane. Vance was dead. He had been viciously murdered. And she was suspected of killing him. Cass wanted to shout out to the world that she had been robbed, cheated. Cass was trapped. Silenced. A prisoner of Marsha Newman. Was Marsha the Leader? No. Marsha was never the Leader. She was the brilliant functionary who reported to the Leader. In the wedding picture of Marsha and Jane – then John – she gazed up with a look of adoration – beyond adoration – worship, as if she had discovered the person who would lead her to the promised land.

Cass took the yellow pad and began writing.

47

MARSHA PULLED ON HER SEXIEST panties, a far cry from the stretched-out and stained hand-me-downs she had been forced to wear as a child. She gazed at the heap of outfits that she had thrown on the bed after trying them on, wanting to look perfect for Noah. The possibility of love dazzled and terrified her. Had she ever really been in love before? Mostly she had been adoring, seducing, hating, aspiring, like with Vance, an out of balance relationship. Then Noah appeared, her miracle man. They were equally matched. Smart, experimental, passionate.

She wriggled into the blue velvet pants and matching sleeveless top. They fit her perfectly, hugging every curve. They also slipped off easily. But she would take it slow. Mrs. Noah Lazeroff. She did not want to jinx that dream.

She had followed the Leader's instructions. For starters, she had isolated Cass, the snoop who feigned innocence, and prepared for the Big Meeting. At the last minute the Leader had insisted that it happen that weekend, refusing to wait another week. The big pow-wow would not last longer than three hours. Discretion was crucial. Members of the inner core of the Brains would then swiftly scatter.

Marsha had met all of the Leader's demands, but she refused to put off tripping with Noah. He would be the first man to make love with her in her small house with the lab hidden in the basement. She had created a border of white stones on the path leading to the house, like big pebbles used by Hansel and Gretel in the fairy tale. Those stories had helped her to survive growing up in Scranton, Pennsylvania.

She had not been a sweet kid. She had never been granted the niceties of a little girl. When she asked her mother to buy her panties with days of the week on them, her mother laughed at her. "Who do you think you are? The Queen of Sheba?"

She gazed at the shelves of books she had so neatly catalogued. Her parents could not afford books, and she stopped bringing them home from the library. Her six siblings would destroy the precious volumes, scribble over the pages or rip them out.

When she hit a confused adolescence, she could not even sip a bottle of soda through a straw like a girl in a magazine ad without being tortured. Her brother Felix would accuse her of masturbating with the Coke bottle. Vile. Disgusting. She learned to fight. Later she realized that seduction better suited her purposes.

Now she was half living the dream. Everything was in readiness for Noah. She loved his name. Noah. She said it over and over again. Like a chant. Noah. Noah. Noah. Noah.

She had decorated her small house in the style of urban elegance, with a soft, comfortable couch covered with beautiful pillows she had collected on her travels. She plumped the pillows. There were expensive chairs. And things she had craved as a kid that had been denied her. A music box. A doll's house with exquisite tiny furniture.

The bell rang. She hurried to the door. Noah's cheeks were red from the cold. He smiled at her and handed her a bouquet of flowers. "Perhaps these could serve as inspiration for the journey."

She unwrapped the flowers and gasped. "White roses. My favorite flower. Thank you."

She took his jacket. She found a blue vase in the kitchen, placed the roses in it, and put the vase on the coffee table. As she did, she looked away from him. She had to look away, because if she looked straight at him, she would get too excited.

He would trip first. While the Big Meeting took place, Noah could wait in the small guest cottage she had built in the back. Afterwards, they would have the follow-up discussion that would last long into the night. She would offer Noah the guest room. But she would not try to seduce him. Tomorrow they would talk about his journey at length over dinner and wine. She would cook one of her specialties, Steak Diane with mushrooms.

The next day she would trip. The following day they would talk all day, about her trip, about his trip, about life. After four days together, they would be so close they would have to make love. There was no other possible expression of this event, something she now regarded as a psychic marriage/honeymoon.

He stood by the fireplace. She walked over to him.

"You look lovely," he said. "You're wearing blue. It becomes you."

"Men like blue." She drew closer to him. "Why? Why do men like blue?"

"Maybe it reminds them of good things. Blue sky. Blue water. Blue eyes. You have unusual eyes. Green. Mysterious."

"Probably my best feature. The rest is the result of hard work and cosmetics."

"Don't underestimate yourself. You are a striking woman." He took a step towards her. "Shall we get started? I have thought about it, and believe that you should go first. I will guide you."

"Why me first?"

"Ladies before gentlemen."

"No," she said. "That's impossible. It's not part of the plan."

"Perhaps we could talk first. Let me get to know you better."

"I have another idea." Her crotch was dripping. Frank Sinatra was singing *Fly Me to the Moon*. "Don't you love the old songs? Let's dance."

He took her in his arms. She moved her body closer to his, like she used to do in her old days as a seductress. So wonderful after two years without a man – unless she could count that one abortive experience – to dance with Noah. Tears sprang to her eyes.

She could not hold it back. It seemed like nothing else mattered. Forget LSD. Forget international meetings of Brains. They danced in sync, perfectly, beautifully. She looked up at him. "Make love to me."

"Don't you think that would be better saved for after the trip?" Noah did not miss a beat.

"Will you promise to make love to me if I go first?" The old Miranda was resurfacing. Pushing guys to the wall. Keep it light, she told herself. But it did not feel light and delicate and flirtatious. It was a powerful need. If he refused her, what would she do?

"I promise that we will make love if you will go first, and permit me to be your guide," Noah said.

"Yes." She put her arms around him and held him close to her. She could take LSD and still attend the Big Meeting with the Leader. She was a seasoned LSD tripper. If anyone commented on her condition, she would explain that it was her last Brainiac journey in preparation for giving herself totally to the Brains.

"Yes." What a wonderful feeling to let a man take control. "Yes. Yes. You tell me what to do." She could not resist rubbing against him. She wanted to grab his crotch but she would not do that. The song ended. She pulled back from him.

The black eye mask was on the table.

"Do you want me to wear the mask?"

"Yes. After you take the LSD, I want you to know that I am here and will be with you during the entire trip. We will start with your lying down and the mask on. But you do not have to stay there. You can walk around. And please remember to go with the experience. Even if you are frightened. You are safe."

Marsha sat down on the couch. The LSD tablet sat in the middle of a small green plate. She picked it up, sipped water from a green glass, and swallowed. She placed the black mask over her eyes. She had programmed the music. Bob Dylan sang *Lay Lady Lay*. "Why wait any longer for the one you love, when he's standing right in front of you…"

She lay down on the couch. Noah sat in a chair next to her. She had not tripped in a year. She had not made love in two years. She had never been more ready.

48

CASS WROTE, AND WROTE SOME more. Her pen paused as she remembered finding Vance murdered, a knife through his heart. Reliving it on her trip. Trying to save him in real life. Then trying to kill him on the trip. She needed to trip again and find him. No. She needed to find his killer and avenge his death. She felt it powerfully, the bitter rage. Forget a trial by jury. She would kill Vance's killer. She felt a black hatred that was beyond reason.

The sobs started. She was crying and writing. She would be crying for the rest of her life. She had never known real grief before. When her adored father died, she had felt deep sorrow but not this over-whelming, all consuming grief. Now she understood Greek women donning black for a lifetime. The black dresses were a way of enclosing their late husbands with them. Their essence. Greek women would weep desperately fifty years after a death at the mention of a name.

She took the yellow pad and put it under the mattress. She lay down. She did not feel like herself, the energetic, aggressive journalist who relished beating down doors and scheming to get a story. Sobs wracked her body.

She woke up smelling tomato soup. Ginger was sitting on the floor.

"Hello there," Ginger said. "How are you feeling?"

"Not terrific." Cass sat up. She grabbed a tissue and mopped her damp eyes. "I would like to get out of here. Why am I locked in this miserable room?"

Ginger arose from the floor and sat in the chair. "Not to worry. It's for your own good. Dr. Newman does this for people who have had a bad trip. You are locked in to be sure you will not hurt yourself."

"How could I possibly hurt myself? I can't jump out the window. It's locked."

"You could run out that door and run in front of a car, or jump in the lake. There's a lake near here. And a river. Right now I suppose you could hang yourself or cut your throat or do all sorts of unpleasant things. I'm here to stop you. So why don't you relax. You must be hungry. Eat. Enjoy. You will feel better. There's tomato soup and a grilled cheese sandwich under that lid. I asked them especially to keep it warm, because who needs a cold grilled cheese sandwich. And there's an apple. And chocolate cake. If you don't like any of this, I will contact the kitchen and ask them to make something else for you."

"And how will you contact the kitchen?"

"With this." Ginger held up a cell phone.

"Why don't you let me use that phone? I need to make some calls and my phone has disappeared."

"Your phone is being kept safe. That's for your protection."

"That's a crock, Ginger, and you know it. Are you part of the conspiracy?"

"What conspiracy?" Ginger registered surprise.

"You tell me. You were involved. You helped defeat Ramsdell and aided his ultra-right opponent. It's a conspiracy to alter the consciousness of Americans, and then the world. And you're experimenting with me."

"You are so wrong!" Ginger's pale mouth scrunched up. "The Brainiacs are totally for the good. Look, you've had a bad trip. But everything's going to turn out fine. Believe me."

"How about your phone, Ginger dear?"

"Unfortunately, it's a phone with a closed circuit. Like I can only reach the kitchen and so on."

"I would like to speak with Otto. Isn't he supposed to follow up with me?"

"Otto asked me to apologize to you that he cannot speak with you today."

"Shouldn't he be reaching out to help me out of this so-called bad trip?"

"Otto cannot meet with you. So I am here in his stead to work with you, to talk with you about your Brainiac trip. I have been in training, and Dr. Newman feels that I am well-qualified to assume the part of guide. Especially with you. It's one reason that I was made your go-to person from the moment you came here."

"But what has become of Otto?"

"Otto's helping to plan a meeting. It will be like a United Nations of individuals involved with psychic research."

"You mean there are others than the Brainiacs."

"Definitely," Ginger said. "The Brainiacs are pioneers. But this has the potential to be a worldwide movement for the good. And different individuals and organizations have been getting into the act." She frowned. "It's far from a conspiracy. It's open and above-board. This Ramsdell who bent your ear is just a sore loser. Now have some tomato soup." Ginger placed the tray on the desk and moved back to sit on the floor. "After you finish with that, if you like," Ginger grinned. "I can order you a martini, if you so desire it. Booze is permitted after a trip, but not before it."

"Tell me, Ginger, do people come back and take a second trip?"

"Not only second, but third, fourth and fifth and so on. Tests show that psychedelics do not affect the brain, although we call ourselves Brainiacs."

"Just let me freshen up before I try that soup." Cass went into the bath-room and splashed cold water on her face. Everything had been taken from her except her comb and a lipstick. She reached into her jacket pocket for the comb and worked through her tangled hair. Then she took out her lipstick, the tube that Vance had sent her. She had brought it with her as a talisman. This would be the first time she had used it. Her "regular" lipstick remained in the make-up kit in her handbag that had been taken from her.

Her hand shook as she outlined her mouth. If it wasn't quite her color, a deeper red than her usual shade, it hardly mattered. The lipstick dropped to the floor. She bent down to pick it up. The red baton had broken off. She picked the lipstick tube off the floor, then carefully scooped up the red chunk with a tissue. It was about half the size of a usual lipstick. She looked down into the tube. Something was there in the space usually filled by the red cosmetic.

She reached into the pocket of her jacket and found a paper clip. She bent the paper clip open and used it to reach into the lipstick tube. Gently, she pried the object up out of the tube and held it in her hand. Vance had imbedded a flash drive, the computer device capable of saving thousands of words in the lipstick tube. In his letter, Vance had told her to "take care of it." She closed her fingers tight around the flash drive. It had to be his manuscript. He had saved a copy and entrusted her with it. He was there for her. She could not let him down. A sob escaped her throat.

"Soup's getting cold," Ginger called out. "Hey, I hope you're not going to start crying again."

"In a minute." Cass pushed the flash drive back into the tube, carefully added the lipstick baton, and used it to paint a red mouth. She closed the lipstick and placed it in the zippered inside pocket of her jacket. She felt now as if she was now armed with a stick of dynamite.

She splashed more water on her face and returned to the room.

"Wow," Ginger said. "You look much more upbeat. What a difference a lipstick makes."

Cass sat down at the desk, took a spoonful of lukewarm soup, and bit into the grilled cheese sandwich. She was hungry.

"Don't ignore that chocolate cake," Ginger said. "It's absolutely luscious."

"Perhaps you would like half a piece. It's way too much for me."

"Are you sure?"

"Absolutely. Do you by any chance have a knife I could cut it with?"

"Sorry," Ginger said. "Knives are forbidden at the Brainaics. Perhaps you noticed that there are none in the dining room."

"And why is that?" Cass used a spoon handle to divide the cake in half and gave the plate to Ginger.

"You never know how people will react to an LSD trip," Ginger said. "The Brainiacs veer on the side of caution."

Cass ate her half piece of cake off a napkin. "I am feeling so much better. You were right about eating. It makes a difference. Now I don't want a martini, but if you could order a thermos of coffee from the kitchen, because I have this enormous coffee hunger, then we could really settle down and talk."

"Excellent." Ginger opened her phone. "Oh, it's thrilling to be your guide. You are such a special person. I promise not to disappoint you."

49

MARSHA HAD NOT COUNTED ON where the journey would take her.

First to hell. She went down. She burned. She pulled the eye shade off, screaming. Noah talked with her. He helped her. She went back. She met her mother, the woman whom she remembered as most resembling a witch. She looked like a beautiful young girl. She embraced Marsha. She told her she loved her. She regretted that there had been no time for her.

Then the other scene and she was screaming no, no, don't do it.

She came around again and Noah was there.

"It happened," she said. "It happened anyway. I didn't want it."

"Remember it," he said. " Then let it go."

She went back and she died. She was totally obliterated, dissolved into atoms and those specks that were once her scattered. Blackness. The void. She could not scream because she had ceased to exist.

"Go back," he said. "Go back. Give birth to yourself, the new Marsha."

She became an infant. Then a child. She rediscovered a dazzling world. A place of freedom and love. As a kid she loved everyone. Even suffering abuse, she would create hand-made gifts for everyone in her family. Her love had been displaced. She had become hard and driven, a woman who wanted to feel nothing. Now she wanted to feel everything. She wanted love. The decision had been made for her.

At 3 P.M., she removed the eye mask and sat up on the couch. Noah was sitting in the yellow Italian chair across from her. Initially she had wanted to grab him and push him into bed with her, to use him the way she had used so many other men. But she did not want that anymore. When Noah made love to her, she desperately wanted the love to be real.

"I'm so happy you're here, Noah." Marsha felt her smile glow and grow as she gazed at him, silly, as if she would never stop smiling. "And I want to talk about everything, but not now."

"I think you had a remarkable trip," Noah said. "I don't want it to fade before we discuss it."

"It will never fade," Marsha said. "But I have some things I must take care of. Commitments that I had tried to ignore. But they are important." She wanted to grab him and just go for it, right now. But once they were in bed together she would not want to stop making love. "Could we meet tomorrow, at 10 A.M., right here?"

"Why – why sure." Noah looked confused.

"If you want, you could stay in the smaller house in the back of this one, and read or whatever."

"Thanks, but I think I'll take a stroll around the Brainiac campus and then explore Woodstock."

"Perfect."

"Are you all right? You said some provocative things."

"I'm a hundred percent fine. I have never been better. Now I must go. It's urgent. Call it life or death." She brought him his coat and helped him on with it. "Leave. Please. Go to the barn. Talk. Discover the Brainiacs. Meet everyone. We have nothing to hide."

"Has Cass Cooper been here?"

"Cass Cooper? Of course not. What a ridiculous idea. If you don't believe me, I suggest you go look for her yourself."

Cass had settled back on the bed, pillow propped behind her, in hopes of creating a cozy atmosphere in which to have a dialogue with Ginger. She needed to gain Ginger's trust. Ginger had taken a fold-up table out of the closet and opened it. A large thermos of coffee and a plate of cookies sat in the middle of the table, along with a bowl of red and green grapes. Ginger had also brought her guitar and a game of Scrabble back to the room.

"So tell me, Ginger, what's this experiment about? Locking me up." Cass smiled and refilled her coffee cup. The coffee was helping to return her to normalcy. "I hope this isn't some form of brainwashing."

"Of course not!" Ginger looked dismayed. "Dr. Newman is into the brain, but definitely not brainwashing. Oh, no. You see, it's like this, Cass. May I call you Cass, now that I am your guide and not just your go-to person?"

"Of course. I prefer it to Mrs. Cooper, which is so formal."

"You wanted to undergo the Brainiac experience because you felt isolated. It appears that when you tripped, you felt further isolated. You encountered your husband but could not reach him, causing fear and alienation."

"Who passed this information along to you?"

"Otto. He listened to you and recounted your experience to me with the utmost compassion. To help you. Dr. Newman advised that we actually isolate you. Put you in a situation where you could not resort to your usual means of escape. You could not reach a friend. You could not return to your familiar apartment. This would force you to face yourself and to confront your feelings. By accentuating them. Underscoring them. Exaggerating them."

"That's a crock. I am experiencing grief."

"Now you're talking! Grief is extraordinarily isolating. That's why people gather in groups. There are grief circles."

"Are you my circle, Ginger?"

"I'm a start."

"Group therapy has never turned me on."

"Then what?" Ginger asked.

"I need to kill my husband's killer."

"Wow. This is news." Ginger plunked on her guitar.

"First I must nail down this person's identity. Perhaps you can help. Suppose we play Sherlock Holmes and Watson."

"That does titillate me. How will we do it?"

"I will ask you a question, and you will give me the best possible answer."

"Okay, I am willing to try."

"Do you consider Dr. Newman capable of murder?"

Ginger frowned, turned her head to the side, plunked a few chords on the guitar. "It's like this. She talks tough. She might even be capable of giving the directive to another person to carry out a murder. Like hire a hit man. But to do it herself? No. Underneath it all, there's a heart beating. She herself might not even be aware of that fact. But occasionally I have heard it ticking. Tick Tock. Tick Tock. Next question, please."

Marsha watched Noah leave. It hurt, but if she played her cards right, she would begin a new life with him. Like the poet William Blake wrote, "If the doors of perception were cleansed, everything would appear to man as it is. Infinite." Yes. Infinite love. Marsha shivered with delight and anticipation. In her new life with Noah, she would read poetry, visit museums, indulge in all the real-people things she had denied herself.

She would also require a new name. What would she call herself? She had always been partial to the name Maya, which meant illusion in Hindu. So much sexier than Marsha. She would become Maya Lazeroff, wife of psychologist Noah Lazeroff. They would live in a spacious apartment on Manhattan's Upper West Side and give unpretentious, witty, talked-about dinner parties.

Other women would be green with envy.

As for Cass Cooper, she continued to be a problem. She could not let Cass ruin her life. Okay, so she had wrecked Cass's marriage but where had it gotten her? Instead of embracing her, Vance had rejected her. Cass had not sunk her emotional teeth into Noah yet, or had she? She was involved with Noah, Jane had told her, after being tipped off on the relationship by the bartender in Charley Blue's.

Marsha went down to her lab in the basement and locked the steel door behind her. She went into the small kitchen next to the lab, made coffee, and ate a banana with a spoon full of yogurt, and a whole wheat English muffin. She watched her diet, with an eye towards her figure and her health.

She had installed a sound system in Cass's attic room that enabled her to record conversations and play them back. She could also listen in. First she rewound the recording to play back the time before Ginger entered the room. She listened to Cass weeping and then shouting when she could not get out of the room. Good. She had been plunged into an emotionally precarious place of vulnerability. She would be ready to spill her guts about everything and everybody including Noah. Marsha munched on the whole wheat muffin that she consumed with just a tab of unsalted butter. Salt was a killer. She avoided it.

Marsha put her piece of muffin down. Cass was making murder sounds. She would seek revenge for Vance's death. Mrs. Goody-Two Shoes had dropped her act to reveal her true vindictive self. Cass had asked Ginger to help her identify Vance's killer. So Cass knew things. She was doing eenie meenie minie moe, making sure she avenged Vance's death by identifying Vance's murderer. That put Cass into heavy doo-doo. A horrible expression, heavy doo-doo. A relic of her tortured youth in Scranton. Much as she wanted to wipe the slate clean, remnants remained of that miserable existence clogged in her gut. She was not sure if Cass should live. Otto had told her everything she needed to know about Cass's LSD trip. Could Otto be trusted? Could anybody be trusted?

Otto had returned to his cubicle and folded away the silk fabrics and robe used to create atmosphere for Cass's trip. He liked wearing the robe. It made him feel like a true guru. He embraced the entire atmosphere of mysticism. Of Buddhism and Hinduism, but now he was ready to cut his spiritual losses, to leave Dr. Marsha Newman, once Miranda Nightingale. How many other identities had she had tucked away?

He opened his suitcase. He would pack up his silk robes and fabrics and depart. He would return to India, a country where people lived their spirituality. He had saved a few dollars, and had inherited a few more. He could make it in India. He relished the idea of travel and discovery. He felt at home in the great country of India which was unfortunately polluted, poor and troubled but offered a reality that almost paralleled magic mushrooms.

He regretted having to abort his exploration of her trip with Cass Cooper. That was Marsha's command. She insisted that Ginger, her protege, talk with Cass. He wanted to warn Cass about Marsha. She was trouble. But he would be putting his own head on the block. Now he needed to attend to the Big Meeting that would take place almost immediately, a week earlier than Marsha had planned. The Leader had commanded it. It would be totally closed to the Brainiac staff, and be held in Marsha's inner sanctum in the basement of her house.

He was in charge of making name tags for the people attending. There would be six of them. The name tags struck him as ridiculous in such a small group, but Marsha said that they would facilitate a smooth communication. This super-important meeting would be brief, a total of three hours. The leaders would come, and then go. For the ridiculous name-tags, they would use aliases. Otto wondered if all of this mystery was truly important, or was it Marsha's idea of a good time. He already knew one person who was coming, who would go under the tag of Benjamin. It was Fazi. He recognized his picture on Marsha's desk in her office. She had quickly covered it when she saw him looking at it. He would be glad to get away from Marsha the Strange.

Cass was tucked up in the attic. Marsha had fed Ginger some story about isolation as therapy that Ginger appeared to believe. We do believe what we want to believe. Otto yearned for a true world, but conjectured more and more that it did not exist. Old Plato hit the nail on the head those thousands of years ago. We are in a cave, and permitted merely to glimpse a shadow of the real.

Otto wanted and deserved more than he was getting with the Brainiacs.

He created a tag for a woman and called it Gertrude at Marsha's suggestion. Of course Marsha would pick a completely unglamorous name for another woman. She was such a bitch. Could the Gertrude tag possibly belong to Jane Endicott, ex-spouse of Marsha. The two of them were thick. If they hadn't once been married, they could have been brother and sister. That kind of relationship would probably work better for Marsha than marriage. He imagined Marsha as an intimidating person in a marriage partnership. Unless she was under the spell of a person like Vance Cooper, who totally awed and outclassed her. Awe. That was the Brainiac byword. And now Marsha had discovered Noah Lazeroff. Why and where was that going? Could Noah be part of the inner circle?

As for Jane, had she recovered? She could have faked catastrophic illness. Jane was a power. Big and bad. She appeared so innocuous but was capable of the worst.

Otto laughed to himself with bitter irony. The Brainiacs could have been so beautiful, not the muddle that he saw evolving around him. Marsha and her cohorts were preparing to play a dangerous game with people's minds. Otto felt that his own mind and soul had been messed with.

Tomorrow he would be gone. For good. He had a key to the gate, but he really did not need it. He knew that it was open. Marsha had lied to Cass, claiming that she must climb over barbed wire to leave. That short of nasty trick amused her. He would not miss Miranda or Marsha. He hoped never to see her again. He would go quietly. He knew too much. He knew that.

51

C ASS WAS DROWNING IN COFFEE and dizzy from sucking up stale air. "Did you ever meet Jane?" Cass asked Ginger.

"Jane? You mean Jane Endicott?" Ginger picked up her guitar and plunked. "I met Jane briefly when she came to visit Dr. Newman. An attractive woman. Stunning, as a matter of fact. So tall and slender. She could have been a high fashion model, but Dr. Newman said that she was a librarian."

"For such a brief visit, she made a powerful impression on you."

"Of course. I was curious. Because she had once been married to Dr. Newman. Before she transitioned from John to Jane. They were divorced but remained close. Why are you interested in Jane?"

"Jane actually confessed to murdering Vance."

"On your trip with Otto?" A riff on the guitar.

"In real life."

"She confessed to you? In so many words?"

"She pointed to herself." Cass imitated Jane's gesture.

Ginger imitated Cass. "Like this?" Ginger held a finger to her head.

"Yes. Hmmn. You are a clever mimic. Now that I observe you, I realize that Jane could have been pointing to her head, not herself. Possibly to her brain. She could have been trying to tell me that a Brainiac killed Vance."

"Wow!" Ginger flashed a chord on her guitar. "You do go for the jugular. I thought this was a game."

"Call it a serious game."

"Brainiacs don't kill. Suppose Jane was telling you that a big brain killed Vance – a super-smart person. Possibly a genius."

"What do you know about the Brains with a capital B?"

"Nothing. Is there a Brain organization? Like Mensa for people with super IQ's? Never heard of them. I have no clue. What else?" Ginger reached for Cass's cup. "Have another cup of coffee. I think the caffeine is good for you. You stopped crying. I was really worried about you." She handed Cass the cup of coffee.

"I'm feeling better." Cass patted the pocket containing Vance's flash drive.

"You were reminding me of these heroines in old movies who perish from love. How sad to go on an LSD trip and end up dying for love. Just sobbing and withering away. Like in Wuthering Heights. I do miss the tube sometimes. Because I enjoy looking at movies. Just like you. We have that in common, like a bond."

"You have an unusual mind." Cass sipped coffee. "Are you sure this is the right career for you? Psychedelics?"

"I'm considering other options. Maybe TV journalism." Ginger twanged at her guitar. "So maybe Jane didn't confess to killing Vance. This is a fascinating game. If I were on a jury I would vote to exonerate her. Of course she could have been a killer. She was able to assume different roles. Man to woman. Librarian to horticulturist."

"Horticulturist? That's a new one on me."

"Dr. Newman yearned to have a green house. It seems that as a kid she had always wanted to live around flowers, and vowed that she would have them when she grew up. So Jane Endicott totally researched and found out how to raise different flowers including Dr. Newman's favorite. White roses."

"White roses. Tell me about them."

"What do you want to know?"

"Does the white rose mean anything special to the Brainiacs?"

Ginger grinned. "That's a Brainiac secret. And I can't give away secrets."

"Oh." Cass stood up and walked to the window. "Ginger. Can you please open that window? I need to breathe some fresh air."

"Sorry. But it's permanently closed because of the heating and air conditioning system. So I couldn't open it if I wanted to."

Cass stood at the window gasping. "I feel like I'm going to crack. I can't breathe."

Ginger put down the guitar. "Ooh, I hope you're not having an anxiety attack. My mother has them. I know the cure. You breathe into a brown paper bag. I have a bag with me. I always carry one for my mother."

Ginger reached into her capacious leather bag and brought out a small brown paper bag. She opened it and held it to Cass's mouth. "Now take deep breaths and think serene thoughts."

Cass pushed away Ginger's hand. "I do not need a paper bag. Tell me about the white rose. Are you really interested in TV journalism? Cooperate with me and I'll help you."

"I guess I'm not giving away any big secret. Although keeping it confidential made me feel like an insider, a special person entrusted with special knowledge. The white rose is the Brainiac symbol."

"Why – that's charming. Tell me more."

"It's so pure. Like it goes along with intuitive consciousness and the new world order of truth and beauty. You concentrate on the rosebud, watch it open, like the universe opening before you, and finally reach its center, a blazing heart."

"That's absolutely poetic. You could set it to music and play it on your guitar."

Ginger smiled. "It's everything – the beauty of the rose, and awesome truth."

As Ginger talked, she reached again for Cass with the paper bag, attempting to put it over her mouth.

"Please stop with the paper bag. I am being gaslighted and you are part of the conspiracy against me."

"Gaslighted. What do you mean?"

"People have been screwing with my head. In the movie Gaslight, Charles Boyer convinces Ingrid Bergman that she's only imagining sounds in the attic, when they are real. He is up there searching for jewels. And he is a killer. I do not need to be locked up for self-protection. Who made the white rose the symbol of the Brainiacs?"

"I don't know. Dr. Newman is the creative force behind everything. She could have made a fortune in advertising."

"Or murder."

"Cass. Cass." Ginger plunked at the guitar. "You are troubled. You *have* seen too many movies."

"Ramsdell alluded to some kind of illicit group with a sexual orientation that Jane had been fomenting. Sex trafficking. Underage kids. Do you know anything about it?"

Ginger sat quietly strumming on her guitar, her expression pensive.

"What are you thinking about Ginger?"

"I don't know. Sad stuff."

"Sad sex stuff?"

Ginger's face reddened. Perspiration popped. She put her guitar down, picked up a tissue and mopped her forehead and cheeks. "It's something I would rather not discuss."

"It's important. Sex trafficking with innocent kids is evil. If you know something, you must speak up."

"She tried to recruit me. She wanted to enlist young men and women to work supplying sex. Preferably sixteen and under. She thought I was younger because of the freckles and stuff. It would pay well. A young guy or gal would travel – go all over the world, wherever needed." Ginger's voice broke. "Like if they wanted five young gals and two young guys for a couple of rich old coots in Morocco, we would be flown there to do whatever."

"And how did you respond to her offer?"

Ginger sniffed. "I threw up. Just downright puked. I hadn't planned it but there I was, vomiting. Then I heard that there were drugs and people being forced to do stuff. That really gave me the heaves. "

"Have you heard anything about Jane's physical condition?"

Ginger strummed a chord on the guitar. "She was a friend of yours, wasn't she?"

"We were close friends. Once."

Ginger looked solemn. "While you were tripping, I worked the switch-board. A doctor from Bellevue called Dr. Newman about Jane. I explained to her that I was her personal assistant and she gave me the message. Jane Endicott did not make it. She had emerged from a coma. She was talking and eating. And then -poof – she was gone. A nurse found her in the morning. Finito."

Cass sat down on the window seat. Although she half-expected it, Jane's death upset her. Jane was amoral. Jane was bad. And yet Jane had been a friend. "What was the specific cause of her death?"

"The doctor did not say. It's going to hit Dr. Newman hard. I wrote her a note and left it at the switchboard. They had their differences, but basically she and Jane were peas in a pod."

Marsha finally reached the Leader on the phone. "The meeting cannot take place tomorrow," Marsha insisted. "There's too much going on. Cass Cooper is still here. She's locked up in the attic room but we cannot keep her there forever. Yes, there are permanent ways of disposing of her. She could plunge into the cold lake or succumb to poison as you suggest. Otto would have to bear witness to that if the police were suspicious. Of course he would balk but ultimately he would be forced to cooperate. But why do you lay that responsibility on me? It's your job."

They moved off of that subject and went on to the Big Meeting. The Leader insisted that the meeting go on as planned. She only half-listened as the Leader talked on. "Yes. We will have the Big Meeting." Marsha did not try to hide her impatience. "Have I ever failed to pull the rabbit out of the hat?"

She hung up the phone. She felt a residual loyalty, even as she planned a radical move that would destroy the Leader. But wasn't she entitled? It was she – genius Marsha Newman-- who had put together the formula that could change the course of history. And she was also entitled to eradicate it. And crush the Leader. If she stayed with the Leader, she could grasp enormous power. Become a famous woman like Cleopatra or Eva Peron or Margaret Thatcher. Thrilling. But she would not have what she desperately desired. True love. Noah's love.

Marsha opened the note that Ginger had left at the switchboard for her.

Jane was dead.

Marsha did not cry. She believed profoundly in "Don't get mad. Get even." She did not need to hear any more about Jane's death. She knew the Leader was responsible. The Leader cared not one whit about Marsha's feelings. This intolerable action reinforced her plan. If she ever harbored any doubts about punishing and abandoning the Leader, they were finished.

Her new commitment was not to world domination but to love. She pictured Noah in her mind, heard his voice in her head. She would become member of the human race with a husband of her own. She would take up married life with a vengeance, with a different lifestyle than when she had been married to Jane/John. Forget sex orgies and experimentation.

She yearned for upper-middle-class respectability. She might even play bridge, although she had always looked down on that pseudo-intellectual pastime as loathsome and pathetic. It would be part of her new image. She would choose a charity, serve on committees and meet other women for lunch. She would learn to like women, or at least tolerate them. She would not flirt with their husbands and have hot affairs with them, unless she became outrageously tempted and slipped, for which she would forgive herself.

The hell with the Leader.

Only one possible obstruction remained in her path to glory. Cass Cooper.

52

CASS TOOK OFF HER PUFFY jacket and made a fist. If she wrapped her fist in the sleeve, she could smash it through the window.

Ginger grinned slyly and plunked on her guitar. "The window's made of unbreakable glass. Thought you should know that before you tried to smash it open. One tripper did that and really hurt herself, like cut a vein. That's when Dr. Newman had the special glass put in. This room is in complete readiness for a person who has had a bad trip."

"I suppose the walls are also sound-proof, so if I yelled my head off nobody would hear." Cass had seen plenty of prison movies but never personally experienced this sense of claustrophobia and rage.

"Yes." Ginger crossed her long legs akimbo on the floor, as if preparing to meditate, and frowned. "Dr. Newman appreciates the fact that people need to let off steam, to express themselves. But others within hearing range could find shouts and sobs disturbing. And the windows are some kind of darkened glass so that one can't see in. It could be embarrassing to be observed."

"How prescient of Marsha." Cass had the urge to explode into hysterical laughter, like when on a long hike weird things keep happening and you're so close to getting there, but exhaustion sets in. "Since when is jail therapeutic?"

"You will be fine. You'll see. Later you'll understand when you glow with new health, like your psyche is renewed." Ginger smiled with exaggerated innocence. "That's what the Brainacs are about."

"Do you really believe all this stuff, Ginger, or is it unadorned bullshit?"

Ginger 's face stiffened. "You need to get a grip. Lighten up. Put on a happy face."

Cass stood by the window. A black Mercedes with New York plates on it had driven up to the barn. A tall, broad-shouldered gentleman emerged from the car wearing a camel hair coat, and carrying an attaché case. It looked like Donaldson. He turned his head. It was Donaldson, obviously come to her rescue. What a prince. She would never call Donaldson stuffy again. He stood and looked around, glanced up at the windows but of course he could not see her. The dark window glass installed for protection shielded Cass from his view.

"Donaldson! Donaldson!" She pounded on the window, knowing that her cries would not be heard. Even if she screamed and shouted her head off with a string of threats and obscenities, he could not respond. "It's Donaldson, my lawyer, Ginger. He's looking for me."

"Did you tell him you were coming here?" Ginger appeared to be in another world as she plucked away on an obscure folk tune. Ping. Ping. Ping.

"Yes. You must go and tell him that I'm trapped in this ridiculous room."

"I would do that." Ginger grabbed a pillow from the bed and now sat on the floor with the pillow behind her. "But I am not permitted to speak with Donaldson Frye unless Dr. Newman gives me the go-ahead."

"Donaldson Frye has no connection with the Brainiacs."

"Wrongo." A riff on the guitar. "Mr. Frye is an important person on the board of the Brainiacs."

"That's impossible. He has no interest in psychedelics."

"But he's heavily into Buddhism and meditation, and often advises on these practices as paths to personal transformation. He's a man of many parts. I love the way he looks, with his tweeds, except when he's in his Buddhist regalia."

"He dislikes Dr. Newman intensely. He has told me that repeatedly."

"I've heard they have their differences." Ginger picked up the guitar and played the classic *Greensleeves*. "Like he's a lawyer, not a psychologist or philosopher or physicist, but he's important. Very important. He's a thinker. He prefers to keep his Brainiac connection private for professional purposes. Like if you're looking for a criminal lawyer, you might not want a guy who's kind of unconventional. The Brainiacs could present a problem to some uptight types."

"And who gives you all this inside information?"

"Otto." Ginger scrunched up her mouth. "He's my lover. We share everything. But of course Dr. Newman can't know that. She's terribly jealous. Another gal looked at Otto and Dr. Newman fired her on the spot. Not that she's in love with Otto, just that she has to be the Queen Bee. Do you get it?"

"I get it. Listen, Ginger. You would be a terrific TV reporter. I have contacts at ABC and NBC." Cass kept her voice steady. "So let's make a deal." Cass's hands shook. She opened and closed them in hopes of stopping the tremors.

"You're making fists with your hands. I hope you're not planning to punch me."

"I would rather hug you. Here's the deal. You tell Donaldson Frye that I'm here, and I will help you. Is that so difficult?"

"Yes and no."

"He's a friend of long-standing. He was my late husband's closest friend. We have a bond which I'm sure trumps any Brainiac involvement. He's looking for me."

"He might be here for another reason. Mr. Frye told me in one of our brief conversations allowed by Dr. Newman that he likes the country life.

Often he will say he's going up to his ski lodge in Vermont, when actually he's coming here."

Cass looked out the window. Fazi stepped out of a black limo and walked towards the barn. "Do you know Fazi Fakhouri?"

"Not personally, but I have seen him. He's madly rich and exotic. Don't worry about Dr. Newman telling Mr. Frye that you're here. She tells him everything."

Snug in her lab, Marsha heard Donaldson pound down the stairs. He was one of the few people who had a key to her lab. She set the Brains formula bubbling away.

Donaldson put down his briefcase and sniffed the air, whiffing in the astringent fumes of the formula. "What's going on here?" His face was red and he breathed heavily. "I thought you had completed work on the formula, that you had actually tested it on a few people and it worked. That it completely turned their heads around."

"True." Marsha moved to a high stool.

"Congratulations." Donaldson looked relieved. He pulled off his coat and sat down in the canvas chair. He had dressed for the occasion in a striped blue and green silk kimono jacket. He wore small gold earrings. A heavy gold and black cross in a Byzantine design hung around his neck on a gold chain.

"The law and order formula works." Martha smiled. "Those who took it emerged with a different consciousness and a desire for a new world of rules, of borders, of conformity. Everyone will have a place and stay in that place. The Blacks will return to Africa, the Indians to India and so forth. That will be the ideal."

Donaldson took a large, clean white handkerchief out of his pocket and dabbed at his eyes. "How amazing. Our society will transform. Forget the Brainiacs. They are finished. Of course they will continue to be our façade. It's the Brains that count, and you, Marsha, are important."

"Have you completed the plan for implementing the Brains formula around the globe?" Marsha asked.

"A main source will be through drinking water. There will be other ways, food certainly, anything the public ingests. It will be particularly easy to implement in poorer countries. Of course we will work with responsible international leaders."

"Divine." Marsha clapped her hands in a show of enthusiasm and thought about Noah.

"It's a new world, and we came so close to losing everything. It still enrages me that Vance learned about the Brains."

Donaldson was beginning to annoy Marsha. "Vance apparently put everything he knew about the Brains in his book, and then destroyed the manuscript. How did you accomplish that, Donaldson, through persuasion or threat?"

"He did it on his own. Survival trumped grandstanding. He realized he could be endangering his own life. After five years in prison, he needed to live free. Without anxiety. Pity that he learned about the Brains. I suspected you as the traitor who told him – you would have done anything to gain his attention."

"That's nasty, Donaldson." Marsha frowned. "Why would I kill the goose that laid the golden eggs?"

"Because you're brilliant, but you're also unpredictable and a sex addict."

"It's a little late in the game for insults."

"I then realized that Jane, double-sexed and two-faced, was the treacherous mole who told him about the Brains. And later revealed my involvement. After four martinis at the Pont Verte, Jane spilled." Donaldson sighed heavily. "Unfortunate. Vance called me that night after he talked to Jane, called me in Vermont – said he would forget the whole insane Brains business, as he put it, if I would close down the Brains. Otherwise he was ready to blast the Brains story out to kingdom come."

"Why his sudden turn-around? He had destroyed the memoir telling about the Brains at great emotional cost."

"Because, he said, he was so pained about *my* involvement. He reminded me about our long-standing friendship, dating back to child-hood -- taking our first steps together. How could I foment this evil oper-ation?" Donaldson toyed with the cross hanging around his neck. "He did not understand."

"I worry about you, Donaldson. You could have negotiated with Vance. Instead you tore down from Vermont and stuck a dagger in his heart."

Donaldson's jaw clenched. "And interrupted your futile, last-ditch attempt at seduction. He was going to remarry Cass, a reality you could not accept." Donaldson smashed his fist down on the table. "We need to go forward, not to look back."

"Was it necessary to eliminate Jane?"

"I needed to stop her sex trafficking scheme. Corrupting youngsters. It defies every tenet of morality including those of the Episcopalian church." Donaldson's black eyes turned darker as his lips compressed. "But the treach-erous bitch is still alive."

"You didn't deal her the final blow?"

"No."

"Bellevue called. She didn't make it. She's dead."

Donaldson shrugged his shoulders. "Rest in peace."

"I cared about Jane."

"Get over it."

"You're aware that Cass Cooper is here."

"I will take care of Cass."

"I'm so happy we're in sync on that point," Marsha said. "Now why don't we go into the next room and sit by the fire. I will make tea and you can have another Scotch. The smell of the potion is getting to my sinuses."

Cass pulled Ginger up from the floor, grabbed her guitar away from her, and twisted her arm hard. "Now give me the keys." She pushed Ginger up against the wall.

"I can't," Ginger cried. "Dr. Newman will kill me."

"She might kill you if you don't. Give me the keys."

"I can't." Ginger looked terrified.

Cass smashed Ginger's guitar over her head. Ginger crumpled to the floor. Cass went into Ginger's enormous bag and dug out a ring of keys. Ginger crawled on the floor after her. She grabbed at Cass's ankle. Cass pulled her up and held her.

"Which is the key to this door?" she demanded.

Ginger pointed. "The blue key."

"And how do I find Dr. Newman?"

"Probably in her house. It's the red key." Every freckle stood out in Ginger's pale face.

"Where is my laptop and my phone?"

"In the locker outside the door. Use the yellow key."

Cass grabbed her jacket and unlocked the door. Outside, she closed the door and locked Ginger inside. She needed to catch up with Donaldson and warn him about Marsha, the woman who killed Vance and Pru and left the white rose symbol behind. Only Miranda/Marsha was egotistical enough to want to sign her acts of murder. Donaldson had been taken in, along with herself and so many other people.

She opened her phone, called Detective Adams in New York and left a message. "I am in Woodstock at the Brainiacs. I have identified the killer."

She turned on the path to Marsha's house.

53

Marsha poured a crystal glass three quarters full with Scotch, dropped in two ice cubes and handed it to Donaldson. She sipped chamomile tea from a delicate China cup. Donaldson swirled the Scotch and drank. "To you, Marsha. To a new world."

"I'll drink to that." Marsha stood up, took a long match, and touched it to the tinder and papers in the fireplace. "It's been quite a trip, hasn't it?' She took a sip of tea. "It was unfortunate about Pru, wasn't it. I know all about it."

"How do you know?"

"Pru told Jane about your freak-out, and Jane told me. Jane told me everything. How you used Call Jane, and they sent you Pru. And how you went back to your house with her, and you couldn't – emn – quite manage it. You were drunk. She noticed the picture of you and Vance. You were smashed and started crying about killing the only man you had ever loved."

Donaldson's ruddy face paled. "How dare you?"

"So you got worried. You thought she knew too much. She would talk. It was probably unnecessary. Pru could have been bought off. And you did not have to kill Vance. It was your damn ego. I tried to stop you. But while Vance was alive, you would always be second best, even if you ruled the world. You just could not take it."

"He was going to blow our cover."

"We could have fought him. The world is waiting for the Brains. People crave the Brains. You've heard the old cliché – escape from freedom. You really fucked up, Donaldson."

"It's over. Cass will take the rap for it. And she'll be dead. Let's stop talking about it."

"I loved Vance."

"He did not return your affection, something you can't seem to accept. It was unfortunate about Vance, but he owed me, in many ways. He lost a minor fortune for me with his Ponzi dealings. But he did not care. He was ready to tell the world about the Brains, paint us with a dark brush, to totally destroy a movement before we even got started. To kill the Brains, the spiritual salvation of our planet. I once loved him, as a man, as a friend, but that changed."

"Why do you lie to yourself, Donaldson?" Marsha asked. "You were hot for him. And he told you go to hell."

"Don't try and make me a homo. I am completely straight."

"I would not get so exercised. The word homo has nasty connotations. It's offensive, politically incorrect. You should not use it. You're probably bi. Why don't you congratulate yourself on having this special talent. It's like being double-jointed."

"I don't like your sarcastic tone."

"I couldn't care less. You will have to go forward without me, and without the Brains. The formula has practically evaporated. I created it, and the Brain recipe – as I call it -- is burning in the fireplace. The Brains are over. You can tell that to your coterie and world rulers."

Donaldson's face was bright red. He put down the Scotch glass. "You are joking."

"I'm serious. Your life as the Leader is finished. You have nothing to lead."

"I could kill you, Marsha."

"What good would that do you? The game is up. I have fallen in love. I want to change my life, not the world."

"And who is this paragon whom you hope succumbed to your charms?"

"Noah Lazeroff."

"It will never happen."

Cass walked in to confront Marsha and Donaldson.

"This is a private meeting," Donaldson said. "It's business."

"Murder business," Cass said. "I tried to push my suspicions away, Donaldson. I didn't want to believe that you were a treacherous, two-faced bastard."

"Regardless -- whatever I did was not personal. It was for the greater good of mankind."

"You even went to all the trouble of beating yourself up – breaking your own arm – to appear innocent. Then you told me that on the night of Vance's murder, you had met your neighbors, Betsy and Bill Coleman, for dinner in Vermont. But they were no longer a couple. Betsy had left her husband for your ex, Irene. You were not having dinner with them. You were driving down from Vermont. Vance trusted you with his life."

"Vance had transmogrified into a pigheaded reformer."

"It was so easy for you to play the innocent party. Your DNA and foot-prints and fingerprints were all over your house. Who would suspect? It was your gold earring. Your muddy shoe. Vance was totally unprepared to fend you off. Even at your worst, he believed in you."

"And Donaldson was so disgustingly arrogant," Marsha seethed. "He insisted on leaving behind the white rose, the symbol of the Brainiacs."

"It was my symbol, my creation," Donaldson said.

"It was not to be used for your evil purposes," Marsha responded.

"Call me sentimental," Donaldson said. "The Brainiacs exposed me to a new world. I embraced it. Then I saw where it would lead, to irresponsible hippies, to a world without borders, a homogenization of society. We need the Brains. We need borders. We need walls. We need control. "

"I tried to stop you," Marsha cried out. "I begged you not to kill Vance." She turned to Cass. "Donaldson was in love with Vance. He bought the portrait and insisted on hanging it in the main room of the barn, to taunt me every time I walked by. And he killed Prudence. And then Fozer. Mr. Super-Cautious trouble-maker. And he was supposed to be our Leader." She spit out the word with contempt. "What a loathsome, self- absorbed, stuffy, narcissistic piece of shit."

"Getting involved with you, Miranda/Marsha, or whatever your name is was my first big mistake," Donaldson said. "Always trying to play the hot babe. Leaving those bikini panties behind after Vance had pushed you away."

"They were special, just like the pair I wore when Vance and I first made love. You came on to me because I loved Vance." Marsha's mouth twisted angrily. "That one attempt at so-called love-making with me was a total disaster. You were always trying to best Vance and it never happened." Marsha spat out the words. "You will always be second best at everything. Teaming up with Jane was less than admirable. You and your shared inter-national ring of sexual perverts."

"You mean Saint Jane?" Donaldson said contemptuously. "She was determined to tear down every sexual inhibition known to mankind. Fine. But I could not tolerate her sex trafficking with youngsters. It's immoral. I had to stop her."

"You killed people I loved," Marsha wept. "You are one pathetic impo-tent bastard who cannot really love anybody. "

Donaldson reached into his pocket and pulled out a small revolver. "Your taunts go over my head, Marsha. You might have a good mind but you lack that all-important something known as class. I hope you two ladies will not become too exercised about this answer to our problem. The world will understand when I tell them, Cass, that you killed Marsha, believing she had killed Vance, and then shot yourself self to death. Pathetic and totally believable."

"But that's absurd, Donaldson," Cass protested. "I can understand my killing Marsha. But why kill myself?"

"Depression," Donaldson said. "Self-hatred. All those girlish things."

Marsha stood up. "Bow out gracefully, Donaldson. And drop the ridiculous gun. It doesn't suit you."

"Sit down, Marsha," Donaldson shouted. "And please be quiet. Both of you. I cannot stand this chatter. I am doing something significant. You attempt to stand in the way of a new world order." Donaldson raised the gun again, aiming it at Cass. "I suppose I should make an appropriate speech, like sorry to destroy our friendship. But that isn't going to happen."

A noise on the staircase. Donaldson whirled around and aimed his gun as Jane came down the stairs. "Do not aim the gun at my head," Jane said. "I do not kill so easily. I am a Brain. Now isn't that fascinating? The choices we are allowed to make. You actually tried to kill me because I deserted the Brains. But I changed my mind, big-time."

"We received a message that you were dead," Marsha said.

"I left the message," Jane said.

"Why were you blabbing to Vance?" Donaldson held the gun on Jane.

"Vance, once the libertine, was Vance reformed. He threatened to turn me in because of my Youth Sex program. I told him that my money was going to support The Brains. And you were the Leader. I knew he could not survive. We're still in business, Donaldson."

"A lot of good that does us," Donaldson raged. "The formula is finished."

"The formula is alive and well in my hands. I did not trust Marsha. I copied the formula." Jane reached into her pocket, pulled out a piece of paper and held it up. "We can be co-leaders of the new world. You and I will make history together."

"Co-leaders. How nauseating. This world isn't big enough for both of us." Donaldson shakily aimed the gun at Jane.

"Both of you are ridiculous losers," Marsha said. "I know all of your tricks, Jane. The formula you have is false."

"You are vile," Donaldson said. "All of you. Vile and perverse. I can't live in a world with the likes of you and your twisted minds."

Footsteps sounded on the stairs. Donaldson turned his head. As he did, Cass dove for Donaldson's legs, bringing him down. She grabbed for his gun but Donaldson was quicker. Donaldson twisted around. He pulled Cass up and reached his strong hands out for Cass's neck. Noah came down the stairs and leaped towards Donaldson in a running tackle. Donaldson went down again. The two men struggled for the gun. Noah pulled the gun from Donaldson's hand.

Detective Adams came into the room.

"We've been tracking you, Donaldson. We were on to you since the first pack of lies you told us about where you were on the night of Vance Cooper's murder. Your story sucked big-time. That led us to pay particular attention to you in the matter of Prudence Duluth's death."

Donaldson stood up and rearranged his cross and the now rumpled silk jacket. He smoothed his hair. Adams read Donaldson the Miranda Act. ".….and you may contact an attorney."

"I am the attorney," Donaldson said.

"Donaldson Frye, we arrest you as the prime suspect in the murders of Vance Cooper, Prudence Duluth, and Bugsy Fozer." He snapped the hand-cuffs on Donaldson, and then turned to Marsha.

"Ms. Newman, let me read you your Miranda rights." After reading them to Marsha, he said, "You are arrested as an accessory in the murder of Vance Cooper."

"I am innocent and will prove it." Marsha put her hands out. "But go ahead. Snap them on. My crime was getting to know Donaldson Frye. Can I have a moment to speak to Noah?" she asked.

"Go ahead." For once Adams looked more animated than exhausted.

"I had such hope for us," Marsha said to Noah. "I loved the vibe. So what do you think? I'm planning to change my name. How do you like Maya? It's Hindu for illusion."

"It suits you," Noah said.

"But I don't suit you," Marsha said. "You were just playing me."

"I admire your mind."

"That's a stab in the heart, Noah," Marsha said. "All my life men have been admiring my mind. I need love."

"Give yourself a chance," Noah said. "Become the new Marsha."

Jane turned to Cass. "Life is full of surprises, isn't it. I was a man, and then I was a woman. A librarian and an entrepreneur. I believe in human potential. I believe in total sexual freedom."

"How does that fit in with control and borders?" Cass replied.

"The world is full of contradictions. Haven't you realized by now that most of what is considered evil is condoned by society. If I'm sent to prison – and I don't plan for that to happen --I will reread Proust. His work, too, is filled with devils and angels."

Cass handed a ring of keys to Detective Adams. "Speaking of mixed bags and would-be angels, there's a young lady named Ginger locked in the top room in the big house. Maybe it's time to let her out."

54

Cass put the final period on her piece *Cures for Cataclysmic Living*.

She had struggled with the article and labored over it since her return from Woodstock. The Brainiacs and the Brains were the story. She told it all, or almost all. So much of it would remain underground, buried in her heart. The hoops she had jumped through. The doubts. The pain. That moment on LSD when Vance was close to her – so close and yet unreachable. He would always be an enormous and precious part of her.

Her phone rang. Dev Lal. "*The Confessions of Vance Cooper* will hit The New York Times Best Seller list this Sunday. We published the book at warp speed and it was worth it. Don't be late for the party tonight. It's going to be an amazing celebration."

"I'm thrilled. Vance worked the miracle, didn't he Dev?"

"The two of you did it together. Two insane wonderful people and a lipstick tube."

Cass took a shower and got dressed. She would wear her black and gold jacket.

It was Noah's favorite.

The sometime lover. The passionate friend.

Life was good, and getting even better.

203 § 32-2568